THE OTHER INHERITANCE

REBECCA JAYCOX

THE OTHER INHERITANCE

REBECCA JAYCOX

First printed by Rocking Horse Publications, 2014
Reprinted by Aelurus Publishing, January 2017

Cover design by Molly Phipps

ISBN 13: 978-0-9956325-5-4

www.aeluruspublishing.com

DEDICATION

This book is for you, Mom. You always believed.

Acknowledgments

The Other Inheritance took eight years to get published. During that time, I met a lot of people who helped and influenced me. Their encouragement and support kept me going. The life of a writer is lonely and full of dark self-doubt. These individuals kept the light shining.

My mom and dad. They were the best parents a girl could ask for, and they knew when it was time to let go and let me fly.

My granny and gramps, who indulged my fascination for science fiction and watched Star Wars with me every Sunday for a year when I was 12. My grandmother's pride in me still brings me to tears.

My husband Gregory, who gave me time and space to write and kept telling me to forget those rejection letters.

I want to thank my writing partner, Philip Perez, who has been with me since the first draft and the six more since then. You rock! My other writing partner, Carolyn Goldhush, who is the best editor I've ever worked with and can pull catchy copy like a magician pulls a rabbit out of a hat.

To my friend George Sirois, thank you for introducing me to Rocking Horse Publishing and supporting me every step of the way. Debbie Manber Kupfer, thanks for the countless FB conversations and internet handholding. Kim Piotrowski, you're an amazing artist and friend and you brought my characters to life. Linda and Andy, you always told me when my manuscript was shit, and I appreciate that. My cover designer, Molly. Thank you for bringing the wonder of the Other to life. Last, but certainly not least, I want to thank Jeff Collyer and Aelurus Publishing for giving "The Other Inheritance" a new home. I'm convinced we can do great things together.

x

CHAPTER 1

"*D*id anyone ever tell you that you're a cliché?" seventeen-year-old Reggie Lang asked. She was hunched in an antique, high-backed chair. Her chestnut hair spilled over her shoulders, her splattering of freckles barely visible in the firelight.

"Am I?" he said.

The man on the other side of the hearth stretched his long legs out toward the fire. A scar puckered his right cheekbone, slanting down to the sharp blade of his nose.

Reggie took in his tough leather boots and duster. "The Hell's Angels called. They want their motorcycle back." His rough exterior stood at odds with the delicate furniture and pink-veined marble fireplace.

He laughed. "Hell's Angels? Never heard that before."

"Really? The leather look of doom isn't deliberate?"

He tugged at his coat, designed for function, not fashion. The light from the fire picked out grooves and scrapes that pitted the hide. "It's for protection."

"From what? Don't tell me you're a rebel with a cause."

His amusement faded. "I have a very important cause. And you're a key part of it."

Reggie wrapped her arms around her knees. Wariness shone in her large brown eyes.

"I'm a key part of your cause? Does this mean you're finally going to tell me what I'm doing here? These little chitchats are getting on my nerves. Tell me what you want from me or leave me alone." Three nights now, they'd been meeting, and he refused to give his name or any answers.

"I'm here to help with the changes you're going through. To help you understand your place."

"My place? Who are you to tell me about my place? For all I know, you're just some pervert who gets off by harassing teenage girls," Reggie said, pushing herself to her feet.

"I'm not a pervert. Never accuse me of such things again." His anger surprised her.

Reggie's eyes narrowed as she searched his, but she found no signs of a lie. She sank back down into the chair. "Sorry, I have to watch out for myself."

"Understood. Now, would you like to know what changes I'm talking about?"

"Stop jerking my chain and tell me already."

"Yes, let's start with the incident in class," the man said.

Reggie's stomach clenched. "I don't know what you're talking about."

"Really, Reggie, surely you remember?" He leaned forward. "How'd you feel when your touch brought that dead frog back to life?"

Sucking in air, Reggie woke from the dream and frantically untangled herself from her sheets. Her thin t-shirt was soaked, and smelled like smoke. Her hands shook as she hugged herself. She didn't want to think about what had happened in biology class. Reggie hadn't told anyone, had ignored her teacher's questioning glance, her classmates' curiosity. Her lab partner Mark Millan had looked at her with wide eyes, his pimpled cheeks unusually pale. The frog had reeked of formaldehyde. There was no way it could've been alive, yet the moment she'd poked its body with her finger, it had leapt off the table.

Her right arm began to tingle again, remembering the strange burst of energy that had shot through her into the frog. First the butterfly she'd found caught in a spider's web and now the frog. Her lack of knowledge, of control over the situation terrified her.

"Whatever you're selling, I'm not buying," Reggie whispered into the darkness, extending her middle finger toward the ceiling and flipping off the man.

Her feet hit the cold wooden floor, and she padded out of her room past her mother's bedroom. Her mother had taken a few sleeping pills around nine, and Reggie had smelled whiskey on her breath when she'd kissed her goodnight. Shivering, she walked to the bathroom. Maybe there were a few pills left.

"No!" she said. No way was she starting down that path. She turned to stare at her mother's door and shook her head. She didn't need pills; she needed to talk to someone. Walking past the bathroom, Reggie went downstairs and grabbed the phone. She'd call John. He'd be angry, but she didn't care.

Pale moonlight filled the large kitchen. Reggie ignored the light switch and settled into a seat. The chrome table and chairs, a retro set from the 1950s, would have been fashionably hip if the red cushions hadn't faded and the chrome didn't wear rust spots. Reggie was debating getting a slice of cold pizza for comfort before she called John when she noticed the sheet of paper stuck to the refrigerator by a magnet. Her mother had an appointment with her psychiatrist tomorrow. What was he doing to help? As far as Reggie could tell, he just loaded her mother with more antidepressants and continued to ignore her increasing drinking problem.

Shaking her head at another aspect of her life she couldn't control, Reggie punched in John's cell number. He answered on the sixth ring.

"Reggie, it's freaking two a.m.!" John grumbled, his voice rough with sleep.

"I'm impressed you can read your caller ID," Reggie said. Her fingers played with one of the cracks in the vinyl seat cover. "Sorry to wake you up, man. I couldn't sleep."

"Now I can't either," John said. "Is your mom okay?"

She stared at her hands. They had stopped shaking. "Yeah, she's as okay as she ever is, I guess. I just had a—I just had a really bad dream."

"You woke me up because of a dream? Don't you have a teddy bear or something you can hug?"

"John, I think there's something wrong with me," she confessed.

"Nothing's wrong. You're letting a stupid dream get to you." She heard him yawn.

"Maybe." Reggie hesitated. "Can you come by my house before school? I want to show you something."

"Sure, whatever, can I go back to sleep now?"

"Just promise me you'll be here early. Okay?"

"Yeah, yeah, I'll be there early," his voice became fainter.

"Seven-thirty," she said loudly.

"Dammit. Yeah, seven-thirty." The phone went dead.

Reggie turned off her phone and went to look at the appointment for her mother. Damn. It was for nine a.m. She'd have to get her mother up early. Reggie put water and coffee into the coffee pot and set the automatic timer. She trudged back to bed, hoping for dreamless sleep.

CHAPTER 2

*D*eep in the forest behind Porth, the small city Reggie lived in, a shimmering patch of air stretched between two large oak trees. The trees were gnarled and ancient, their curved branches framing a makeshift doorway. It was like looking into a muted, two-way mirror. On one side was the normal forest, awake and alive with nocturnal creatures feeding and being fed upon. The other side of the mirror reflected a similar image.

With one striking exception.

Standing on the other side was a tall man; his hard stare trained in the direction of Porth, which lay in the valley below. He stretched out a hand to reach through the shimmer and a thunderous boom echoed through the forest, followed by the sound of sizzling flesh. Blue energy crackled from the indention of the man's handprint in the barrier. Smoke trickled from his fingers.

"The magic holds," the man murmured.

He turned and flicked his fingers. A young man appeared next to him, standing above the older man's impressive height. Moonlight illuminated his bronze skin and green eyes of deep jade. Black hair hung past slightly pointed ears. He wore a gold collar with tiny figures performing acts of labor carved into the metal.

The older man surveyed the younger. He gestured for him to put his hand through the doorway. With a slight hesitation, the young man cautiously touched the surface. The barrier sighed as energy parted, allowing his long fingers to meet the air of Reggie's world.

"Now is the time, Asher, when I demand payment in full," the older man said. "I personally took you out of the House for my own, educated you, saved you from the Pits that are fitting to traitors' children. Without me, you'd be wasting away in some mine, waiting to die." He added weight to his next words: "You can finally be free; your family can be free if you complete a task for me."

Asher's eyes narrowed in doubt. "All the debt, Master? All of my family, not just me? I want things spelled out clearly."

"Yes, all. This task is very important to me. If you can complete it, I'll free all of your family," he repeated. "And restore a place in society for you."

"What do you need me to do?" Asher said. Andrius Drake, Master of the Mages Council and head of the Military of Two Cities, wasn't known for his mercy.

"Don't look so concerned. I'm not asking you to kill anyone." Andrius reached into the pocket of his traveling cloak and pulled out a plain gold locket and handed it to Asher.

Asher took the locket and opened it. Inside was a photo of a young girl, pretty, with brown eyes and long brown hair. Not so much a girl as a young woman; she wasn't much younger than Asher. He traced the picture with his thumb.

"Lovely, isn't she?" Andrius observed, looking at the photo with Asher. "Now, I've done my best to beat that irritating morality from you, but you insist on clinging to your guilt, so you'll be happy to know I don't want you to hurt her."

Asher broke his gaze from the picture. "You don't?"

"No, she's very important to me. I want you to find her, observe her, and when the time is right, bring her through the barrier to me."

"But isn't that against the law? No one has been allowed to cross over or bring anyone back through the barrier in almost twenty years," Asher said. He flinched as the collar heated, burning his skin.

"You forget yourself, boy. I make the laws, and I can break them when I choose to," Andrius said, and Asher's collar glowed with the force of his anger.

Chapter 3

The third house on Cherry Lane was a shabby Victorian on a street that curved up a gently sloping hill. Below Cherry Lane sat a row of antique stores, old-fashioned soda shops, and jewelry boutiques. This was the historic part of Porth, where all the awnings were green and white striped and the pristine sidewalks were full of polished pine benches. The Victorian homes were the oldest in the city, most of them neat and well kept. Reggie's home was like a big glob of paint spoiling an otherwise perfect canvas. Once a beautiful blue and white jewel in the curving necklace of homes, its paint was now crumbled and faded, the wood warped.

Reggie stood in her lawn, putting on thick rubber gloves before moving a dead beetle onto the boards of the front porch that wrapped around the house. Sunshine warmed her back as she bent over and arranged its body. John would be here soon, and she wanted everything in place. She wasn't certain she could bring the beetle back to life, but she'd managed to jump-start both the butterfly and the frog. Reggie straightened and turned, her eyes flitting over the lawn. The grass was out of control this spring, growing much more rapidly than the rest of the neighborhood. She'd mowed it two days ago and it was already shin high. Glancing at her wristwatch, Reggie went back into the house, tossing her gloves on the couch. She needed to wake her mother to remind her about her appointment. The stairs groaned as she bounded up them. Swinging open her mother's bedroom door, she stepped inside.

Heavy drapes hung on all the windows and dimmed the morning sunlight. Dirty clothes strewn across the floor muted Reggie's footsteps, and her mother, Arlene, lay in a queen size bed, wrapped in a faded floral comforter. The only space untouched by clutter was the polished rosewood nightstand where a picture of Reggie's father, Sebastian, was in a silver frame. He was smiling, his dark brown hair shining in the sun as he lay out on a picnic blanket.

Reggie walked to the bed and stared down at her mother whose mouth was slightly agape, her breath a soft rasp. She paused, not wanting to disturb her mother's rare moment of peace. Lips tightening, she grabbed the blanket and yanked. Immediately, her mother squeezed into a ball, shivering, then blinked, her eyes bleary with sleep and the remnants of alcohol.

"What the hell did you do that for?" Arlene mumbled, then more loudly, "What time is it?"

"It's after seven, Mom," Reggie said. "You have a doctor's appointment today at nine, so you need to get up now. I have to go to school."

Staring at her daughter, Arlene slowly sat up. She observed Reggie's neat, trim figure clad in a T-shirt and faded jeans. Her eyes filled with guilt, and she pushed herself to the edge of the bed and put on her slippers.

"You look nice this morning, baby. Have you had breakfast?" she asked, stretching to her feet.

"Yeah, I put coffee on for you too, and I put out a corn muffin. I bought groceries yesterday, so there are cold cuts and cheese in the fridge. Oh, and I bought some fruit, so eat a few apples or something." Reggie made an "after you" gesture with her hand, she wasn't leaving the bedroom until she was sure her mother was leaving it.

10

"Hey, isn't that my line?" her mother joked as she walked out the door.

"Yeah, I guess it's supposed to be," Reggie replied, wincing when her mother flushed. Be nice, she said to herself. She needed her mother to be at the kitchen table eating when John came.

"I promise to eat an apple with my muffin," her mother said. A hesitant smile curved her lips.

Reggie smiled back. "I promise to take an apple to school with me."

Her mother beamed, her relief evident, and Reggie allowed the tension between them to melt. Following Arlene to the kitchen, she sat her mother down at the table and poured coffee into a huge mug. She added milk and sugar to the steaming liquid and placed the mug in front of her mother.

"Be careful," Arlene warned when Reggie yelped and blew on her scalding fingers.

"I'm fine. Drink and then muffin and apple, okay?"

"Yes, ma'am," her mother answered, sipping her coffee.

A loud knock sounded at the front door. Reggie tensed, and she looked at her mother who was staring off into the distance.

"That's John, I'm riding with him to school today." Reggie started from the kitchen when her mother's voice stopped her.

"Anything I should know about you two?" Arlene asked.

Reggie inwardly groaned as she turned. Arlene's light hazel eyes were suddenly sharp as they scanned her daughter. Her mother showed interest at the oddest, most inconvenient times. "No, Mom, we're just friends," she assured her.

Reggie walked back and planted a light kiss on Arlene's forehead, squeezed her shoulder, and then hurried through the house. As she headed toward the door, the knocking grew more insistent. She gripped the door handle, breathing deeply.

11

John waited on the porch looking sleepy, rumpled, and a little pissed off. His black hair hung perfectly straight over his forehead and his slightly slanted eyes were the color of polished onyx.

Reggie stood in the open doorway and gave her best friend a sheepish smile. "Sorry to get you up so early."

John's face relaxed and he grinned. "It's okay, you know me and early don't get along. So what's up?"

Reggie closed the door behind her and moved out onto the porch.

"Hey, you're not even going to give me a Pop Tart?" he said as he watched the door close. She rolled her eyes and grabbed his arm to steer him toward the dead beetle.

"Focus. I need you to listen, okay? There's some strange stuff that's been happening lately. And I don't know what to do."

John gripped her forearm. "Is your mom's drinking worse? Should I tell my mom, maybe she can help—"

"No! I mean, Mom is still—but this isn't about her. Now, about my dream last night—"

He released his grip. "This is about a dream? Dammit, Reggie, here I am worried that something's seriously wrong—"

"Forget the dream. I brought a dead frog back to life! Stop looking at me like that." Reggie cringed when she saw John's shocked expression.

"So it's true? You brought a frog back to life?"

"People have been talking about that? What did you hear?"

"That asshole Mark Millan is telling everyone you used voodoo or black magic on your frog. He's saying you're into some dark shit."

"Great. Not only am I the kid with the alcoholic, depressed mom, now I'm practicing witchcraft and sacrificing chickens." She paced back and forth in front of the beetle.

"Well, I've been to your room plenty of times and I haven't seen any dead chickens, so what's going on with you? And why didn't you tell me before now?"

Reggie stopped. "I was scared. I don't understand what's happening to me. I hoped this would all go away. But I guess it's not, because the frog isn't the only thing I've brought back to life."

John's eyebrows shot up and he sagged against the porch railing. "It's not?"

She shook her head. "I don't know how to make it stop!" She pointed at the beetle in front of them. He looked down. "That's why I brought you here, to show you what I can do."

"Show me."

His calm acceptance alarmed her. "John?

He glanced up. "Yeah?"

"You're being really chill about this."

John shrugged. "We're best friends. Who else are you going to tell this to?"

She swallowed the sudden lump in her throat and nodded.

Reggie approached the dead beetle, her eyes searching its hollow shell. A dull throb began as she reached out toward it. The closer she came, the sharper the throbbing. Energy surged within her pushing to get out, her skin a poor casing for her power. She sensed the drowning emptiness of the beetle, the essential spark of life gone.

"Here we go," Reggie breathed.

She bent down. Slowly and gently, she touched the beetle's brittle shell with her finger. She felt a static charge, a painful release of energy that shot from her into the beetle, leaving her empty. The beetle's legs shuddered, clattering against the floorboards, and then a faint squishy, sucking sound, as if its organs were growing fast. After a few moments, the beetle twitched, trying to get off its back. Reggie flipped it over, watching as it scrambled away toward the porch stairs. Weariness soaked her bones. She heard a loud exhale above and looked up, realizing John had been holding his breath. Their eyes met.

"Holy shit!" he whispered.

Reggie sank to the floor, wrapping her arms around her legs, and putting her head on her knees. John squatted down next to her. "You okay?"

"I don't know—it feels strange, like when I touch dead stuff, I feel I'm losing some of my life force. I don't know how to explain it." He rubbed her back.

"Don't take this the wrong way, because I know you're upset, but that was the coolest thing I've ever seen."

Her head whipped toward him. "What?"

His eyes glowed with excitement. "You have a super power! You're like—like a comic book superhero or something."

"Screw that."

"Why? Do you know how many people want a super power?"

"I don't need something else messing with my life. My plate is piled this high, okay?" She raised a hand to eye level. "My power isn't something useful like super strength or telekinesis; I'm bringing dead things to life! And in my dreams, there's this guy who says I'm a special part of his master plan. I don't want to be a part of anyone's plan but my own!"

John was silent for a moment and then squeezed her shoulder. "Let's push the power thing aside for a second. Tell me about the dreams."

Reggie sighed. "You're going to think I'm crazy."

"Kid, this whole thing is crazy, so spill."

"After the first time I . . . brought something back, I met this guy in my dream. He knew my name and started asking me questions, but he wouldn't answer any of mine. Then last night he tells me I'm important, and he wanted to talk about the frog."

"Hmm, do you think you made him up, like subconsciously?"

She lifted her head. "Maybe, but there's a fireplace in the room where we meet, and every time I wake up, my clothes smell like smoke. The fireplace in my house is full of junk, never been lit."

"So if this guy is real, what does it mean?"

"No idea. None of this makes sense."

John laughed, a nervous warble. "I guess science really can't explain everything."

"Don't say that." She grimaced.

"Reggie, you have super powers! How do you explain that?"

Finding strength, Reggie pushed to her feet. "I don't want them! Having no control over it? Uh-uh. I don't need this."

John leapt to his feet. "I'll help you figure this out. It's going to be okay."

She paced back and forth. "Right, I need to do something. We need a plan. We'll tell Ms. Lamb during study hall we're doing a science project for the district science fair. That should get us out of there. Maybe there's something on the Internet about people who have my . . . ability."

"Your super power."

"John!"

"Or your magical power, that would be equally cool." When he saw her frown, he grabbed her arm, pulling her to a halt. "Keeping it light, kid."

It suddenly hit her. She'd told John everything and he'd stayed. She raised a fist, knuckles out and he lightly bumped it with his own. "You're made of awesome sauce, you know that?"

"Obviously. Come on, we need to get going."

"I'll grab my backpack." Reggie walked toward the door when John's voice stopped her.

"Hey, you remember my dog Einstein? If this is a lasting power, he's buried in our backyard, and I miss him; do you think—"

"I'm so gonna kick your ass."

John laughed. "I'll shut up now."

CHAPTER 4

*R*osemont High School tried to disguise what it really was. Teal and white banners hung from the cafeteria ceiling, encouraging school pride. Playful cartoon characters painted on the walls of the hallways in neon colors advertised the joys of education. But no amount of color or false pride could transform the gray and white cement block walls into something they weren't. This was a prison. And although Reggie loved learning, she was trapped with inmates who didn't like that she was different.

Reggie passed Mark Millan, surrounded by his gang of friends. They stared at her. She stared back, her expression flat. Mark smirked at her, crossing himself.

"Jackass," Reggie muttered.

Josh Reynolds—Mark's first henchman—flipped his Zippo lighter open and shut, yelling out, "Hey, voodoo girl, raise anything from the dead lately?"

She flipped him off and continued walking, the sounds of their laughter lapping at her footsteps. She reached her locker and briefly rested her hot face on the cold, green metal. Shaking herself, she spun the dial on her locker and opened the door, shoving her books inside. She was angry she'd let Mark and his gang get to her. In the end, people like them don't matter, Reggie reminded herself.

She repeated this mantra in her head, but her skin prickled. People were watching. Normally, she avoided being part of the rumor mill, but in high school, rumors ran like water. If she kept her head down, people would forget and this would pass. She was smart, she made good grades, and one day she'd escape to a college far away from here.

Among this unwanted drama, thoughts of her new power invaded her mind with predatory determination. She'd lied to John that morning. A part of her, albeit a tiny one, was excited about this mysterious ability. The larger part was terrified that the life she'd threaded together was going to be ripped apart at the seams.

When she entered study hall, she spotted John slouched in a desk at the front. His backpack rested on a seat next to him. He removed it when he saw her, and she slid into the seat.

"You got the excuse ready?" he asked. "I wanna get out of here."

"Give me some credit. I've even made our project relevant for the issues we're facing today," Reggie said.

John rolled his eyes. "Whatever. Just make it good so we can leave."

She raised her hand in the air, impatient for Ms. Lamb to notice her. Ms. Lamb, the resident study hall teacher, was settling into her desk. Her eyes softened when she focused on Reggie. "Yes, Ms. Lang?"

"John and I," Reggie thumbed in his direction, "are working on a science project for the district fair, and we wondered if we could study in the library for this period."

Ms. Lamb paused as she leaned back in her chair. Reggie waited, trying not to notice that Shelley Michaels was leaning forward in her chair to eavesdrop.

"What's the project on?" Ms. Lamb asked.

"Uh, the use of algae as a new source of energy."

"More save the planet stuff? Original," Shelley said, as she tossed long blond hair over her shoulder. "I thought it would be on the regenerative ability of frogs." She sat diagonally from Reggie, smirking.

Reggie turned back and met her gaze. "I thought you'd be doing one on the regenerative ability of crabs." Snickers bounced around the room.

Shelley's mouth curled in rage. "You're just a jealous, drunk's—" she began, but Ms. Lamb's angry voice drowned the oncoming insult.

"Ladies! Enough!" Ms. Lamb shouted. She motioned to the door with her head. "Reggie, John, go to the library. Shelley, why don't you go back to studying since that's the reason we're here?"

Reggie and John slid from their seats, hastily grabbing their things. Reggie felt the twin lasers of Shelley's eyes. Shelley would make her pay for that dig later. Once outside the classroom, John burst out laughing.

"Too bad Lamb interrupted. That was starting to get good. I expected a hair pulling, bitch-smacking showdown."

Reggie elbowed him lightly in the side. "I don't pull hair. Hey, can I come over tonight?"

"Don't you have kickboxing?"

"Yeah, but I'm going to skip it." John stopped. She turned, waiting for him. "What?"

He made a show of looking around. "Making sure hell hasn't frozen over. You never skip kickboxing. If there was a hurricane, you'd find a way there."

Reggie offered a brittle smile, absently fingering the scar along her hairline. "Well, this takes priority now. I want to research more at your house tonight."

CHAPTER 5

*R*eggie stepped off the bus and began walking to her house. She and John had discovered nothing. They'd searched sites ranging from science to folklore to necromancy. She guessed the latter wasn't PTA approved, as she'd received an access denied message at every attempt. She'd have more privacy at John's house where his mother only censored for porn.

As she trudged up the hill to her home, she felt a tug of paranoia in her stomach. Her heart beat faster. She forced herself to keep the same pace as her eyes casually swept the neighborhood, and her ears filtered the sounds of passing cars and birds for anything unusual. Nothing. Her muscles remained tense. Four years of martial arts training kicked in, and she shifted her weight forward. Fear swamped her as she remembered being assaulted when she was thirteen. Her fingers touched her ribs. Images flitted across her mind: blood, the emergency room, and her mother's hysterical sobs. But her physical wounds had healed, and she pushed the memory away.

Her security wouldn't be so easily taken again. Now she was prepared. If Shelley Michaels was hiding, waiting to jump her, she was in for a nasty surprise. Reggie focused on her surroundings once more. Although she couldn't detect anyone, her paranoia lingered. To hell with acting casual, she thought. She jogged up the hill, taking a fast turn into her driveway. Chalky white gravel crunched under her feet as she sprinted across it and up her front porch steps.

"Mom!" she called as she shut the front door behind her, flipping the lock. "Are you home?"

"In here," came a muffled voice from the kitchen. Reggie dropped her backpack and hurried to the kitchen.

"Hi baby, how was school?" Her mother sat on a chair; her thin frame wrapped in a satiny bathrobe printed with big tropical flowers. Two bottles of prescription pills sat in front of her. Reggie hated the sickly yellow bottles.

"Same old, same old. How was the doctor?" she asked. She opened the fridge and took out a pitcher of iced tea. She gestured at the tea to her mother who shook her head.

"Same. Just refilled my pills and asked how I was doing, wanted to know how you were. I told him you were my angel, that I never have to worry about you because I know you're smart," Arlene said. Her smile glowed with love and affection, and Reggie knew she meant what she said.

Her mother didn't understand that sometimes Reggie wanted to be the kid, not the parent. She felt a stab of envy for John with his fussing mother and concerned father. "That's because I have my pitchfork in my other pair of jeans," Reggie teased.

Her mother laughed. "So, what are we having for dinner tonight?"

Reggie poured her tea and sat at the table. "Actually, I'm going to John's house for dinner and to study, so you're on your own tonight."

Sadness swept over Arlene's face. "Well, Regina," she said with forced brightness, "you tell John's mom 'hi' for me, okay?"

Reggie swallowed back tears at the sound of Regina and reached for her mother's hand. "Sure. We'll hang out tomorrow night, okay? I'll order pizza, and we'll watch Breakfast at Tiffany's."

Arlene's face lit with a genuine smile, and she squeezed Reggie's hand. "Sure, sweetness, that sounds nice."

Reggie grabbed her glass of tea and pushed away from the table. "I'm going to my room, unwind for a bit before I go to John's. I'll tell you when I'm leaving."

"Okay, I might go for a walk in the neighborhood, clear my head," Arlene said. She reached for one of the bottles, examining it.

It would take more than a walk to clear her mother's head, but Reggie replied, "Sure, Mom, the fresh air would do you good."

She ran up the stairs and closed her bedroom door, leaning against it for a moment. She placed her tea on a white wooden desk with faded pink flowers painted along its edges. Her bed stood in the middle of the room, sporting an old-fashioned wrought iron frame also painted white and a navy blue comforter hanging over the sides. Reggie had bought the blue comforter in defense of the overtly feminine room.

She flopped on her bed, sighing with pleasure as the mattress dipped and cradled her weight. Wrapping herself in soft navy folds, she snuggled into her pillow and closed her eyes. She promised herself she would only rest for a minute, but sleep pulled her under.

Once again she sat in the high-backed chair, her face turned toward the heat of the fire. The man sat across from her, his eyes probing her face. Reggie was surprised at how comfortable she felt, despite his scrutiny, as if she knew he held the answers she sought.

"I like your duster. It's pretty hot," she said, breaking the silence.

His eyebrows shot up and his following laughter made her smile. He ran a hand over the leather. "Well, that's not what I was expecting, but thank you. You're usually much more . . ." he paused, searching for the right word.

"Bratty?" Reggie supplied

He laughed again, the deep sound soothing her nerves. "I was going to say hostile. I don't think you're a brat. You've had a busy day. How did your research mission go? Did you find out how you revived that beetle?"

"No, but I plan on looking again tonight. Or maybe I wouldn't have to look if you'd just explain what's going on."

"Are you sure you're ready to know?" he asked.

Reggie gritted her teeth, holding onto her rapidly diminishing patience. "Yes! You told me you were here to help me. Well, here I am, Professor, enlighten me!"

"You're right. I did tell you I was here to help you." He sighed. "It's just people from your world are conditioned to think one way and information that doesn't fit their worldview is usually taken badly."

"Is something wrong with me?" she whispered.

"No," he assured her. "You're different than most people, but nothing is wrong with you. You see, you straddle two worlds. And the Other is finally showing you its face."

Reggie leaned forward, her elbows on her knees. "I don't understand. What two worlds?"

"Do you remember anything about your father?"

Surprised at the change of subject, she shook her head. Half-formed ideas flitted through her mind, but nothing took hold. "Not really. He went hiking in the woods behind the city when I was really young. He went missing. He was really handsome. He's smiling in all the pictures I've seen. I mean, he seemed like a happy guy." Reggie smiled briefly and then looked away. "My mom completely fell apart after he was gone."

"I'm sorry," the man said gently.

She looked at him as tears stung her eyes. She shrugged, embarrassed. "So what are you getting at? That my dad has something to do with what's happening to me? He's dead."

He fingered the scar on his face. "This might be hard for you to understand. Your father wasn't from here. He never was supposed to come here, but he was always headstrong, too curious for his own good, and very powerful," the man said with affection. "And once he met your mother . . . I knew he was never going to be whole living in our world again."

"What do you mean came here? Where is here? Who are you? What's your name so I can stop calling you Biker Guy!"

The man raised two large hands, palms flat in a conciliatory gesture. "Biker Guy? I've seen the motorcycles here, and I don't care for them, too smelly and loud. But you're right, it's time I introduce myself. Perhaps it's safe now. First choose a subject; your father or me."

"I want to know everything about my dad, since my mom won't talk about him. But even more than that, I need to know about the source of my information. So let's start with you."

He nodded in approval. "Wise choice. I knew Sebastian couldn't have made a stupid child."

The sound of her father's name almost made her forget her priorities. Reggie pushed temptation away and focused. "Thanks. Now spill."

"My name is Rhys Griffith. I'm your guardian. I'm here to offer you guidance and protection, to teach you. Your father and I were best friends," he explained. "He asked me to watch over you if anything happened to him, and I'm here to fulfill that promise."

She digested his statement, tasting bitterness. "Wow, Rhys, you're seventeen years too late with that, but thanks anyway."

She stood up to leave the room, but realized the futility of the gesture.

"Sit down," Rhys ordered.

Reggie sat. "Fine. Finish."

"I've been watching over you for years. How do you think I know so much about your life? I know you've had a difficult time, but I couldn't interfere. I didn't want to draw attention to you that might put you in danger."

"Put me in danger? Have you met my mother? I'm amazed I made it past elementary school!" Speaking those thoughts aloud made Reggie feel guilty, but she pushed past the guilt and focused on her anger.

"Your mother wasn't always this bad. I knew you weren't starving and you had shelter. Your mother is a good person—"

"I know my mother is a good person," Reggie interjected.

"Just a fragile one," Rhys finished. "Besides, the kind of danger I'm talking about is the deadly kind."

"If meeting you, my guardian, puts me in so much danger, why haven't you stayed away?"

"Because now I don't have a choice. And even now I haven't dared risk contacting you physically. Only in the Dream Realm do I feel secure enough to speak to you, and I'm still afraid I'll be caught."

"Why would someone want to hurt me?" she said.

"Because of your power, Regina; it's finally coming into being. As long as it was suppressed, no one would notice you, but now that it's out . . . well, let's just say that even where I'm from, one can sense the magic if one knows what to look for," Rhys explained. "You're the last of your kind, Reggie. You are your father's daughter."

"Whoa, magical power? I'm asleep right now. Is any of this real? Maybe John's right, and I made you up in my head to give me answers. Crazy answers!"

"You're not crazy. You've inherited your father's magic, his ability to draw power from the earth. How do you think you brought those creatures back to life? You have a gift that needs to be cultivated carefully, a gift—"

"A gift?" she interrupted. "I'm making dead animals come back to life, I've become an even bigger outcast at school, and now you're telling me that this freakish new power puts me in danger! What kind of gift is that?"

"Your father's gift," Rhys said. "It's your heritage, a part of you that you can't escape! You never got to know your father. You never got to meet him. Well, here's your chance to find out who he really was."

"Why was my father magical? Was he—was he human?"

Rhys regarded her a moment before answering. "Your father wasn't this world's idea of human because he was a magical being."

"Magic isn't supposed to be real." Reggie rubbed her throbbing head.

"Reggie, do you really believe that, after all you've experienced?"

"This is just a lot to deal with." She pulled her knees to her chest, wrapping her arms around her legs and resting her chin on her knees.

"I know it is, but unfortunately there's much more you need to hear," Rhys said. "I wish I could ease you into this, but the truth is we're running out of time. You are in danger, and I can't come there to help you, so you need to come to me."

She lifted her head. "Come where?"

"There are a small number of places that have doorways between your world and mine. Few people from your world know about them, but people from mine used to cross over often. They had to be discreet, of course, and they couldn't interfere with the order of things in your world. Soon after you were born, a war broke out and my people no longer crossed over. Some can still move through the doorways, but I can't breach the barriers. You can."

"What doorways? Where do you live?"

He took a deep breath. "Your reality, well, we refer to it as the Real. Magic no longer exists, except in the imagination. Science and technology are gods there. The Earth doesn't have the same importance for the people in the Real as it does for my kind. I'm from the Other, a place with a very different set of rules. Our magic, our society, is based on the elemental powers in nature. Each of us is born with different gifts, different strengths. Magic is our source of power. And this place, where we are now, is the Dream Realm. The Dream Realm is neutral ground, the only place where a bridge can be formed between the Other and the Real without physically crossing through a doorway. I can establish a link with your mind in the Dream Realm and communicate with you."

"There are three different realities? And one just exists in our dreams?" Reggie shook her head, meeting his eyes. "I can't go to you. Who's going to take care of my mom? I can't ditch school and my life to go off to some mythical place! Even for my own safety, and I'm still not convinced I'm not safe here."

"I'm afraid your mother will have to take care of herself and school will have to wait, because the danger to your life won't." Rhys sighed, stood up, and began pacing back and forth in front of the fireplace, his duster swirling around him. "Reggie, I need you to listen to me. As I said before, you have the ability to draw power from the earth, from the elements. This power is much greater than bringing a dead beetle or frog back to life. And this talent you have to revive things, it's unusual, to say the least. You've never had the proper training or the right environment for your ability to fully reveal itself.

"There's someone seeking you. He's extremely dangerous. He destroyed your people and he's not happy to discover you're alive. He'll find you and send his agents to bring you back to him. He'll kill you. He destroyed your father, and I made a promise that I wouldn't let him destroy you. You're the last of your kind that is alive. Your kind is a threat to him. Please, Regina, you need to let me help you."

"How do I know that you're not the man who killed my father? This could be a trap. I don't know you! You're just some guy who shows up in my dreams. Maybe you want me to come to you so you can kill me!"

"I never hurt your father, and I never would hurt you!" Rhys vowed with passion.

"Prove it! Tell me something about my father that only I would know. Then maybe I'll believe you."

Rhys rested his elbow on the marble mantelpiece. His eyes glowed with urgency, but his voice was patient when he spoke. "When your father met Arlene, it was late spring and she was walking through the forest. She was dirty and completely lost, and Sebastian told me he fell in love with the freckles on her shoulders."

Struck speechless by the story and the sound of her mother's name, Reggie struggled to find her voice. "What did he say to her?" she asked hoarsely.

"He didn't want to frighten her, so he asked if she was lost too, and suggested they work together to find their way back," Rhys paused, a smile curving his lips at the memory. "And this

29

part reminds me of you: your mother picked up a large stick and told your father that if he tried anything with her, she would bash his brains out and rip off his nuts. He managed to convince her, on the hike back, to have dinner with him and the rest is, as they say, history."

"Okay," she said. Her mother had told her a similar story, minus the nuts part. "I believe that you knew my father, now tell me who wants to kill me."

"Trust me, this man is a magic heavyweight, and he doesn't want me speaking to you. The magic I use to keep him from invading our connection is delicate. Normally, this location would be private to prying minds. Unless you're invited in, it takes a lot of power to rip into a Dream Construct. When I want to speak with you, I focus on your name, your essence, until I can forge a link. Then I create a Dream Construct where we can meet. So speaking his name is risky—if he concentrates, he can hear me say his name, even whisper it, and find us."

"That's not good enough, Rhys. I have a right to know. How can I trust you if you won't tell me?"

Their eyes locked. Rhys glowered at her but finally bowed his head. "You do have the right to know. His name is Andrius Drake, Master Mage of the Mages Council and Commander of the armed forces of Two Cities. He's a very powerful and ruthless man, and through my own intelligence networks, I've discovered that he's aware of your presence and is searching for you."

"Master Mage?" Reggie shook her head in denial. "Why would someone like that look for me? I can't be that important! I still don't understand what all this means—"

Suddenly, the air surrounding her began to ripple like the after-effects of a rock being thrown onto the smooth surface of a lake. A quiet buzzing started, grew with the intensity of a motorboat assaulting her ears. Reggie trembled as Rhys grabbed her, pulling her toward him slowly as if the ripples had current. His tall frame bent around her body, blocking her view and offering what protection he could as a wave of icy pain crashed into her. She screamed, and he shuddered.

"He's here," Rhys shouted in her ear. "He's breached my defenses, you need to leave now! I'll contact you again."

Oh God, she hurt. She felt like shards of ice were being thrust into her skin. Blackness began to descend. "Wait!" she cried. "How will you contact me?" She needed Rhys. He was her only guide through this terrifying new world, and she battled to stay conscious.

"I'll send someone from my world to you. Now wake up!"

Reggie clutched at him. "Promise? Promise!"

"I promise! Wake up!"

A dark whirlpool sucked her down and out. Reggie's eyes opened, meeting blackness. She couldn't breathe. An impenetrable layer wrapped around her body, drowning her, and she thrashed around in panic. Clenching the layer in two fists, she was surprised to feel softness. Reggie stopped moving. She relaxed her grip and cautiously felt along the material. The cocoon she was trapped in was her comforter. Shaky laughter burst from her as she began to unravel herself. Finally, cool air hit her face, and she gulped in its sweetness.

"What have I fallen into?" Reggie whispered. Sitting up, she discovered she was no longer on the bed but on the hard wooden floor. Between dreaming and waking, she must have rolled off. Pain shot through her lower back. Her chest was tight with the force of her breathing.

"It was just a dream, they can't get you here," she said aloud, trying to convince herself. But when she attempted to stand, the world tilted and she landed back on the comforter with a soft thud. The pain radiating from her temples to her toes was a stark reminder that nothing was what it seemed anymore. Dreams were all too real. Maybe Rhys was right; maybe she wasn't safe here anymore. Tucking her knees to her chest, Reggie rocked back and forth, tears rolling down her cheeks.

Chapter 6

*R*hys Griffith felt Reggie slip through his arms and return to her own reality. His protective spell had been shredded. Now Andrius Drake strode toward him through a gaping black hole. A foul odor like rotting meat preceded the dark mage as he raised his hand to attack. Rhys braced himself. Andrius' magic hit him hard, but Rhys' leather duster was warded with defensive spells and absorbed most of the impact.

Rhys connected his mind to the Earth, harnessing its energy. "Entangle!" he commanded.

Vines with large, curved thorns shaped like hooks burst through the floor of the dreamscape and wrapped around Andrius' legs, digging into his flesh. Rhys watched with satisfaction as blood stained the dark mage's pants.

"You use their magic almost as if you were one of them. Almost. Rhys, old friend, this will only stop me momentarily," Andrius said, amusement infusing his voice.

"As will anything you throw at me. You're not the only one who can inflict pain."

"You've already led me to her, and now I've cut off your communication. I must thank you for that."

"She's strong, like her father," Rhys said.

"And look what happened to him. Goodbye, Rhys."

Rhys watched as a hazy shadow swirled around Andrius, pulling him from the room. Rhys curbed his rage as he quickly cut his dream connection. He woke abruptly, his eyes meeting the slanted ceiling of his cabin in the Other. Slowly he stood up, stretching his limbs to work out the dull aches that still resonated. He smiled, knowing that Andrius had his own wounds. The smile faded. Reggie was in even more danger.

Rhys stepped outside the cabin. An icy breeze rolled off Hornsbay, which lay a mile to the east. Faded sunlight softened the rough edges of the makeshift village in front of him. Rhys and his followers had fled to Hornsbay Forest and settled here after the war with Andrius. The dark mage may have won the war, but they still carried on the Resistance from the safety of the forest. Barracks occupied the east side of the settlement and civilian homes occupied the west. In between lay a school, a small hospital, and a large storage shed that held supplies that were rationed out to the villagers.

Rhys wove through them to the center of the settlement where two men and two women sat in a circle, eyes closed in concentration. They served as the perimeter guard, their purpose to stop Andrius' soldiers from entering the forest. Fiona, their leader, possessed the greatest magical ability. She linked their four minds together to cast the defensive spell that created an opaque mist, which formed a barrier between Andrius' soldiers' camp on the edge of Hornsbay Forest and the Resistance force. If the soldiers ventured into the mist, they would lose all sense of direction and memory of why they were there. Remaining too long in the mist would then bring on paranoia, and eventually madness. Many soldiers infected by the spell had ended up killing each other.

Fiona would switch the guard in fifteen minutes, but Rhys needed them to hold the spell longer. Any break in routine was the weakest part of their defense system.

"Fiona," he whispered. "Fiona," he repeated a little louder, careful not to startle her. Her eyelids fluttered open, and she fixed him with a dazed stare.

"Mmhmm," she murmured. She rocked her body from side to side.

"Don't switch the guard until I come back. I have business to take care of," Rhys said.

Her eyes focused and she nodded. "Of course. Should we be worried?"

"I don't think so, but I'm not taking chances." Rhys gave her a reassuring smile and strode swiftly away from the village and deeper into the forest. He paused, tuning his ears past the rustling of creatures in the undergrowth. Rhys dropped his mental shields and opened his consciousness. There it was; a painful noise that was half wailing, half shrieking, and all hopeless rage and despair. It amazed him that the animals in the woods had found a way to ignore the sound without magic. Concentrating harder, Rhys found the particular sound he sought and moved toward it.

CHAPTER 7

*A*sher crouched into the shadows of the hedges separating Reggie's yard from her neighbors', watching as she came out of the house. Suddenly she jabbed the air with vicious strikes, her fists hitting the same spot again and again. Her precision shocked him. He reminded himself not to be deceived by her slender, fragile appearance.

Andrius had assured Asher that he wouldn't have to hurt her, just persuade her to come back with him. But Asher hadn't expected her wariness. It would take a lot to convince her, and he refused to use violence unless it was a last resort. He dreamed of murdering his master daily, but the thought of harming this intriguing girl repulsed him.

Asher needed an opportunity to approach Reggie and he didn't want his otherness putting her off. He had to adjust to the strange smells and sights of the Real. He had enough human in his blood to pass as one, but the gold collar was difficult to disguise, and he'd spent most of the previous day observing the behavior of others so he wouldn't seem out of place. Reggie stepped off the porch and sprinted away. Asher moved from the shadows and silently hurried after her. Increasing his pace, he caught a glimpse of her down the hill. He would deduce how to meet her later; right now he just needed to keep up.

Chapter 8

*R*eggie sat on John's front steps. Her body ached. John sat quietly beside her, shoulder to shoulder. She'd just finished telling him about her latest nightmare. They stared out at the street lit with harsh fluorescent lamps, Reggie's eyes on the shadows. The darkness never used to bother her. She knew bad things were just as likely to strike in daylight. Evil didn't have a preference, just an appetite.

"So I was right about the magic thing," John finally said. "I really hate being right."

"I should've swiped a kitchen knife before I came here. I'd feel safer with a weapon."

"Do you think this guy Andrius' agents are here?"

"After Andrius tore into my dream and started—they might be. I made sure Mom double-locked everything before I left, made up a story about a prowler in the neighborhood. She was so freaked I'd get jumped again it took me forever to leave."

"You don't look so good." John asked. "How do you feel?"

"Like I was body slammed by an MMA fighter, but I'll be fine." She rubbed her arms for comfort. "John, maybe you should keep your distance for a while. I couldn't take it if something happened to you."

He leaned closer, catching her words. "You know I won't. You can't handle this on your own. It's too much with your mom and everything. I can deal."

She knew it was selfish, but she was grateful he wouldn't leave her. Her throat tightened, and she nodded.

"Reggie, do you trust Rhys?"

"I know it's hard to swallow, but right now what Rhys told me is the only thing I have to go on. And he knew all that stuff about my dad and mom that no one else knows."

John slung his arm over her shoulder. "There's no other way he could've found that out?"

"No, it's not like Mom goes around telling that story. She has a hard time talking about Dad," Reggie said. "And Rhys tried to protect me when Andrius attacked us. He didn't have to do that; if he wanted to hurt me, that was a great opportunity."

"True. Well, doing research is pointless now." He swept the street with his eyes. "That somebody could be watching us creeps me out. So what now? You just gonna wait around until Rhys' guy contacts you?"

"I don't know what to do. I don't have enough information." She bit her lip. "You know what, let's keep looking. Maybe this Other exists on some website we haven't looked at yet. If I don't do something, I'll go crazy!"

John scraped the toe of his sneaker along the concrete. "Let's look tomorrow. I'll walk you home." He stood up.

Reggie looked at him. "I know I'm in pain, but I can manage."

He arched an eyebrow. "I know, ass-kicker, but I'd feel better."

She decided not to be stupid, and nodded. They walked out of John's neighborhood and into an area filled with small family businesses and coffee shops. They crossed the street as the bright red pedestrian light blinked. Dashing across the intersection, they made it onto the opposite sidewalk. Tires screeched behind them, followed by a sickening thud.

Reggie whirled and watched in shock as a man rolled off the hood of a black SUV and hit the pavement. Other vehicles slid to a halt, while some swerved to avoid the still figure. Reggie saw the panicked driver looking for an escape route. Running into the street, she wove through the cluster of cars toward the SUV.

"Hey! Hey, asshole! Don't even think about it!"

The driver's window was down, and a man stuck his head out, his face wild. "He came out of nowhere. It was a green light!"

"Yeah, then you've got nothing to run away from, and I've got your license plate number." Reggie reached the side of the vehicle. She felt John grip her shoulder. "Don't let him go anywhere," she told John, and then knelt on the ground by the victim. He was lying on his side, his body still.

John leaned against the driver's side of the car and whipped out his cell phone. "He's not leaving, are you, buddy? Hello? Yeah, I have an emergency . . ."

Touching the young man's neck gently above his shirt collar, Reggie checked for a pulse. A strong, steady beat tattooed her fingertips, and she sighed in relief. She moved closer and spoke in his ear. "Hey, can you hear me?" A hand shot out, gripping her wrist, and she jerked back in surprise. The man moaned as he rolled onto his back. Green eyes met hers. She'd seen a cat once with eyes that same deep shade, but she'd never seen anything like that on a human. "Sorry, sorry, you startled me. How many fingers am I holding up?"

His cloudy eyes cleared as they focused on her. "Two," he answered correctly, his voice colored with an unfamiliar accent. Recognition flitted across his handsome face.

"That proves you can count. I hope it means your head's okay," Reggie said. "No, don't sit up!" He had braced his weight on his elbows in a jerky motion, and she put a restraining hand on his solid chest. "I don't know how badly you're injured. Can you tell me where you hurt?"

He remained propped on his elbows. "My side hurts . . . and my head a little, but I think I'm okay." He looked down at her hand, and she moved it. "I need to get up."

"A car just hit you! You need to stay still until an ambulance gets here. You might have internal injuries or something," Reggie protested, her hand going back on his chest. Warm muscle moved under her fingertips, and she quickly pulled her hand away.

"I don't think that's likely," he replied, but his breathing was labored.

"Best not to take chances. I'm Reggie and that's my friend John." She waved in John's direction.

"I'm Asher," the man said. He balanced his weight on one elbow and offered her a large hand. She shook it, impressed and exasperated by his manners. His palm was warm and callused, as if he regularly performed manual labor. "What kind of name is Reggie?"

Reggie dropped his hand. His eyes never left hers. "It's short for Regina. Please lie back down."

Asher shook his head. "I need to get up."

"Now's not the time to play macho man! Just wait until the EMT gets here. John, how long?"

"They said ten minutes, probably less," John said. He stood behind her now, peering over her shoulder. A small crowd of people had gathered, forming a ring surrounding them and the SUV. The driver couldn't get away now.

She turned back to the stranger. "See, only ten minutes. Do you need to call your family?"

"Macho man?" he looked confused, and Reggie flushed. "I don't have any family here. I'll wait, but I'm standing. Can you help me? I'll do it with or without you. It will just be easier with you."

"Okay, take it easy," she said, exasperated. "John, give me a hand?"

"Sure, but I don't think it's a good idea." John moved to Asher's other side.

They both slid a shoulder under the crook of his armpits and together lifted him as gently as they could from the pavement. But he was heavy, and they could only lift him so far.

A hiss escaped from his lips as he leaned against the SUV. "You okay?" Reggie asked, looking for signs of blood.

"No, but I will be." Warm green eyes searched her face, and he started to speak but then glanced at John and stopped.

Reggie watched the driver slide out of his vehicle, slamming the door. John stepped in front of him. "The cops are coming." A faint siren wailed in the distance, growing louder. "Stay right there."

She looked back at Asher and guessed he was nineteen, possibly twenty. She still couldn't place that soothing, melodic accent. "Are you sure you don't want to sit down? You don't look so good." Even in the dim light his skin looked ashen. She shivered in the damp air, wishing the ambulance would hurry.

"I'm positive." Asher smiled. "Don't worry, I'll be fine. I just need a minute."

Reggie just shook her head. She saw blue and red lights dance across Asher's face as the sirens' volume blasted her ears. Two EMTs spilled out of the ambulance, pushing a stretcher. They hurried to the scene, followed by a couple police officers.

"Everybody stay put until we get your statement!" an older officer yelled as he walked over, his gut sloshing as he moved.

A skinny, short paramedic reached their circle first. "Who's the injured party here?" he asked.

Reggie pointed to Asher. "He is."

John grabbed her elbow and they moved out of the way. "I guess we're stuck here."

Reggie nodded. An urge to stay near Asher tugged at her. His eyes were on her as he answered the officer's questions while the paramedics examined him. "I don't have identification on me, I'm sorry," she heard him say.

"Reggie, they're insisting I go with them. Can you come with me?" Asher called to her. He looked uncertain and frustrated.

"Sure, if they'll let me." She understood his predicament; it was scary to ride in an ambulance alone. "Excuse me, officer? Excuse me, sir, but can I ride with him to the hospital?"

The older officer turned to her. "Have you given your statement, miss?" She shook her head. "Are you immediate family?"

"No."

"Then you'll have to stay put until we get to you." His lined face was stern. Reggie nodded.

"Come on, sir, let's get you checked out," a paramedic said. She and her partner walked Asher to the ambulance. Asher looked back at Reggie, his eyes panicked.

"Wait, can't she come with me? I need to talk to—" his voice was cut off as the paramedics loaded him into the vehicle and shut the doors.

"They're taking him to St. Luke's. You can see him when you're finished here," the police officer said with a reassuring smile.

Something didn't feel right. The way Asher looked at her as if he knew her. The guy just got nailed by a car, it's nothing, she told herself. But the feeling sank into her gut like an anchor too heavy to pull up.

Reggie hated hospitals. She hated the smell of disinfectant that barely disguised the odor of disease. She hated the stark white walls and the harsh, bright lights. As she walked to the front desk, she tried not to think about the last time she'd been there, and she focused on Asher. The way he looked at her, his familiarity. She knew she needed to make sure he was safe. He'd seemed so lost.

Reggie stopped in front of the receptionist's desk and wiped damp palms on her jeans. The receptionist wore bubblegum pink glasses and sat behind a sliding glass window.

The glass door slid open. "Can I help you, miss?" she asked.

"Yeah, there was an accident victim brought in here about an hour ago, he'd been hit by a car. His name is Asher."

"Last name?"

"I don't know," Reggie said. The woman raised an eyebrow.

"If you're not family and you don't have a last name, I really can't—" the woman began.

"Look, I was there at the scene and helped him until the paramedics came. I just want to make sure he's okay." Heat crept up her cheeks.

The receptionist studied her and then sighed. "Let me see what I can find."

"Thanks," Reggie said, rocking from one foot to the other as the woman slid the window closed and picked up her phone.

After a few moments, the door slid open. "Your guy is interesting. He claimed he didn't remember his last name, didn't fill out any forms, and left before the doctor released him."

"He just left? After being hit by a car?"

"I'm sorry, I hope he's okay," she said.

"Me too." Reggie drummed her fingers on the desk, her lips pursed. "Thanks, I appreciate it." She gave the woman a polite smile.

"Sure."

Reggie left the hospital, wondering where Asher was now. Was he lying on the side of the road somewhere? None of my business, she thought. Her responsibility ended here. She forcefully pushed her worry to the back of her mind.

Chapter 9

Black charcoal stained Reggie's fingers and the palms of her hands as she smeared shadowy contours on her still life drawing in art class. Two days had passed since her nightmarish encounter with Rhys and Andrius and her meeting with Asher. Reggie knew the events were unrelated, but they kept mixing together in her mind. And Rhys was gone. Now when she slept—when she could sleep—all that awaited her was a deafening silence. Her pain had faded, but her paranoia grew. She needed answers now more than ever. Did Andrius know where she lived? Would he hurt her mom? And when would Rhys' guide show up?

She glanced down at her drawing and grimaced at the mess she'd made. She needed a break. Shuffling to the sink, she moved past Josh Reynolds, his Zippo lighter snapping shut with an audible click. Josh was built like a spider monkey, all arms and legs. He was part of Mark Millan's posse of bullies, and since the frog incident, Reggie had become their new object of torture.

Ignoring Josh, she continued to the sink at the back of the room. She was reaching for the faucet handle when she saw it. A moth lay on its side, the weight of its fuzzy body resting on one large wing while the other wing stuck out at an angle. Its abdomen was flattened. Mint green wings dotted with light pink reminded her of a pastel watercolor. Reggie felt a kinship with the creature. She couldn't control her situation, but she could help the moth. Without thinking, she stroked one of the velvety wings.

An electric jolt sizzled up her arm, robbing her of what energy she had left. Gasping, she watched the moth as it twitched. A muffled curse spun her around, and she locked eyes with Josh Reynolds. His lighter dangled from his fingers, slack-jawed like its owner.

"Shit," she whispered, fear growing at his horrified expression. He looked from the flapping moth to her, his eyes wide.

"You really are a freak."

Josh shoved her out of the way, reaching for the moth with a clawed hand. Realizing his intent, her fear of discovery vanished and blind rage took its place. Jerking him away from the moth, Reggie swept her heel behind his ankle and toppled him to the floor.

Josh lay sprawled on the tiles for a moment. "Bitch!" he spat, scrambling to his feet.

He lunged toward her, and Reggie readied for impact when a large figure rushed between them, catching Josh hard.

"That's enough!" Mr. Williams, the art teacher, shouted as Josh struggled against him.

"She's a crazy bitch, she's—" Josh began, but Mr. Williams' cold voice stopped him.

"She's half your size!" He removed his hands from Josh's shoulders and looked at her. "You okay?"

"Yes," Reggie answered him, staring down at her sneakers.

Mr. Williams nodded, looking them both over. The classroom had gone silent. Reggie kept her eyes trained on the floor, waiting for Mr. Williams' judgment.

"Josh, you're coming with me to the principal's office, now! You can explain to her why you were trying to hit a girl," Mr.

Williams said, and a few snickers scattered across the room. "Go sit down, Reggie. I'll talk to you when I come back."

"Okay," she said.

"Josh, let's go." Mr. Williams gestured to the door.

"Your ass is mine," Josh hissed at her as he walked by. Reggie stared back at him, her expression icy.

She watched them leave and then returned to her seat. She kept her head high, locking eyes with each person who looked at her. Showing weakness wasn't an option. Sliding into her chair, she picked up her charcoal and began drawing again.

After Mr. Williams came back, he asked her to stay after school to help him clean up the studio. Now almost four o'clock, it was time to go home, rest, and meet John for another research session. Grabbing her backpack, she took a side exit out of the building.

The faculty parking lot was abandoned except for a few cars. Reggie rummaged through her backpack for her old MP3 player as she crossed the lot. The dream of owning an i-anything was still out of reach. Every penny she earned from her summer job went toward her college fund. Her head buried in her backpack, Reggie tripped on a lump of asphalt and fell hard on her knees. Cursing, she started gathering the books now spread out around her. Footsteps approached from behind, but she ignored them until they stopped a few feet away. A warning shiver chilled her skin, but she calmly rearranged the books in her pack to hide her fear.

"My, my, we're a clumsy little bunny, aren't we?" came the syrupy voice of Shelley Michaels.

"Little bunny—don't you mean little freak?" Mark Millan replied. Reggie got to her feet slowly and turned around. Shelley stood next to Mark, with Josh Reynolds flanking her other side.

"Told you I'd get you back." Josh bared his teeth at her, playing with his lighter.

Reggie stared at the lighter. Her heart thudded in her ears. They couldn't know she was afraid. "Shelley, you're coming down in the world. I didn't think you'd be caught dead with these two. An A-lister hanging with the B crowd? What will everyone think?" She shifted her pack from her shoulder to her right hand.

"You're not even on a list. You're not even a blip on the radar," Shelley said, and the two boys laughed. Mark and Josh moved away from Shelley's side, loosely boxing Reggie in. Josh slid the lighter into the pocket of his jeans.

"And you, Mark, Shelley's been making fun of you since kindergarten. Did she flash you her tits? Did you get a little something in the janitor's closet? I guess it's classier than the boy's locker room," Reggie said, eyeing the two boys.

"You bitch!" Shelley hissed. "You're just a psycho with a drunk mom who does weird shit to animals!"

Reggie caught Mark and Josh in her peripheral vision closing in on her as Shelley charged forward. Gripping her backpack, she swung right, hitting Mark in the face. He yelped, and his bulky frame folded. Her elbow crunched into the cartilage of Josh's nose. Reggie felt power rise within her. Suddenly Josh howled as yellow flames shot from his pocket. Shelley stopped. For a heartbeat, she and Shelley stood there stunned, watching Josh dig for the lighter in his pocket with one hand while patting the flames with the other. Droplets of blood flew from his nose with his frantic motion. Breathing hard, Reggie wondered if she could have possibly caused the fire to—but that thought was cut short as Shelley recovered from her shock and surged forward again.

If Reggie could get through Shelley, she was pretty sure she could outrun the rest. Long, pink manicured nails formed into claws aimed at her face. Blocking with her left arm, she ignored the slicing pain of the tiny daggers and delivered a solid punch into Shelley's face. Shelley's scream rang in her ears, and Reggie turned to run.

She made it two whole strides before Josh lunged and grabbed her ankle. The pavement slammed into her, knocking the breath from her lungs as she skidded to a stop. Pain shot across her knees and side as hands jerked her back up. Josh's bleeding face met hers, his expression feral like a rabid animal. Mark's stout, strong arms entangled with hers from behind.

"What did you do to me?" Josh said.

"I'm going to scar that pretty face of yours!" Shelley shrieked.

Reggie watched as Shelley drew her fist back. She tensed, waiting for the blow. It never came. Josh's body was thrown into Shelley and together they toppled over like stacked dominos. Mark released Reggie and she fell to her knees again. Sucking in air, she glimpsed a tall figure rush at Mark with blurry speed. If Mark tried to defend himself, it was a wasted effort. His body sailed through the air, landing twenty feet away.

Reggie looked over at the crumpled forms of Shelley and Josh. Josh began to stir, his eyes wide as he blinked and attempted to sit up. Her view was blocked as the stranger bent in front of her and dragged Josh away, his feet dangling unnaturally. She shrank back at the gurgling sound he made.

"Come near her again, and I won't stop until I've beaten you into a broken, bloody pulp. Do you understand?" The voice was rough with menace. Josh emitted a squeak. "What was that? I can't hear you."

"Yes," Josh choked out. His body fell at the stranger's feet.

Faded denim filled her vision as gentle fingers touched the side of her face. "Are you okay?" the stranger asked.

Reggie looked up into Asher's green eyes. Shocked, she said hoarsely, "I've been better."

"Here, let me help you up. You might have broken something," Asher said, lifting her to her feet. She grabbed his forearms for balance, hissing at the sharp sting in her palms.

"Thank you." She resisted the urge to cling to him. "I don't know what they would've done if you hadn't . . ." Her throat clogged with tears, and she wrapped her arms around her body.

"We should leave." Asher glanced around the parking lot. "It would be bad if someone found us." He picked her backpack off the ground and slung it over his shoulder.

Reggie nodded. She was relieved to see him, but she had questions. Like how he had managed to throw a two-hundred-pound teenager after being hit by a car? And how had he found her?

Asher moved with a nimble quickness toward the sidewalk leading off campus. She followed, but was hobbled by pain in her knees. Suddenly two strong arms scooped her up; one tucked under her knees, the other curving across her back. Surprised, Reggie gripped Asher's neck. His body bulged with muscle, warm and firm against her.

She dropped her hands and pushed against his shoulders as he carried her. "I can walk."

"But you can't walk fast enough," Asher said.

Reggie admired his speed as he darted down the sidewalk, the school fading from her vision. Asher took a sharp turn a few blocks away into a residential neighborhood.

"You're really tall," she observed, watching the ground whirl by.

"I apologize, it's a fault of mine."

She laughed. "Look, I'm grateful that you saved me, but I need some answers. And you can put me down now. People are staring."

Asher stopped and looked into her eyes. The space between them seemed to shrink. She glanced away. He lowered her with care, keeping her backpack.

"Better?" his voice was soft.

"Yeah." Reggie began walking slowly, and he fell into pace beside her. "You move good for a guy who got crunched by a car."

"I have a few broken ribs, some bruising. It's nothing," he shrugged, his eyes on the sidewalk.

"Asher, I've had a few broken ribs. You can't move like that. You threw someone across a parking lot! You have magic healing powers or something?" It was a joke, but her heart galloped when he flinched at the word magic. She grabbed his arm.

"What?" he asked. "Why are you looking at me like that?"

Reggie's eyes widened. The night of the accident flashed by, and she heard Rhys' promise that he would send a guide. And who'd shown up directly after? Asher. She'd always known something was different about him with his mysterious accent and eyes. The feats of strength he'd displayed. The way she was drawn to him that wasn't just about his beautiful face.

"You're Rhys' guide! That's why you've been following me. That's why you wanted to talk to me the other night. You're from the Other!"

Asher sputtered, "How did you—?"

"Rhys told me he'd send someone, just not when. I'm so stupid. I should've seen it sooner!"

Asher mussed his black hair, and Reggie discovered that his ears were pointed. "You're not stupid. How could you have known?"

He closed his eyes, lifting his face to the sky. The afternoon sunlight glittered off a metallic object poking out from his shirt collar. Reggie squinted trying to see what it was, but his head snapped back and his gaze bored into hers. "I've been following you for a few days. I wasn't sure how to approach you because I didn't want to frighten you. I didn't know how much . . . Rhys had told you, and I couldn't risk you not believing me."

"I guess your dream contact has been cut off too?" Reggie asked softly. He was far from home and alone in a strange place. She'd be scared shitless.

"It's been difficult. I'm sure you have a lot of questions for me—"

"You have no idea! I don't know where to start—"

Asher picked up her hands, silencing her. His touch was delicate as he examined her palms. His eyes roved over her body, lingering on her bloody knees and the scrape on her face. "I'll tell you what I can, but first we need to bandage these cuts. How far is your home?"

"Ten minutes by bus." Reggie was uncertain about taking him to her house, but he already knew where she lived. "Can you tell me on the way?"

"We shouldn't discuss this in public. People have been watching since I stopped. If we start talking about magic and other worlds, there might trouble." He nodded in the direction of a middle-aged man who stood in the driveway nearest them. His eyes moved from Reggie to Asher, his face stamped with suspicion.

Reggie combed her fingers through her hair, covering the injured side of her face. "Yeah, I guess you're right. The last thing we need is the cops."

"How far is this . . . bus?" Asher grimaced. "It wouldn't be my first choice in transportation. If we were in the Other, I'd simply pick you up and run. I'm still fast here, but I'm less so. The energy is different, and I don't know my limitations. I don't like it."

"That sucks, not knowing what you can do anymore. I'd hate that," Reggie said. "Come on, the bus is just a few blocks away."

Chapter 10

*R*eggie led Asher into her driveway. Her pain had gone from boil to simmer, but the glimpses she'd caught of herself in the window of the bus weren't pretty. Sober or not, her mother was sure to flip.

Asher ran his eyes over her body again and her stomach dipped. "You need to clean your wounds."

"They won't kill me. Listen, if my mom comes out while we're talking, let me deal with it. I'm going to have to explain this." She pointed to the side of her face and then her ripped jeans. "And I'm going to have to explain you."

"Tell her the truth."

"Tell my mom I got jumped by bullies? Sure, let's just push her over the edge."

"What do you mean?"

Reggie didn't like talking about her mother with anyone except John. "Nothing. I guess I can tell her a version of the truth."

Asher eyed her then shrugged. "Okay."

"As for you, you came, you saved, and you took me home. If my mom asks why you're still here, I've invited you for pizza as a thank you."

"I appreciate the gesture," he said dryly.

She felt her face redden. She stopped him in front of the porch. "Seriously, Asher, thanks for stepping in before those jerks ripped me apart. I got lucky this time, not like last time.

Feel this." She reached for his hand, placing his fingers along her hairline.

He caressed the thin, jagged scar. "What happened?"

Reggie shivered. "When I was thirteen, I got jumped in the bathroom at a mall by some older girls. They slammed my head into a mirror, kicked the shit out of me. All for a measly twenty bucks."

"They're the ones who broke your ribs?" She nodded and he dropped his hand, balling it into a fist. "I wish I'd been there to stop it."

"Me too. Come on." Reggie winced as she climbed the steps. She felt him watching and gave a limp smile. He frowned.

Reaching out to cup her cheek, he ran a gentle thumb over the scrape. She sucked in air through her teeth. He arched a brow. "I didn't save you just so you could get an infection. Go on, clean up, I'll wait for you."

Reggie looked at his crossed arms and stubborn mouth. "Fine. I'll sneak inside, get the first aid kit and bandage up out here, okay?"

"It's an acceptable compromise." Asher smiled.

She rolled her eyes. "I'll be right back."

The front door swung open, and her mother stepped onto the porch.

"Honey! I thought I heard you out here. Why are you so late?" Arlene's words were clear, lacking their habitual slur. She cradled an oversized coffee cup in her hand.

Her mother was sober, and Reggie was injured, with a stranger. "Hey, Mom—"

"Who are you?" Her eyes shifted between Reggie and Asher in confusion before focusing on Reggie's face. Gasping, she tossed the coffee mug over the porch railing and pulled Reggie close. "What happened to you?"

58

"Ease up, Ma, I'm sore," she said, and her mother's grip loosened. "Some kids jumped me after school, tried to take my backpack."

Her mother snared her in a crushing grip again. "Are you okay? Do you need to go to the emergency room?" Reggie watched Arlene glower at Asher. "Who the hell are you and why are you with my daughter?"

"Mom, this is Asher. He saw me being attacked and saved me. Then he got me home. Thanks to him, I'm not in the hospital."

Asher's eyes were wary as he looked at Arlene. He shuffled his feet. "I just did what anyone would've done."

Arlene released Reggie, taking both his hands in hers. "Not everyone would've helped her. Thanks for stepping in and saving my baby," she said, her eyes glistening.

Asher's shoulders relaxed, but his smile was strained. "You're welcome." Letting go of Arlene's hands, he shoved his own deep into his pockets.

Taking pity on him, Reggie called to her mother, "Mom, I need to clean up. Is it okay if Asher stays for dinner?"

"Of course, it's the least I can do to thank him." Arlene dashed a hand across her eyes. "Come inside, the both of you, and I'll get the bandages."

"Okay, Mom, just stop crying." But Reggie basked in her concern, in the rare feeling of not being in charge.

They followed Arlene to the kitchen. "Sit down. I'll be right back with some gauze and peroxide."

"Mom, the first aid kit is in the upstairs bathroom," Reggie told her as she slid into a kitchen chair. Asher took the seat next to her.

"Okay." Arlene disappeared through the kitchen archway.

Reggie lowered her voice. "We have some time. Tell me your deal." At his questioning look, she amended, "You know, your role in all this."

Asher moved his face closer to hers. "My role is actually small. When I was chosen for this mission, I wasn't given a lot of information about who you were, just enough for me to find you. I'm in the service of the Mages' Council, a courier of sorts."

"So finding me is part of your job? I was under the impression that I'm a big, dirty secret."

"You are. I'm not explaining this correctly." Asher braced his elbows on the table. "The political situation in the Other is unstable right now. There's a Resistance trying to overthrow the current government and establish a new one. Rhys is part of the Resistance. The Mages' Council is not."

"But if you work for the Council, why would Rhys send you?"

"I might serve the Council, but I don't agree with their laws or the way they enforce them. I was in the ideal position to come for you."

"Oh, I get it. You're a double agent."

"You could call me that. I'm a rebel sympathizer."

Reggie shook her head. "Won't the Council notice you're gone?"

"I'm supposed to be traveling right now on an errand for the Council. No one will notice if I'm gone for a few days. It's the perfect cover."

"What happens if your cover is blown? What happens to me if I'm with you?"

His throat muscles worked as he swallowed. "I can't fail this mission." Asher dropped his eyes, staring at the table.

She clasped his shoulder, wanting to comfort him. He glanced up at her in surprise. A loud crash caused them both to jump. "Mom, are you okay?" she yelled.

"Fine, the damn towel rack fell!" her mother called back.

Reggie turned back to Asher, noticing his carefully neutral expression. "Tell me how I fit into this."

He shrugged. "I just know I'm supposed to bring you back. That Rhys wants you and that you're very important."

"Yeah, Rhys wants me alive, and Andrius Drake wants me dead. What about the Council? They after me too?" He cringed at the sound of Andrius Drake's name.

"What do you know about Andrius Drake?"

Footsteps sounded in the hall, interrupting Reggie's reply. A few seconds later, her mother walked into the room. She held up a bottle of hydrogen peroxide and a plastic bag full of cotton balls.

"Okay, start with this. I'm going to find some bandages and ointment, they've disappeared." Arlene placed the bag and bottle on the table.

"Thanks, Mom, you're the best." Reggie ripped open the plastic bag as her mother left the kitchen.

Asher grabbed the bag from her hand. "Here, I'll clean you up. Do I use this?" He gestured at the bottle of hydrogen peroxide. She nodded.

"I can do it myself."

"I know you can, but you've had a rough day, and I want to, okay?"

She wanted to tell him rough days were normal, but his tender expression stopped her. "Okay."

"Lean closer. Andrius Drake, you know about him?" he repeated as he saturated a cotton ball, dabbing her injured cheek.

She hissed and he murmured an apology. "Unfortunately we've met but—wait! If we say his name, can he show up here?" Her body trembled.

"No, he can't enter this reality," Asher assured her. "Finished, now let me see your knee. Has he been stalking your dreams?"

"He crashed my dream with Rhys and attacked us. I don't know what he did, but it hurt like hell."

"He's a very powerful mage. He likes to inflict pain." He glanced up, seeing her panic, and quickly added, "Honestly, he can't come here." Scooting back his chair, he reached for her injured leg, hooking it over his lap.

"Good." Reggie's body relaxed into his touch until he spoke again.

"But his agents can. You must come back with me," Asher said as he cleaned her knee. "Your family, your friends will all be targets. He can trace you from the Dream Realm. He'll send his soldiers and won't stop until he captures you."

"Are his soldiers already here?"

Asher stilled. "I don't know. But you shouldn't wait around until they find you."

"Can't you protect me? I can't leave my mom. I'm all she has, okay? I have my life to think about!"

"I understand your need to protect your mother, but I'm thinking about your life and hers. I can't stay here and neither can you. Whatever magic you have that is attracting all this attention, it's not going away. You know that. Come with me."

After her encounter with Andrius in the Dream Realm, Reggie knew she'd have to leave. She'd escaped only because Rhys had shielded her. When Andrius' soldiers came, she'd have no defense against them. No way to protect her mother or John. They'd only be safe when she was gone. "Yeah, okay."

"I know this is happening very fast, but I believe you'll be safer in the Other." He reached for one of her hands lying on the table. His other hand remained on her knee, and he rubbed his thumb against her skin.

Reggie pulled away from him. "Let me tell you what I can do."

"What does that have to do—"

"If you're going to be ass-deep in alligators with me, you should have all the facts, or at least as much as I know. Maybe I can do different stuff in the Other, but what I can do here is kinda creepy."

Asher frowned. "Tell me."

"I bring dead things back to life. Bugs, and a frog once," she said, embarrassed.

He stood up so abruptly his chair rocked. His skin blanched white, his eyes wild.

"What? What's wrong?"

Asher tore his gaze from hers. "I wish I didn't know."

She blinked back tears. "I really am a freak if you react this way."

"Reggie, I don't think you're a freak. It's just that your kind is a legend in the Other. I never, ever thought I'd live to see an Aether Mage."

Rhys' words came rushing back to her. The last of her kind, he'd told her. "Is that what I am? An Aether Mage?" She rolled around the name in her head relieved to finally have an identity.

"Yes, I believe so. The power you have . . ." Awe soaked his voice.

Reggie's skin prickled. "Raising dead bugs doesn't seem very powerful."

"You give life. That's the pinnacle of power."

"'Cause someone needs an army of bugs?"

"Do you really think your magic only extends to giving life to insects?"

"You tell me. I have no idea what an Aether Mage can do!"

"You possess a connection with the Earth and can control its four elements: Earth, Air, Water, and Fire. That means you can wield and manipulate life forces," Asher explained. "I've heard rumors that some Aether Mages developed special abilities, like reanimating the dead. You have a rare talent. I also think your magic hasn't developed more because this reality dampens it."

Her mind replayed the image of Josh's pocket shooting flames. "You think my magic will be stronger in the Other?"

"Yes. The Real blocks most of your magic, but the Other is all magical energy. I'm slower here, and I don't feel connected to the Earth. In the Other, I could've outrun that car. Most importantly, Reggie, Andrius sees you as a threat. That tells you how powerful you really are."

She heard the stairs creak. Her mother would join them in seconds. "When do you want to leave?" she whispered.

"Tomorrow afternoon, I'll come for you. Can you be ready by then?"

"I guess so," she replied when her mother sailed back into the kitchen brandishing bandages and a yellow tube of ointment.

"Found them! Let's order some pizza," Arlene said.

"I'm so sorry, but I can't stay for dinner. Thank you for the offer." Asher stood, looking at Reggie. "I'll see you later."

"Later," Reggie echoed. He hurried from the room.

"What was that all about?" Arlene asked.

Reggie shook her head. "Nothing. Let's order the pizza, pig out, and watch Breakfast at Tiffany's." She'd pack her things later. Right now she needed to spend time with her mother. Maybe for the last time.

Arlene's grin stretched across her face. "Sounds great, baby."

An hour later they were curled up on the sofa, Reggie's head on her mother's lap. Arlene's fingers brushed against the scrape on her face with tenderness. For a moment Reggie felt like a little girl again, when falling asleep on her mother's lap was a habit, not a rarity, before her mother had started drinking. Then a shadow fell across her vision as Arlene stretched over her, pouring a glass of whiskey with her free hand. Reggie hoped her mother couldn't see the tears curving down her cheeks.

Chapter 11

*R*eggie's attic was like a shrunken third floor, where the servants would have slept when the house was in its prime. Pieces of furniture littered the large room, mixed liberally with cardboard boxes with labels like "Toys" scrawled across in Magic Marker. It was close to midnight, and John stood next to Reggie while she rifled through some boxes.

John sneezed. "What are we doing up here?"

"Before my dad disappeared, he and my mom used to go camping. I need a bigger backpack. I want to see if Mom kept any of her old supplies. I don't know if hotels are in my future." After her mom had passed out on the couch, she'd called John and explained the situation, gathering her things together. Guilt dug its teeth into Reggie, but she shook it off.

"Do you trust Asher's story? You just met him."

Reggie looked at his grim face. "He saved me from those assholes. He hasn't tried to hurt me, and he knows what I am. You should have seen the look on his face when I told him what I could do . . ." she trailed off, remembering the reverence in Asher's eyes. "I believe him."

Turning away from John, she spotted a cluster of boxes under a rusted daybed. Maneuvering around the debris and cobwebs that clung to the surfaces like Silly String, she dropped down in front of the bed. John landed beside her. Together they pulled out a large box.

"I don't like you running off with this guy," he said. "It's not like you to trust a stranger. You won't have anyone to watch your back."

"I don't have a choice. I have to keep Mom and you safe." Opening the sagging cardboard lid, she rummaged through the box. "Andrius' soldiers are coming for me, and I don't know how to fight them."

He was quiet for a moment. "I'm going with you."

Shocked, she stared. "What?"

"I'm going with you."

"John, your mom would flip if you went missing!"

"Our moms can take of each other until we get back. I know you're scared, this way I'll have your back."

"Listen to me—"

"I'm coming, end of discussion. If I go and help, we'll be back that much faster. No one will miss us too much."

"Okay." Reggie let the lie comfort her. Reaching out, she hugged him fiercely.

John released her. "What are we looking for again?"

Reggie dug in the box, discovering the drab, olive green army backpack that belonged to her mother. She pulled it out, showing it to John. "This."

Rising off the floor, she sat down on the daybed and opened the pack. Maybe there was a Swiss Army knife or a flint she could use. She tossed out a few old T-shirts, a broken compass, and plastic cups, before her fingers brushed against something cool and metallic. Startled, she dropped the backpack, springing up from the bed.

"What's wrong?" John asked.

"There's a gun in there!" Reggie pointed at the open pack.

"Why would your mom have a gun?" John peeked into the backpack.

"No clue. She hates guns!" Reggie picked the backpack up, sliding her hand inside toward the gun as if it were a poisonous snake waiting to strike. She pulled out an old-fashioned six-shooter and laid it carefully on the daybed. She found a box of shells in the backpack too and placed them next to the gun. Her hand curled around the gun's smooth, wooden handle. It was an uncomfortable weight.

"What are you doing?" John said.

"Checking if it's loaded."

Pointing it toward the wall, she fumbled until the chamber popped open. Empty. Her breath whooshed out.

"Here, put it in the box." John pointed to the warped cardboard.

Reggie hesitated. She didn't know much about the Other and what she did know was unsettling. She wasn't confident that once she entered the Other she'd even know how to use her magic. It didn't come with a manual. But this was a real weapon. This didn't need magic. She stuffed the gun back in the army pack along with the shells.

"Reggie, what are you doing? You don't know how to use a gun! That's dangerous."

"That's what the Internet is for." Reggie held up her hand. "Until I figure out how to use my magic, I need a weapon."

Chapter 12

Reggie and John followed Asher through the forest behind Porth. They'd abandoned the trail long ago, winding their way through the tall evergreens, oaks, and tangled undergrowth. As she walked alongside John, she acted like a sponge. She absorbed every scent, every flower, every shift in color, in case she didn't return.

They began climbing a small hill when Asher stopped. "Can you feel that?"

"Feel what?" John asked, stumping his toe on a tree root. "Damn! I felt that."

The birds were louder here, their chirps shrill. "I don't feel any—" Reggie gasped as an invisible force nipped her skin. "What the hell?"

John touched her arm. "You okay?"

"Don't you feel it?" Reggie asked. John shook his head.

Asher stood still, his eyes closed. "He can't. But just listen closely."

She concentrated until she heard it: a low, steady humming that sounded like it was emitted from a large magnet.

"I hear it! Is that the gateway?" John said.

"Yes. We're almost there." Asher started walking again.

"Reggie?" John prodded.

Shaking off her increasing tension, she shot him a reassuring smile. "Let's go."

Two ancient oak trees rested at the top of the hill. Their knotted branches dipped low, curving toward each other to form an irregular, oval-shaped doorway. The oval shimmered and waved like heat bouncing from the desert sand. A seemingly identical forest was reflected through the gateway. The humming grew louder, the sound vibrating through Reggie's chest. She couldn't look away from that dancing patch of air.

"Are you ready?" Asher asked.

Reggie pulled her eyes away. "As ready as I'll ever be."

Asher turned to John. "You won't be able to cross over, you don't have—"

"Magic in my blood, blah, blah. I'm still gonna try. If there's any chance I can go through the rabbit hole, I'm going!"

"It's your choice." Asher went to Reggie, placing his large hands on her shoulders. "You'll feel some pressure when you pass through. It's more uncomfortable than painful. But when you actually enter the Other, I'm not sure how it will affect you. I'll go first, so you can watch me."

Reggie nodded. John inched closer to her. The air sighed and the humming faded as Asher stepped through the doorway, the barrier bending to let him pass. When he landed on the other side, he turned and beckoned to Reggie.

Her stomach churning, she grabbed John's hand and started toward the portal.

"Wait! Let me try first, see if I can make it," he said. Reggie released his hand.

Stopping before the doorway, John stepped into the undulating space. Blue and white sparks exploded from the point of contact his sneaker made with the barrier. John fell back screaming, cradling his foot. Smoke billowed from his shoe, and the stench of burnt rubber blanketed the air.

Reggie dropped to the ground to examine his foot. The sole of his sneakers had melted to a waxy, black substance. "You all right?"

"You mean besides being electrocuted? Yeah, never better," he said, rubbing his foot.

She stood up. "You're being sarcastic, you'll live."

Reggie offered her hand, helping him stand on shaky legs. Glancing through the portal, she saw Asher watching them intently. He gestured to John and mouthed "Goodbye." She clung to John's hand.

"He was right. You really can't come with me," her words tumbled out, unsteady.

"I could try again."

"Sure, your skin didn't melt the first time." Tears burned her eyes.

"I'm sorry, Reggie." He gripped her hand. "I promise I'll look out for your mom."

Reggie pulled John into a tight hug. "Thanks, I'll come back as quickly as I can."

He squeezed back, his voice gruff. "Just be careful. I'll camp out tonight. Make up a story on my way back tomorrow. Now go before I try to talk you out of it."

"I'll see you soon."

"You bet you will."

Excitement blended with fear as she neared the doorway. The unknown called to her, promising answers to her questions. Reggie cautiously touched the shimmering space with her index finger. Nothing. No sparks, no pain, just a shift in energy to allow her entry. Taking a deep breath, she stepped through.

The air was dense, like pushing through a thick vat of clear gelatin, and she was bombarded with images of being trapped between worlds forever in this foggy prison. Focusing on

Asher's blurred figure, she moved toward him. Two steps later, the air thinned and Reggie cleared the barrier, entering the Other.

Her insides began burning like liquid fire was shooting through her veins. She fell, panting. Her magic boiled over and extended past her body, seeking the Earth. She felt her power entwine with the Earth's, amplifying her senses. Smells, sights, and sounds exploded around her in vivid color, as if in the Real she'd existed alone in a dark, soundproof room.

Asher knelt beside her. His eyes filled with worry as he stroked her hair from her face. Even that light touch was agony.

"Stop, that hurts." Reggie forced the words past a raw throat. Blood trickled from her nose.

He withdrew his hand. "Your scrapes have faded. How do you feel?"

Wiping her face with her sleeve, she tried to sit up. Her muscles ached. "Like I got steamrolled. Too much magic inside me, I can't make it stop."

"Do you want it to stop?"

Their eyes met. "No, but I just want it to be less—intense."

"The Real blocked most of your magic, so your body has never been whole before. It needs time to adjust."

"I wish it would hurry the hell up." Reggie wanted to stand, but her legs refused.

"Let me help you."

She raised her arms, bracing her body for contact. He pulled her to her feet in one smooth motion. Reggie stared at the spinning ground.

"Whoa!" Asher steadied her when she slid sideways.

She tried to anchor her feet, gripping his arms. "I've seen my mom like this a few times. God, how can she stand it? Okay, you can let go now."

"You sure?"

"No, but you'll catch me if I fall," she said and he chuckled.

"We need to move on. The border guards patrol this forest, checking the gateway from time to time. I'd prefer to avoid them. Take my arm, I'll help you."

Reggie slipped her hand into the crook of his arm, both grateful for his strength and resenting her dependence on him. Asher guided her into a forest remarkably similar to the one she'd just left. The scent of pine and the perfume from budding flowers clogged her olfactory senses until she felt lightheaded. Pine and—and something feral. Something wild and dangerous coated her tongue. She shivered.

"Asher, do you smell that?" Reggie whispered.

"Smell what?"

"Blood or rotting meat and . . . and shit, I think."

"I don't smell anything—" he began when a piercing howl punctured the air, answered by a dozen other cries.

She stumbled, her muscles locking in place. "What was that?"

"Marsh wolves. But I'm not sure why they're in the forest."

"Shouldn't we be running?"

Asher shook his head. "Running from predators isn't a good idea. It just makes them give chase. We need to hide. What would cause the wolves to come into the woods?"

"Do we need to figure that out now?" Reggie replied. The ground shuddered under her feet, the feral smell growing stronger. The sound of thunder rumbled in the distance, echoed by more eerie howls.

"Wild boar!" Asher hissed. "I smell it now, damn it! The wolves must have chased it from the Marshes."

"Who cares about a pig? What about the wolves? Shouldn't we be hiding?" Reggie whipped her head around searching for something they could crawl into. They were in a small clearing with large trees and sparse patches of weeds.

"A wild boar isn't just a pig! We need to climb a tree. Pray to the Mother that if the boar escapes the wolves, it doesn't come for us. On my back, hurry!" Asher swung her onto his back, and Reggie clung to him as he sprinted to a giant oak tree and began climbing.

The ground below shrank as Asher climbed higher. She could hear the snorting huffs of the wild boar, the impact of its hooves like hammers on the ground, and the wolves' howls closing in. Asher stopped, and Reggie glanced from the ground to the tree, spotting a wide, sturdy limb.

"Are you strong enough to climb up there?"

It took all her strength not to fall off his back, but she gritted her teeth. "I'll try."

She reached for the tree branch, the rough bark cutting into her palm as she maneuvered from Asher's back. They were about thirty feet off the ground, and her vision swayed as she looked down. Her hand slipped. Reggie screamed, but Asher gripped the waist of her jeans, hoisting her back on the branch. Wrapping her arms and legs around the tree limb, she only relaxed when he slid behind her, pulling her against his chest. The wild boar burst into the clearing, wolves baying at its heels. Instead of running past them, the boar skidded to a stop. Its enormous head swiveled toward the oak tree.

Reggie trembled as she took in the scene. Five wolves the size of Shetland ponies, their shaggy coats ranging in color from gray to brown, surrounded the boar. They growled low and rough, their fangs flashing. They were living nightmares. But they weren't as impressive as the boar. Six feet at the shoulder, short, wiry black fur covered a massive, muscular body that weighed at least a thousand pounds. Two huge, sharp tusks curved out from the long snout. Black beady eyes penetrated through the branches, focusing on her. To her shock, the wolves followed the boar's gaze.

Reggie pressed into Asher, and his arms tightened around her. "Why are they looking at us?" She didn't want them anywhere near her.

"They can smell your fear and your magic."

"But how—"

Snarling, the wolves attacked, four lunging at the boar's legs trying to trip it, while the lead wolf went for the throat. For all its bulk, the boar was steel grace. Using its powerful legs, it held its ground, wielding its wicked tusks with deadly accuracy. Thud! Reggie held onto Asher as a three-hundred-pound wolf hit the tree. Rivulets of blood ran down the boar's side. The fallen wolf below pushed itself off the ground, its shoulder sliced open. She choked on the acrid stench. All this fear and anger was too much. The tree shook again.

"Shit!"

"Hold on, I won't let us fall," Asher said.

Reggie's escalating terror affected the animals below. The attacks became more vicious.

"Reggie, listen to me. I know you're frightened, but you need to calm down. They're attracted to your magic and your fear is making it worse. I can feel it too. That's why they're not leaving, that's why the boar isn't running away."

"Right, calm down. I can't be killed by an overgrown pork chop and the Big Bad Wolf. I can't go out like that," she muttered to herself as she closed her eyes. "I can't go out like—" Another wolf slammed into the tree. "That!"

"Dammit!" Asher held onto her. "Wait! The alpha wolf, he hasn't taken a hit. He's waiting. He's different. Can you feel that?"

77

Reggie watched the alpha. There was something different. Too much intelligence shone from its frosty blue eyes, even for a top predator. "That's not a normal wolf, is it?"

Asher's eyes widened. "No, it's not. It's a Changeling Elf."

"A what?"

"Changeling Elf. They're almost as rare as you are. I need to climb down."

"Are you out of your mind? No way, I'm not letting you get killed!"

"Trust me. I know you're still feeling weak, but I need you to hold on. No matter what happens, don't come down, okay?"

"Asher, I don't think—"

"Trust me."

Reggie didn't like it, but she nodded, watching as he scrambled down the tree. Somehow she felt naked without his strength. Asher dropped to the ground silently, his body turned toward the struggle in front of him. The wild boar was still kicking, swinging its massive head. Reggie knew this magnificent animal was trapped because of her. She couldn't control her fear, and it had just been transferred from worry for herself to Asher.

The alpha wolf swung its shaggy head around, looking at Asher, who raised his hands in the air. "I'm not here to hurt you, brother. Please take the hunt from here and let us go."

Reggie held her breath as the wolf and Asher stared at each other, ignoring the violence around them. Suddenly the wolf turned from Asher, leapt onto the boar and tore its throat out. Cringing, Reggie closed her eyes to block the sight, but she couldn't block the smell. Death. She felt the life drain from the boar. Growls rose again. She opened her eyes. The other wolves had taken notice of Asher, but the alpha jumped in front of him. The alpha growled and snapped, and the other wolves cowered in obedience. Reggie blinked as the alpha started changing. Fur disappeared. Bones made a sickening crack as they rearranged themselves into a new shape. Fluids flowed onto the ground. A few moments later, a tall, naked man stood, long wheat-colored hair flowing down his back. He turned and faced Asher, blood staining his face and chest. Reggie saw he had long, pointy ears. An Elf. A very naked Elf.

"Way too much information," she whispered.

"You're not a Changeling," the Elf said.

"No," Asher said, and then he fumbled with his shirt. His back was to Reggie, so she couldn't see what the Changeling was looking at.

"Ahh, I see. And who is your companion? She smells delicious." The Changeling closed his eyes, sniffing the air. The pleasure on his face made her blush.

"You can smell her, or the beast?"

"I can sense her magic, but the beast knows there's something special, something different about her. He likes it."

Reggie watched as the Changeling opened his eyes again, zeroing in on her in the tree. She shrank back against the trunk. The other wolves still hadn't attacked, content to feed on the carcass, and she wondered how the Changeling controlled them.

"She and I shouldn't be here. Is the forest safe for us?" Asher asked, and Reggie sensed the deeper meaning behind the question.

"You're safe from me. I like the way she smells. When you go, I'll forget I saw you."

"Thank you. Have you seen the border guards?"

The Changeling grinned and his face became handsome. "No, I made sure of that. You're safe here tonight, but you'll never make it to the Witch Plains before dark."

Asher nodded. "I know. Thank you again." He didn't move and the Changeling gestured toward her tree.

"You going to get her down?"

The lines of Asher's back tensed, the muscles bunched as if ready to attack. "Are you going to be polite?"

"I smell the Giant, but that's not why I'll be polite," the Changeling answered.

Asher turned away from the Changeling and trotted back to her tree. "Reggie, I'm coming to get you now. It's safe."

Reggie glanced at the sardonic expression on the Changeling's face and didn't know if she believed that, but she was tired of being terrified in a tree. She waited as Asher scaled the trunk, climbing onto his back when he reached her. A few minutes later, her feet hit the forest floor and she almost crumpled to her knees. Asher wrapped an arm around her waist, keeping her steady as they faced the Changeling.

"Aren't you lovely," he breathed, a mischievous glint in his mint green eyes.

Reggie tried to keep her gaze on his face, but her eyes slipped down past his chest and hips. Her eyes widened. He noticed, and his grin grew broader. Rolling her eyes, she said, "Red's definitely your color. You should wear blood more often."

Asher's arm tightened, but the Changeling threw back his head, laughing. "I like you." He took a step closer. She held her ground. He breathed in her scent. "Delicious. Make sure he keeps you safe, but I have a feeling you can do that yourself. Now if you'll excuse me, I have a kill to enjoy before I return to civilization."

"Thank you," Asher repeated, and the Changeling inclined his head.

"Enjoy your bacon," Reggie said, and the Changeling laughed again. "Let's get the hell out of here," she muttered to Asher.

"An excellent idea," Asher said.

CHAPTER 13

"*Y*ou look better," Asher said, as they hiked through the forest, his stride brisk.

Reggie welcomed the fast pace; she wanted to get far away from the kill site. "My magic is sort of evening out, but I still feel too full. Don't know if that's normal." Her entire body vibrated with power.

He shrugged. "I'm not sure. We don't have the same type of magic."

"What happened back there, with that Changeling? What did you show him?" Asher fell silent. He was quiet for so long that Reggie prodded, "Asher, what's going on?"

He looked at her, his face brimming with bitterness. "You and I, we're more alike than you know. We both have mixed blood—"

"Whoa! What does that mean? I'm not human?"

Asher's eyes were green frost, his voice even colder. "Mixed blood is nothing to be ashamed of."

Reggie wrestled with her shock and reached for his arm. "Oh, no! No! That's not what I meant at all, I'm just—I don't understand! I thought both my parents were human. I didn't mean for it to come out like that."

"I apologize; I'm sensitive about it. You couldn't have known about your heritage."

"People have neglected to tell me important things my whole life, I'm getting used to it."

"Do you think your mother knew? About your father, I mean?"

Reggie thought about the gun hidden in her backpack. "Maybe. She rarely talks about him. It's been hard for her."

"It's hard to lose someone you love," he confessed.

"I'm sorry. Was it recent?"

"It seems like it happens everyday."

Surprised by his confession, Reggie sought words to comfort him, but none came. They started walking again, the trees passing by in a slow blur. As the silence stretched, she realized he'd neatly avoided the subject.

"You were telling me we're alike," she reminded him.

He sighed, slowing down. "You have more power than I do, but we share similar genetics. There are three races in the Other: Humans, Giants, and Elves. Elves have offshoots, the Changelings, which you saw tonight. Each race has their own magic, and when the races interbreed and their magic blends together, a new species is born. Aether Mages. You have the blood of three races inside you."

"I do?" Reggie avoided tripping over a gnarled root.

Asher nodded. "There's no exact ratio to become an Aether Mage, it just happens. To prevent it, the races aren't allowed to intermingle or intermarry anymore unless the parties are sterilized."

This time she stumbled. "Sterilized? They can't have kids with each other?"

Asher clasped her arm, steadying her. "Andrius forbade it after the war with the Aether Mages. He wants no one to challenge him for power."

"You guys don't do birth control?"

"We do, but birth control isn't foolproof."

"So what happens if you're caught having sex with a different race and you haven't been fixed?"

"An Elf, maybe seventeen, was studying at the Academy in Two Cities when he met a Human girl. He didn't think anyone noticed that she snuck into his room at night until they were dragged naked onto the street by Special Enforcement guards. They castrated him . . . she disappeared for a while and returned with some interesting scars."

"Then how do you and I exist? There's got to be other people with mixed blood!" Having met Andrius, Reggie knew there was evil in the Other but she never expected this twisted darkness.

"We were born before the war ended. No hybrid who wasn't already in the womb has been born after."

She'd just been bumped to the top of the endangered species list. "You still haven't told me what you showed the Changeling. What are you so afraid of?"

Asher stopped. "Nothing. It's just very difficult for me to explain." His eyes drilled into her, pinning her down. She watched as he flicked open the top few buttons of his shirt, the fabric parting to reveal a gold collar.

"What is it?"

He straightened. "It's a slave collar."

Reggie's voice failed her. He stood watching her, his face hard and blank like marble. "Slave collar? You're a slave?" She recoiled from the shiny metal, horrified.

His whole body stiffened. "Yes, I'm a slave. Does my lowly status offend you?"

She felt like he'd punched her in the gut. "God, no! Asher, I can't imagine what you've gone through, what you're still going through. But this doesn't make me think less of you. I swear, if anything, it makes me like you more."

He didn't speak. He just stared at her. Reggie stepped closer. "Asher, please tell me how this happened to you."

"My parents were on the losing side of war. I'm a spoil to be savored by the victors, made to serve Andrius. Every hybrid was. Andrius fought and defeated the Aether Mages, and he used the rest of us as an example so there wouldn't be any more interbreeding."

"How old were you?"

"I was five when Andrius came for me." Asher's laughter could have peeled paint. "He didn't call what he did to us enslavement. He put us in a house for 'indentured reformation.' I lost my identity. I was just another Indentured waiting for a Loyalist to take me and 'reform' me. They could keep us until our indentured period was over at 21, and we were free again. They were supposed to educate and protect us, but . . ."

"Yeah right, kind slave masters. How did you end up with Andrius?"

"Because of my parents. They had been very active in the Resistance. He personally put on my collar. I remember his smile. He wanted my parents to know he was going to twist me, mold me into his image. I also showed promise, and I think he wanted to know what kind of power my mixed heritage would bring."

"Where are you parents now? Are they . . ." she trailed off, uncertain.

"They were sent to the Pits. No one comes out of there alive. It's a punishment for the worst sort of traitors," Asher said.

"But there's still a chance, right?"

"Don't you think I've thought of that? Dreamed of rescuing them? It doesn't matter if they're alive. I can't get them out."

"I wasn't trying to make you feel like you didn't care." She felt like she was playing a game of emotional Russian roulette, clicking closer to the bullet in the chamber. "Have you ever tried to escape from Andrius? That was a stupid question, forget it."

Asher cocked his head to the side and studied her. "Look at this." A finger stabbed the gold collar.

"They went to a lot of trouble to make it pretty, didn't they? Assholes."

He ran his thumb over the gleaming metal. "I guess it is pretty. See all those symbols. Why do you think they're carved into the gold?"

She shook her head, afraid of the answer.

"They're magical bindings. They represent the labor you owe your master. And if you disobey, your master can punish you." Asher pushed the collar down slightly to reveal skin melted like wax, red and shiny.

"He burns you?" Reggie gasped. She felt coils of power tighten around her.

Asher nodded. "As you can see, I haven't always been the model of obedience."

Her vision spotted. A vise clamped her lower legs, and she looked down. Large roots had burst from the dirt and roped around her ankles and calves, their stalks pulled tight.

"What the—?" She turned to Asher for help.

"I think they're reacting to your anger. You used your magic without realizing it. Take a deep breath, calm down."

"I can do that? Great." Reggie ran through a few breathing exercises that she used in kickboxing. The roots' grip slackened. She bent over and untangled her ankles, watching as they slid back into the soil.

"You must learn control."

"How? Besides, it's hard to have control after what I just saw." She straightened.

"At least I have the satisfaction of knowing Andrius didn't break me. I'm still whole and sane."

"And kind and decent. You saved me."

He shifted away from her. "Anyone would've done the same."

"That's a nice sentiment."

He looked back. "I hope they would've."

She stared at his neck, which was covered again; the seared flesh an imprint on her mind. "Now I really get why you're on Rhys' side. Thanks for taking such a big risk for me."

"Don't thank me," his voice was harsh. "I haven't done anything for you yet."

"Are you kidding me? Not only did you get me here in one piece, you just told me something very painful and private just so I could understand what's going on here. That's the bravest thing I've ever seen."

"I brought you to a world in trouble! Don't be so grateful." Asher paused, taking a deep breath. "Anyway, Changeling Elves are sympathetic to Indentureds, so when he saw my collar he let us go. And he liked your smell. He probably thought we snuck out into the forest to have forbidden sex."

She glanced away as the image flashed through her mind. "Ohhh."

"We need to push on, our light is almost gone. We'll camp in the forest tonight, but I'd like to make it to Two Cities within the next couple of days."

"Is Rhys in Two Cities?"

Asher hesitated a moment. "He's in Hornsbay Forest, hiding out with the Resistance."

"Shouldn't we go straight to Hornsbay?"

He gestured to his collar again. "Andrius can track me anywhere with this. It took me longer to find you than I'd anticipated. Now I'm off schedule. If I don't report back within the next few days, he's going to send someone after me. I really don't want that."

"You want me to go where Andrius is? No way!" Shaking her head, Reggie took a step back.

Asher followed. "You don't have a choice. Reggie, we don't want one of Andrius' Ravens coming after us. I know too many secrets about Andrius to be left unchecked. At least this way we have some control over the situation. I'll hide you in the city somewhere, then report to Andrius. When he sends me out again, I'll collect you and take you to Hornsbay."

"How long will that take?"

"Not long. He sends me out frequently."

She looked at the abomination circling his neck. "I don't want to be anywhere near Andrius."

He gave her a wry grin. "Me neither. Come on, I have a deadline to make."

She sighed, resigned. "How much farther?"

"When it gets too dark to see, we'll make camp."

"Any more crazy animals we should worry about?"

"If there are, you'll be the first one to know."

"That's comforting."

Chapter 14

*M*egan crouched by a row of thick hedges growing between Reggie's yard and a neighboring home on Cherry Lane. The yellow porch light cut a swath of illumination across the shaggy lawn. She shifted, relieving her tingling limbs. Two hours of waiting, and nothing. Digging into the pocket of her trousers, she pulled out a photo. Rhys had told her that Reggie Lang was important. That bringing her safely to him was top priority. She didn't look like much, just another pretty girl. But when it came to magic, appearances were often deceiving.

The front door swung open, banging against the side of the house. A woman emerged. Probably late thirties, Megan calculated. Definitely Reggie's mother; the resemblance was strong. The woman sat on the front steps, her fingers curled around a bottle of amber liquid.

Megan carefully crawled out of the hedges. She backtracked to the front of the graveled drive leading to Reggie's house. Twigs and dirt clung to her clothing, and she frantically brushed at them with her hands. It would be suspicious enough to approach Reggie's mother without looking like she'd been rolling in mud. Perhaps she wouldn't notice in the dark. The woman remained on the porch, the bottle resting between her feet now. Megan advanced toward her, her steps exaggerated and loud. The woman's eyes were glazed as she glanced at Megan.

Megan smiled. "I'm so sorry to disturb you, but are you Mrs. Lang?" She remained along the edge of the light.

The woman blinked. "What?"

"Are you Mrs. Lang?" Megan repeated, hearing the slur in the woman's speech.

"Oh, yeah, yes, I'm Arlene Lang," the woman said, suddenly moving into action. She grabbed the bottle between her feet and put it behind her, standing up. Wiping her palms on her jeans, she thrust her hand toward Megan.

Megan took her hand, deciding it was safe to use her real name. "Megan Treston, it's nice to meet you."

"Nice to meet you too. I'm sorry if I'm a bit of a mess." Arlene smiled and then narrowed her gaze. "Why did you say you were looking for me again?"

"I didn't, actually. I'm looking for Reggie." Megan watched Arlene's face closely.

"Reggie?" Arlene blinked, becoming more alert. "Oh, well, Reggie isn't here right now. What do you want with my daughter?"

Megan flicked through the files in her brain. "We're in kickboxing together. She missed a few classes, so I thought I'd stop by and check on her."

"You do kickboxing with Reggie? Oh, she loves that! No, she hasn't been in a few weeks, she's been busy."

"Aren't we all? When is she coming back?"

"Not until tomorrow. She went camping with a friend," Arlene replied, her face crumbling.

Megan pushed on quickly. "Camping? Really, where?"

"In the national forest. Excuse me, but I need to go inside and get some things done. I'll tell Reggie you stopped by when she comes home."

Megan watched the woman sway on her feet like a reed. "Sure, thanks."

"G'night." Arlene picked up her bottle and turned to go inside.

"Goodnight," Megan answered, feeling uneasy as she stared at the woman's back. The thought of Reggie in the forest, possibly so close to the gateway, unsettled her. The woods were vast, stretching over hundreds of acres. If she wanted to find Reggie by tomorrow, she'd better start looking tonight.

CHAPTER 15

Shadows lengthened along their path as the afternoon sunshine vanished behind the trees. Reggie sensed the stirrings of nightly creatures, her body keen to the shift.

"We're going to camp here," Asher announced, stopping ahead of her.

Reggie glanced around. Giant pine trees provided a decent shelter and moss covered the forest floor. "What can I do?"

"Do you know how to make a fire?"

"Nope."

"Then pick a place you want to sleep, and I'll gather some kindling."

"That I can do."

Ten minutes later, Asher had built a gentle glow. The heat warded off the spring chill. Reggie tore open a protein bar as Asher sat across from her, munching on dried fruit.

"Asher?"

"Hmm?" he murmured.

"Where are we going tomorrow?"

"The Witch Plains."

"Witches are real, then."

"You're surprised?"

"Not anymore. Why are we going there?" Reggie asked between bites.

"We need transportation to Two Cities," he replied.

"Do you guys have cars, or am I gonna have to learn to ride a horse?"

He stopped chewing, staring at her. "A horse? No, we'll travel by ley lines. I can't really explain them, it's better if you see how they work."

"You're going to say that a lot, aren't you?" Reggie said, finishing off the bar.

Asher laughed. "Ready to sleep? I'd like to make it out of the forest by morning."

Reggie noticed he was more relaxed than she'd seen him before. His shoulders drooped, losing their right angles. Ever since his confession, she'd wanted him to know she understood what he'd been through, that her own life wasn't white picket fences and teddy bears. "Asher, I need you to know something about my mom. The reason I was so scared to leave her."

He tilted his head. "Okay."

"The day you met her, she was having a rare shining moment of sobriety. Things aren't usually   so . . ."

"So what?"

This was hard. "Mom drinks a lot. Takes antidepressants, you know, drugs for depression. I guess being numb is better than dealing with pain, right? I take care of her. I'm responsible for everything. I don't know how she'll make it without me."

"Oh, Reggie." Sympathy painted his face.

"Sometimes it pisses me off because it makes me feel old. I just want to be a kid, you know? I pretend things are normal and hide the truth from everyone. But they know. You've had it worse than me, no doubt, but Asher, I get not having control over your life. I want you to know that."

"Don't do that, compare. From what you say, your life hasn't been an easy one."

"Asher, come on! Andrius enslaved you. You were burned every time you stepped out of line. Yeah, I've had it rough. But despite my mom's problems, at least I know she loves me and she's there. You didn't even have that." She shook her head, disgusted.

He was quiet for a while, the shadows near the fire masking his expression. Finally he took her hand. "Thank you for telling me."

She shrugged. "Seemed fair."

He squeezed her hand. "Fair and I are rarely familiar."

"Well, maybe we can change that."

"You really would try, wouldn't you?" he whispered, his gaze intent on her face. Her heart thudded. He shook himself. "Let's get some sleep."

She swallowed. "Sure." She was plumping up her backpack when his voice stopped her.

"You should sleep by me. I believe what the Changeling said, but he won't be in the forest all night. The border patrol might come back. I'd rather have you close."

Reggie's heart danced a quickstep. She crawled next to him, lying with her back toward him. Separated by mere inches, her heightened senses made her aware of his heat and smell, the combination of healthy male sweat and spicy cloves. The only boy she'd ever been alone with was John, and she'd never wondered what it would be like to kiss him.

"Are you warm enough?" Asher's breath was suddenly soft against her neck.

Reggie shivered. "I'm fine."

She felt the light brush of fingers against her hair, and she tensed with a nervous hope and fear that he might turn her over, but he just said, "Goodnight, Reggie."

"Goodnight."

Reggie stared into the dancing flames, her body strung tight. After a while, she felt Asher relax. Of course it would be easier for him. He was in his comfort zone while she felt like a slug tasked with learning physics. Snuggling into the springy moss, Reggie thought about home. About how her mother was holding up, and how John would deal with her. Finally she began to doze, her mind sucked into deep dreams.

Icy seawater slapped her body into temporary shock. Feeling herself sink, Reggie opened her eyes and looked up. The surface of the ocean was drifting farther away. How had she fallen into the sea? Terror filled her body as quickly as oxygen leaked out. She surged upward, the gray water churning around her. But she was going nowhere fast. If she didn't get air soon, she would die. A strange glow from underneath caught her attention, slicing through her panic like a scalpel. Looking down, she saw a gigantic round bubble, like a membrane, radiating soft green light. Within the bubble were bodies—hundreds, maybe thousands of bodies.

Reggie changed course, swimming toward the bubble. If she could find a way in, maybe she wouldn't drown. As she drew closer, she noticed the bodies were floating, suspended in the membrane. She placed her hands on the bubble, the exterior slick and smooth to the touch. Her cold-cramped fingers couldn't find any edges or entryways. She banged on the bubble with her fist, but the bodies remained still. Their milky eyes watched her.

"Help me!" Reggie screamed, but the ocean swallowed her words. The eyes stared, unblinking. She turned away, treading water and focusing on the surface once more. Could she make it? A loud bang whipped her head around.

A naked man drifted in front of her, face level with hers. Reggie shook her head, but his eyes latched onto hers. Oh, God. Her father's eyes. His fist smashed through the bubble and his fingers clenched her shirt, dragging her toward him. She screamed again.

Suddenly, the cold disappeared. Warmth invaded her bones, soaking up the chill. Reggie opened her eyes. An endless cerulean sky stretched above her. Sitting up, she turned to find her father lying beside her. Fully clothed now, his eyes were shut. The sun's rays picked up copper highlights in his rich brown hair, bathing his handsome face in a soft glow. That was her nose resting on his face. Her throat tightened as a tear slid down her cheek.

His eyes flickered open, soft velvet brown. "Don't cry. There's no need for tears here," Sebastian said, sitting up.

Her tears continued to fall, urged on by his tender expression. "I can't help it," Reggie whispered. "Hi, Dad." She fell into his arms, her cheek pressed against his broad chest.

"Hello, Reggie. My little girl. Shh," her father crooned, stroking her hair. "It's so good to see you."

"It's great to see you too." Her voice was muffled against his shirt.

Sebastian held her tightly. "I know you feel lost right now. A lot of changes are happening in your life. Things you don't understand. I'm here to help you."

"How can you help me? You're dead!"

Her father shook his head. "I'm not dead. But I wouldn't consider what I am as living, either. I haven't walked in years. Since right after you were born. Or felt the sun or the open air or looked into my daughter's eyes." Sebastian ran his knuckles down her cheek. "But the magic and my spirit are still strong enough to reach you here. You've come home, and finally I'm able to see you." He pulled her close to his body again.

Reggie ignored her doubts, giving in to the comfort of his embrace.

"How's your mother?" The timbre of his voice changed slightly.

Reggie stiffened. She didn't want to tell him. She didn't want him to hear the guilt and anger in her voice. "It's been hard for Mom, since you've been gone. We've done our best to deal."

"And have you dealt well?"

"We're not starving, and we still have our house, so things could definitely be worse." Reggie wiped her nose, keeping her voice even with an effort.

Her father tipped her chin up, searching her eyes. "It hurts you to talk about her. What aren't you telling me?"

She shook her head.

"I love your mother just as I love you. I miss her," Sebastian said and Reggie experienced a different kind of guilt.

"I know you do, but you're right. It hurts too much right now." And beyond that twisting pain was the selfish need to have her father to herself. Ashamed, she turned her face against his shoulder.

Sebastian was quiet. "I understand. We'll talk about that more later, yes?"

Reggie nodded.

His body tensed, the arms that had offered comfort turning to steel bands. Raising her head from his shoulder, she stared at his face. Tension bracketed his mouth, and his eyes were glazed in deep concentration.

"Dad?"

Sebastian glanced down at her. "Reggie, you need to wake up now."

Shaking her head, she clenched his upper arms. "No! I don't want to leave you!"

"Sweetheart, it's not safe to be here with me right now. We've lingered too long in the Dream Realm. It can be dangerous here."

Reggie trembled, remembering the pain Andrius Drake had inflicted. And that had only lasted a few seconds. "I know, but we haven't been here that long. I just want to spend more time—"

"I do, too. But I need to keep you safe. I'll come to you again, and we can begin your lessons."

"Lessons?"

"On how to control your ability. I need your help, Reggie. Wake up," he demanded, placing a swift kiss on her forehead.

She fought against his will. "Dad, when will you come again?"

He gave her a reassuring smile, shaking her shoulders a little. "As soon as I can. I love you, now go!"

It was one of the hardest things she'd ever done, but Reggie obeyed her father's command, her mind snapping their precious connection. She awoke with a start, regretting bitterly that she didn't have time to say I love you back.

CHAPTER 16

*R*eggie's muffled gasp woke Asher. Her dream must have been triggering strong emotions, because a wolf's howl rolled over the forest, startling birds in the trees, disturbing animals in the brush. Asher felt the forest's reaction to Reggie's presence crawling over his skin. She rolled toward him, as if seeking comfort. Asher hesitated and then wrapped his arms around her, savoring the warmth of her body. She drew him to her, like a loadstone draws iron. He studied her face. Her eyes jerked behind closed lids, and her fingers dug into the fabric of his shirt.

Guilt wormed its way into his heart like a splinter. This should be a homecoming for her. He meant it when he told her she was finally whole. The Real suppressed a vital part of who she was. Reggie trusted him, and he was going to take her to a monster.

Asher watched as Reggie's eyes popped open, her breathing erratic. "Are you all right?" His arms tightened around her despite himself.

She lifted her face from his shoulder, blinking rapidly. A curtain of chestnut hair slid over his arm. It was soft. "I had a weird dream. It seemed so real—everything's too much here."

"Are these dreams like the ones you had before? Are you in the Dream Realm?"

Reggie's eyes focused on his, then they darted away. "No, just dreams about my parents. I guess I feel closer to them here or something." She gave him a faint smile, blushing when she became aware of their position.

Asher knew he should release her, but he didn't. "I understand what it's like to lose a parent. Try to rest. We have a lot of ground to cover tomorrow."

"Yeah, we do," Reggie said, but she didn't pull away.

Asher stroked her cheek, dipping his thumb to brush her lips. Her brown eyes were wide. Slowly he lowered his head and kissed her.

CHAPTER 17

*R*eggie stilled as Asher's lips touched hers, her heart rocketing in her chest. His mouth was a delicate whisper, gentle and patient. She kissed him back, her lips clumsy compared to his. He didn't seem to mind. His large body was heavy against hers. Twigs dug into her back. But she was afraid to move. Afraid he would stop kissing her. Her arms snaked around his neck, pulling him closer. He deepened the kiss, and Reggie followed his lead.

Despite her absolute certainty that she was completely inexperienced and sucked at kissing, she liked what they were doing. Maybe too much. When his mouth moved down to press against her neck, she became aware of how vulnerable they were, exposed for anyone to see. She gently tugged at his hair, and Asher's head snapped up. Their breathing was unsteady.

Asher leaned back, putting some space between them. "I'm sorry, I—"

Reggie shook her head. "It's okay. I just got nervous. Someone could walk up on us."

His green eyes roved over her face, lingering on her lips. Suddenly his head jerked to the side. "Do you hear voices?"

Reggie propped herself up on an elbow and listened. There it was. Not just one voice, a cluster of them, faint but unmistakable, coming up behind them.

"It's probably a border patrol. They're fools risking the Changeling's wrath. We need to get up now." Asher's expression hardened. "They won't be Andrius' elite patrol either, that makes them more trouble than they're worth."

The voices grew louder.

"I hate this forest and that Changeling! Arrogant son-of-a-bitch! Thinks he's better than everyone else, telling us what to do." A man's angry voice drifted toward them.

"He might be arrogant, but we could've used him to get out of a dull night," a woman responded. "There's hardly a rebel in here anymore. All you want out of life is to bust a few heads."

"Bust a few heads and have a good roll with you. That's all I need."

Loud laughter rang out. Reggie guessed there were three of them. Getting caught by a border patrol was the last thing they needed. She turned to Asher, who was already on the move. Reggie scrambled to her feet.

"Who are these guys?"

"They're Andrius' rejects. They've been banished out here for misconduct or incompetence. Causing trouble makes them feel important. And we can't outrun them, they'll smell the smoke any second now. Dammit!"

"Simon! Do you see a light?" the woman's voice called out.

"And I smell smoke, must be our lucky day!" the man said.

"This won't be pleasant." Asher straightened Reggie's shirt, brushing off dirt and leaves, and quickly combed his fingers through her hair. She arched her brows at him. "Trying to make it look like we haven't been rolling around together."

"Shit," she hissed and began dusting off his clothing. She heard branches snap.

"Listen to me, no one will suspect you're a hybrid. You look pure human. Just follow my lead and play along with whatever I say, okay?" She nodded. He brushed his hair over the points of his ears.

"What are you doing?"

"If we're very lucky, they might think I'm human. But I doubt it." Asher scooped his pack off the ground, taking out a small leather booklet that resembled a passport. He slipped it into the front pocket of his pants. He offered her a bitter smile. "My official papers that allow me to travel without my master."

"Well, well, what do we have here?" a man called.

Reggie twisted around. Three people stepped into the circle of firelight. One man stood in front, another man and a woman flanking him in a triangular formation. The leader's meaty fists rested on his hips, stretching his camouflage uniform across a muscled chest, and a belly going soft. Reggie looked up into a broad, weathered face.

"Don't you know you're not supposed to be here?" the leader asked, a malicious glint in his eyes. "Only rebels and witches come here. It doesn't look good for you." His fingers caressed the knife handle hooked onto his utility belt.

Reggie froze. Asher pulled her into his arms from behind, but he remained silent.

The leader grinned. "Maybe they're in here for something else, eh?" He nodded toward his companions. "She's a cute little thing, young and tender. She's with a boy when she could have a man. Wouldn't you like a man, honey?"

Reggie swallowed her reply as Asher's fingers dug into her waist. She stared, stone faced at the leader, refusing to show fear.

The woman laughed. "I don't think she'd like you, Simon, you're not nearly as pretty as he is. What do you think, Jensen?" Her dark eyes flicked from Reggie to Asher, her hands resting above the knife sheath strapped around her narrow hips.

"Simon hasn't gotten laid in a while. That's not going to change anytime soon. She wouldn't touch him, would you?"

the other man asked Reggie. He looked ghostly, his blond hair nearly white, his skin pale. "And maybe the boy's big everywhere."

Reggie bit her lip, tasting blood. The taunts grew cruder. She wanted to shut them all up.

Asher whispered in her ear, the sound soothing. "Ignore them. Reacting is what they want. Wait them out. They're just Andrius' rejects."

She knew Asher was right, but anger frayed her control. And then Simon stepped toward her.

"Let her go," he ordered Asher. "Come here, honey. I need to pat you down. You might be carrying weapons." He wiggled his fingers, beckoning her to come.

Reggie looked back at Asher. His face was thunderous, but he nodded. She walked to Simon, keeping her hands in front of her.

"Hands on the back of your head. That's it, very nice." Simon circled around her, taking his time. He bent in front of her and began running his hands up her legs, squeezing.

After Asher's gentle touch, Simon's fingers felt like dirt being tattooed into her skin. When he didn't stop at the top of her thighs, her leash snapped. She didn't hear Asher curse at Simon in warning; she just heard roaring in her ears. Then she realized the sound wasn't in her head.

A gale whipped through the trees around them, bending branches and sucking up leaves and debris from the ground in a mad swirl. Reggie stumbled to her knees. They'd all stumbled. An angry howl trailed after the wind. Asher's arms found her once again, muscles flexing as he steadied her. The guards tried to catch their balance, pushing themselves to their feet.

"Reggie, calm down," Asher urged. "You could accidentally kill us!"

"Slumming, sweetheart?" Simon's unwelcome voice slithered between them. "You know what the penalty for that is, don't you?"

Fighting for control, Reggie watched Simon's eyes fill with contempt as they flitted from Asher's exposed ears to her features. He advanced closer, the other guards following. They moved with trained precision, their hands resting near their weapons.

Asher's hold tightened. "Reggie, let me handle this."

"Let me go," she said, gripping his arms with clawed fingers. "If you don't, something worse will happen."

Asher searched her eyes and released her. Reggie stepped away from the safety of his embrace and faced Simon. He was just like the bullies at school. Part of her mind screamed that he could damage her much worse than school bullies ever could, but she ignored it.

"Slumming would be screwing someone like you!" Reggie stabbed a finger in his direction.

"You little bitch! Only whores screw Indentureds." Simon took a step toward her as Asher jerked her back against him.

"You would know. No woman would screw you unless you paid them!" Reggie gestured to Asher. "He's twice the man you are. You're just Andrius' reject!" She heard Asher swear. The guards' faces twisted with fury.

"Pray to the Mother. You've just made things considerably worse," Asher muttered.

"Andrius' reject, am I?" Simon grabbed Reggie's arm, yanking her hard, breaking Asher's hold. "You'll find this reject can still cause a world of pain."

"Go to hell!" Reggie yelled, as she fought against him. His grip around her upper bicep was brutal.

"Stop! Let her go!" Asher moved toward Simon, hands balled into menacing fists. "You have no idea who this is, who I serve. This isn't someone you want to harm."

"Shut up, slave!" Simon wrenched Reggie closer. "Jensen, Friegbert! Hold him!" He and Asher stared at each other. "Say goodbye to your balls, boy. I hope she was worth it."

Reggie watched as the two guards rushed Asher. As scared as she was, she held onto her power. Her magic pushed hard against her skin until it felt like talons scraped her insides. But if she lost her grip on that vengeful force she might kill them. And if this man discovered what she was, he'd take her straight to Andrius and a sore arm would be the least of her problems.

"You're going to regret this," Asher said. The guards each grasped one of Asher's arms, their knuckles white with strain. But Asher didn't struggle. He just stared at Simon.

"We'll see. Check for the Indentured's papers. Let's see where he and the little bitch are going."

Jensen patted down Asher, pulling his documents from his front pocket. "Here you go," Jensen said, tossing Simon the leather booklet.

Snatching it from the air, Simon shoved Reggie in front of him so he could free his hands. He rested his heavy upper arms on her shoulders, pinning her in place as he read the documents. She resisted the urge to stomp on his boot. Her eyes latched onto Asher's. He gave her a slight nod, and she relaxed.

Simon's head jerked up. "You're Andrius Drake's Indentured? And who's this?" he demanded, shaking Reggie.

"This is Ms. Regina Farr, Councilwoman Leona Farr's niece," Asher replied. "I was ordered to bring her to Two Cities for her yearly stay."

Reggie snaked around and looked up into Simon's eyes. "I don't think my Aunt Leona is going to be happy when she hears how you treated me. In fact, she's going to be pretty pissed off."

Simon scowled as he reread the documents. "You might be Drake's servant, but there's nothing in here that proves she's Farr's niece."

"Why would there be?" Scorn seeped from Reggie's voice. "I'm a free citizen. Do I have to make an announcement when I visit my aunt? Are you an idiot?" She hissed as Simon squeezed her again.

"You should stop doing that," Asher said. His eerie calm frightened Reggie.

"I'll do what I want, slave!"

The woman, Friegbert, shook her head. "If she's really Farr's niece, we're screwed."

"Yes, you are," a voice growled.

Simon whirled around, dragging Reggie with him. Outside the fire's light, a pair of ice blue eyes glowed. A blurred figure rushed toward them. Simon released Reggie, reaching for his knife. He was lifted off his feet before the blade cleared its sheath. Reggie hit the ground clutching her wounded arm and looked up.

The Elf Changeling held Simon by his throat with one clawed hand. The Changeling was in a state of partial transformation; his canines were elongated and the edges of his face were like mismatched puzzle pieces. The other guards let go of Asher, charging the Changeling.

"Stop them!" the Changeling shouted to Asher.

Asher lunged for the guards, shoving them to the ground with ease as if they were misbehaving dogs. The smell of burnt sage choked Reggie.

"No spells," the Changeling said as he shook Simon. Blood trickled down Simon's neck. The smell dissipated. Reggie cowered at the Changeling's raw aggression, the absence of humanity in his voice. "I told you to leave the forest tonight. How dare you disobey me!"

"Just doing our job," Simon croaked.

Suddenly the Changeling's fangs were centimeters from Simon's carotid. "I am Brwyn Cavill, Representative of the Witch Plains district. Your job is to obey me!"

"It's illegal to have sex with an Indentured."

"Leona Farr's niece can have sex with anyone she wants. Look at him. Don't you think Andrius Drake gives him to certain allies in exchange for favors?" the Changeling asked.

Reggie turned to stare at Asher, who wouldn't look at her. My God, did Andrius really force him to prostitute himself? But why was she so surprised? Seeing as Andrius burned Asher without remorse, he probably didn't think twice about using Asher's beauty as a tool to further his ambitions. She hoped what they'd shared had been a different experience for Asher. The reasons to hate Andrius kept piling up.

"Regina!" the Changeling called, snapping Reggie back into the present. "Come here, please." He released Simon, who crumpled to the ground.

Reggie scrambled to her feet, her legs like rubberbands. She wondered why he was playing along with their story. As the Changeling watched her, his eyes bled from blue to light green, his facial bones reformed, and a flirtatious grin curved his mouth. He held out a hand to her, his claws retracting. She took it.

"Don't you ever put on clothes?" Reggie blurted then cringed. But he simply laughed, the sound easing her fear.

"I don't mind you seeing me naked, little darling." Brwyn raised Reggie's hand to his nose and inhaled deeply. "Ahh, like a drug." He turned her to face Simon's fallen form, his eyes flashing blue once more. "Apologize to the lady."

Loathing flooded Simon's eyes as he looked up at her. "I'm sorry." Brwyn growled. "Please forgive me, Ms. Farr."

"You should learn how to talk to your betters," Reggie said, wanting a little payback for her bruised arm and Asher's humiliation.

"Ah, yes, and speaking of one's betters, apologize to the young man. It would take ten of you to replace one of Andrius Drake's personal Indentureds." Simon just scowled. Brwyn snapped his teeth. "Apologize!"

"Sorry," Simon spat. He glared at Asher, who stood looming over the other guards.

"Wasn't that civilized?" Brwyn asked, kissing Reggie's hand before directing his attention back to the patrol. "Get the hell out of my sight. The next time you disobey me, the only remains they'll find are your bones."

Simon pushed himself to his feet. With one last glare at Reggie, he sprinted out of the small camp, the other guards following. She relaxed and looked at Brwyn, whose green eyes focused on the purpling mark on her upper bicep.

"I should have killed them."

"They're not worth getting all bloody for again." She gently removed her hand from Brwyn's. Asher stood next to her and she tucked herself into his body, rubbing her sore arm. She was relieved when his arms circled her waist. "Thanks for your help. How did you know we were in trouble?"

Brwyn observed them, a knowing glint in his eyes. "Your magic. It spiked, and my senses were flooded with the most amazing smell. So close to nature, it called to the wolf."

"The wolf?" Reggie asked. "You talk like you're separate beings."

"We are. He's my other half. He told me to protect and his instincts are infallible. I can never let him have complete control of course; he doesn't understand life's little nuances. He smelled your distress and came for you. I was only too happy to follow."

"Thanks to the both of you then."

"Yes, thank you. But it's not over. You humiliated them, they'll want revenge," Asher said.

"They're not stupid enough to go after you themselves. But they'll make sure other guards look for you, and that could make life very unpleasant. What are your plans?"

Reggie glanced at Asher, waiting for him to make the decision. Her mouth had gotten them into enough trouble.

Asher watched Brwyn for a long moment. "I have to go to Two Cities and report back to my master. We'll go to the Witch Plains to catch an airship to Holden's Folly for transfer."

Brwyn smiled. "Now was that so hard? You'll have to stay in Holden's Folly overnight. Go to the Lavender Inn, the owners generally turn a blind eye to that sort of thing." Reggie's face went hot, and Brwyn smirked at her. "You'll be safe. Until you get there, make sure all your documents are in order and stay in separate cabins."

Asher nodded. "We'll be careful."

Reggie kept her eyes on Brwyn's face, trying to ignore his nudity. "The wolf must really like me."

Brwyn leaned forward and inhaled her scent. "He's not the only one. You know, sweetheart, I, too, will be in Holden's Folly shortly. I'd be happy to escort you around, show you the sights."

She smiled. "I've seen enough of your sights. Besides, I have the escort part covered."

Brwyn laughed at Asher's grimace. "Yes, yes, I can smell. You've marked her. No need to get angry."

"He's what—let's not talk about marking people," Reggie said, blushing.

"What is it with young women and tragic heroes? Well, my dear, if you ever get tired of him, let me know. I need to find my clothes and go. Can't have all the ladies distracted."

Reggie rolled her eyes.

"Thank you, brother, for all your help," Asher said, holding out his hand. Bryn clasped it briefly.

"May the Mother be on your side." Brwyn dashed into the forest, a blur of beastly power.

She pulled away from Asher, holding her throbbing arm. "Give it to me straight, how bad did I screw everything up?"

He covered her fingers with his. "How's your arm?"

His gentle concern made her feel guiltier. "It hurts. Another bruise to add to my collection."

Asher sighed and dropped his hand. "It could've been worse. Thank the Mother for the Changeling." He laughed.

Startled, Reggie stared at him. "You're not mad?"

"The way you went after that guard, he wasn't expecting that." He shook his head, grinning.

"I was so pissed, I was afraid that if I didn't say something—"

"You would've lost control of your magic again?" he asked. She nodded. "That's why I let you go. I took a chance that if you could handle this like you would in the Real, your magic wouldn't come into play."

"It didn't, but I still messed up."

"Losing your temper here is dangerous. The things you yelled at the guards could be interpreted as Resistance sentiments. I understand, I hate them too, but you have to keep yourself in check. Now we'll be harassed from here to Two Cities. Never

115

forget that this isn't like your home. You have to be very careful what you say here."

Reggie sighed. "I know. You deal with this everyday. I get it for five minutes and can't keep my mouth shut. God, I feel stupid."

"You're not. A little reckless, maybe. Besides, the guards chose to confront us at a very bad time." His eyes met hers, and the memory of their kiss stretched between them. "Thank you for defending me."

The raw sincerity of his gratitude melted her. "It was the least I could do."

"No one has done that for me before."

"They should have. But in the future, I promise to shut up, even if the person really deserves it."

He laughed. "I'll hold you to that."

"Asher, about what happened between us—"

"We can't talk about it now. We need to start moving again, I'm sorry—"

Embarrassed, she held up her hand. "Okay, I get it. You're right, we should probably go."

He nodded. "We'll talk, just not tonight. Come on. Let's find a different place to make camp. It's a few hours before dawn, and I don't want to sleep here."

"Me neither."

CHAPTER 18

*T*he filmy light of morning touched John's eyelids, waking him. He'd camped close to the gateway the night before, just in case Reggie came back through. Stretching to his feet, John sighed. Reggie could take care of herself, but he still worried. If only he could've gone with her. John doused the small campfire with water from his bottle, covering the smoking embers with rocks. He slipped on his backpack and began the long hike back.

Every minute John drew closer to home, he was another minute closer to telling Reggie's mother the truth. He shuddered. That was going to be one ugly conversation. After walking for half an hour, John spotted a woman speeding toward him. The woman froze like stalked prey. She slowly lifted her head, eyes narrowing on him. Freckles blotted her skin, and her long red hair gleamed like a sheet of copper. She was about his height and reed-slender. He guessed her to be in her mid twenties.

"Good morning," John called. She observed him for a few seconds before lifting a hand.

"Morning." Her voice held a melodic accent that John found familiar. A ripple of unease crawled up his skin, but then she flashed a warm smile. "I'm so sorry to bother you, but I haven't seen anyone else all morning. This may seem odd, but I was wondering if you could help me?"

John stopped in front of her. "Are you lost or something?"

She shook her head. "No, I'm looking for someone who might be in trouble. I have a picture. Do you mind taking a look? Maybe you've seen her?" The woman rummaged in the pocket of her cargo pants, pulling out a photo.

"Sure." John plucked the photo from her hand. His guts froze into a block of ice. Reggie's face stared back.

"Do you know her?" She did have the same accent as Asher. Her lips smiled, while her eyes scanned his face like lasers.

John exhaled slowly, steadying his hands. He needed to buy time to think, to plan. "Uh, no, it's just that I go to school with her. This is Reggie Lang."

The woman's eyebrows reached for her hairline. "Really? Maybe you could help me find her."

"Why are you looking for her? What kind of trouble is she in?"

"Sorry, I'm Megan Treston. I specialize in finding missing children. Reggie's mother called the police yesterday to report that Reggie never came home from a hike. My team is out searching for her now." Megan extended her hand to John.

As he took it, a small charge of power like static electricity passed from her palm to his. It wasn't strong, but John knew it wasn't static. That was magic. He missed the days when all the magic he had to deal with was on his Playstation.

This woman was probably Andrius' agent sent to take Reggie back to the Other. Maybe I can't help Reggie there, he thought, but I'll be damned if I let this psycho get her. "Do you have ID?"

"ID?" Megan echoed. "Sure, here you go." She fumbled in her pocket, pulled out a shiny gold badge, and flashed it.

John caught a glimpse of flames encircled by a ring. It didn't resemble any police badge he'd ever seen on TV, but he kept his face neutral. "Okay. How can I help?"

"Come with me. I really appreciate you doing this. Normally I wouldn't allow a civilian to help in an official search, but since you know her, you're probably my best shot at finding her. You'll be able to recognize her more easily."

"Awesome. Which way are we heading?"

"Back that way." Megan pointed in the direction he'd just come from.

John hesitated, wanting to lead her from the gateway. "I just came from there. I didn't see anyone."

"I've been following the tracks of a hiking party heading this way. Reggie might've been with them."

"Maybe, but people hike through here daily."

"But not many venture off the trail. Time is precious, and this is my first solid lead of the day. I have to check it out."

He was afraid of that. But he couldn't think of a plausible excuse to head back into town. And he couldn't let her out of his sight. "Lead the way."

They began walking up the hill.

"By the way, you never told me your name."

And he didn't want to now. One thing he'd learned from all those magic sites he'd researched, bad things happened when you gave your true name. "It's Jay."

She glanced at him from the corner of her eye. "Jay? What brings you way out here by yourself, Jay?"

"I'm an Eagle Scout. I have a test coming up. So you're a tracker, huh? I guess that's why they sent you." He wanted her to keep talking, give him some clue about her abilities.

"I know my way around a forest."

That cool assurance worried him. "I guess we have a better chance of finding her then."

"I think finding you has improved my odds quite a bit." Megan smiled at him.

CHAPTER 19

*T*he Witch Plains stretched before Reggie in an endless ocean of pale emerald, the shin-deep grass rippling like waves. She and Asher stood on the edge of the treeline. They'd spent the last couple of hours running hard, and she was exhausted. Her wet shirt clung to her skin, clammy and uncomfortable. All she wanted was a hot shower and food that wasn't packaged. And time to think. Between meeting her father, kissing Asher, and being attacked, her mind was a stew of confusion.

She leaned against a tree.

"Are you okay?" Asher asked, his voice polite.

She gritted her teeth at his neutrality. Ever since their kiss and Brwyn's offhand revelation that Andrius lent Asher out to be ridden like the town bike, Asher had shut down, treating her with casual courtesy.

"Fine, just tired. We can go—wait, what's that?"

Reggie spotted a large craft hovering in the air about a quarter of a mile away, standing out like a beacon. A cross between a ship and a blimp, the craft had an observation deck and windows cut into the wooden sides. But what fascinated Reggie most were the black, intricate symbols painted along the outside of the wooden hull and the white, air-filled canopy. The symbols had the sloping elegance of Japanese characters, with complicated swirls and patterns.

"You like it?" Asher asked. "It's an airship. It's the fastest way to cross the Witch Plains. There are transportation stations all along the Plains."

A ramp led from the floating airship to the top of a two-story wooden platform. Wide steps led from the platform to the ground. At the bottom, Reggie saw a modest brick building, and a large crowd of people standing in line.

"It's beautiful." She turned to find him watching her. She grinned. Slowly, he smiled back. "What are those drawings on the side?"

"They're sigils. Magical symbols. They harvest power from the ley lines and feed the engine of the ship."

"You use magic the way the Real uses gas or electricity."

Asher nodded. "It fuels everything here. We're going to take this ley line to Holden's Folly, and then transfer to another ley line. We'll finally be able to get some decent food."

"And a shower? I smell."

"I noticed a strange odor this morning," he said.

"I'm not the only one who's ripe," she shot back, relieved at his teasing.

Asher put his hands up in mock surrender. "True."

Reggie frowned at the airship. "There's something I don't get. You have all this sophisticated magic, so why were the guards using knives last night?"

"Everyone has different levels of magical ability. Some can barely light a candle, while others can blast a hole through a person. And drawing magic from the Earth is tiring. Sometimes it's easier to cut someone down with a sword than to use magic."

"And you never know if the person you're facing is stronger than you."

"Exactly. Come, we've stayed here too long." He glanced behind them quickly, stepping onto the Plains.

His words reminded her of the danger of the vengeful guards. She followed him.

A jolt of pure, raw energy shot up her spine. Reggie's bones felt like liquid. And for the second time in as many days, she hit the ground.

"Are you all right?" Asher's face was close to hers. When she didn't answer, he pulled her against his chest. "Reggie, talk to me!"

She trembled, "Something's inside me, fighting against my magic."

"It's the energy of the ley lines. I feel it too, but I'm used to it. Relax and just breathe. Let it in."

Closing her eyes, Reggie sucked air into her tight chest. She focused on the alien magic inside her, smoothing away its jagged edges, encouraging it to bind with her blood. A few moments later, the pressure eased. She sagged against Asher in relief.

"Better?" he asked, and she nodded. "Ley lines carry great power. They can enhance your natural ability if you know how to use them." He stood, carrying her with him, gripping her arms until she stopped swaying.

"Thanks. Sorry I can't seem to stay on my feet. It's starting to piss me off."

"Can you walk? We do need to move."

"I won't be winning any races, but I can manage." She stumbled forward.

"We'll be there soon, just take one step at a time, slowly. There you go." Asher took her elbow.

Reggie obeyed. After a few steps, her balance returned. Asher stopped suddenly, releasing her arm. He was concentrating on a cluster of people waiting in line. His eyes roved over them methodically, his mouth pressed into a grim line.

"Asher?" Reggie whispered, afraid.

"I'm looking for border guards. I was careless not to look for them before."

"It's my fault. I can't seem to stay on my feet for more than five minutes at a time."

"That's no excuse. I don't see anything, although they could be in civilian clothes, but I doubt it."

"Why?"

"They'd want to publicly humiliate me. Let's buy our tickets." Asher led her down to the line. He stopped, fumbling in his pack. "I need to get my identification."

Reggie observed the line in front of her. The people were all shapes, sizes, and species. An elf family waited together, a male and female, and a little girl. Their ears were longer and more pointed than Asher's, lying close to their head. Eyes the color of pine needles stood out against ivory skin.

Ahead of the Elves were a group of towering figures around seven feet tall or more. All male, their bodies roped with heavy muscle that boasted great strength. She guessed they were Giants. No wonder Asher could tangle with a car and walk away. Different groups peppered the line. There weren't any outright displays of hostility, but she noticed the individual clusters kept close together. A few curious gazes roamed over them, but when Reggie stared back, their eyes flicked away. Then it hit her. Her ancestral line stretched before her. These were her people.

"Found it," Asher said, holding up his identification.

Twenty minutes later, Reggie and Asher walked across the ramp and onto the main deck of the airship. Asher had purchased their tickets with gold coins bearing elemental symbols. She hated not having money, of being even more dependent on him.

"Where's my cabin? I'd like to clean up," Reggie said.

"You're in . . . 3B. I'm right next to you." Asher held up a brass key. "I'll clean up as well, then meet you back here. We can get something real to eat."

Reggie took her key from his hand. "Sounds good to me."

CHAPTER 20

*J*ohn walked beside Megan, trying to think of ways to stall her. They neared the gateway, and soon he'd be able to hear it.

"How long have you known Reggie?" Megan asked, gracefully avoiding rocks embedded in the ground.

"Since middle school."

"You're friends?"

"We've talked a few times. She's nice."

"You're a good man to help a girl you barely know."

"She'd do the same. She's that type of person." John was wary about the fluid way Megan moved. He needed to distract her, find a weapon.

"You have a crush on her, Jay?" Megan teased.

Startled, John tripped on a rock.

"You okay?" she asked

John balanced on one foot, faking an injury. "I think I sprained my ankle. Could you get a stick or something I could use?"

Megan stared at his melted sneaker. "What happened to your shoe?"

Shit. "Oh, I left them too close to the fire. Sucks, huh? How about that stick?"

She searched his face until he felt sweat break out. "Sure."

She picked up a stick. It was thin, but it came up to his chest. "Thanks," he said, taking it from her.

Inclining her head, she started walking again. He hobbled after her. As they lapsed into silence, the terrain steepened. John glanced at Megan. She should already be feeling the whatever-it-was-magic people felt when they neared the gateway. He needed to make his move. He couldn't let her through the barrier.

"How's the leg?" Megan asked, interrupting his thoughts. "Is the walking stick helping?" Her tone was considerably less friendly.

"Yeah, it is. I'm usually not so clumsy. Sleeping on the ground didn't help. I guess you don't get much sleep, being a cop and all."

"I'm used to it. Now I really don't need sleep to stay alert. It's amazing the endurance you build." Her eyes darted briefly to the branch then to his face.

"Do you think we'll find Reggie?" There it was, that faint buzzing sound.

"I think I'm missing some pieces of information, but yes, I'll find her." Megan adjusted her leather satchel, her hands lowering to rest on her utility belt.

Could he take her by himself? She was lighter than him but moved like a martial artist, like Reggie. If he couldn't stop her, at least he could slow her down. Buy Reggie some time.

John stopped. "What's that weird sound?" He tightened his grip on the stick.

"Judging by your shoe, I think you know." Megan had stopped too. "What do you plan on doing with that?"

"Walk. What else would I use it for?"

"You tell me," Megan said, sliding a large knife from her utility belt.

John stared at the curve of the blade. Blood rushed to his head.

"We both know I'm not a cop, but the real question is, what are you?" She began circling him. "I can't sense anything, but maybe you're good at cloaking your magic."

Abandoning pretense, John switched grips on the stick, bringing it around until he held it like a baseball bat. "I'm not letting you get Reggie."

"Did Andrius promise to change your blood, you sniveling little worm? Where is Reggie?"

John jabbed at her with his stick, and she jerked back but kept looping around him, faster and faster. "You're the one Andrius sent!"

"I'm going to find her if I have to gut you to do it." She slashed at him, he swung at her, deflecting the blade.

His heart thundered in his chest. "You're not going to get the chance to hurt her!"

"Ahh, so concerned. Maybe Andrius chose you because you look so innocent."

"I'm Reggie's best friend! And you're a liar. I can prove it."

"Pathetic." Suddenly Megan charged him.

John swiped at her again but missed. Steel parted the skin on his upper arm. "You bitch! You cut me!"

"And I'll do worse if you don't start talking." Scarlet flashed on her blade.

"Cut me again, it doesn't matter. Reggie's safe. Rhys sent someone for her."

Megan's jaw slackened. "What did you say?"

John took advantage of her momentary lapse, hitting her knife hand hard with his stick. Megan yelped but held onto the knife.

"You're too late! They're bound to be miles away by now."

"Son of a bitch!" Megan swore. "Jay, listen to me, I'm the one Rhys sent to help Reggie."

"Why should I believe you?" John challenged.

Megan held the knife in front of her, dropping it on the ground. He watched her kick the handle with the toe of her boot, sending the blade spinning over by his feet.

"Take it." Megan nodded at the blade. "I believe you're Reggie's friend, but you need to tell me who she's with or something very bad is going to happen to her. I'm not going to hurt you. Please trust me." She raised her hands in surrender.

John shifted the branch to one hand, bending down slowly to take the knife. His arm hurt like hell. Megan's eyes held his as he straightened. "This could just be some trick. I don't know what your power is here. Besides, this guy with Reggie, he saved her from getting beat up. If he was so bad, why would he do that?"

Megan shook her head. "I don't think Andrius would want his prize damaged."

"His prize? I thought he wanted to kill her."

"Rhys believes Andrius wants to test her power first. See how he can use her before he discards her."

John's eyes searched Megan's face for answers, but all he could see was worry. "I'm not telling you anything until you can prove that Rhys sent you."

"Jay, I don't have time to—"

"No proof, no deal."

"Okay. But you'll have to put down your weapons and take my hands." She sat on the ground, holding out her hands, palms up.

"What the hell are you doing?"

"Giving you proof. I'm taking you to Rhys."

"How? By holding hands and singing Kum-ba-yah?"

She heaved an impatient sigh. "I'm going to take you to the Dream Realm."

"We're not asleep."

"I still have enough power for that."

"The minute I touch you, you could rip into my mind."

"Not in the Real. Besides, that's not my specialty" She took out her badge once more, pointing at the flames. "See this? Fire is my element."

"So you could burn me to death. Reassuring."

She shook her head. "Hardly. Watch."

Narrowing her eyes, she focused on his branch. Seconds ticked by. Suddenly flames burst from the tip. John jerked back, and the fire quickly died. He looked at Megan. Sweat ran down her face and her shoulders sagged. She focused on the branch again, her teeth sunk into her lower lip. Nothing happened.

"See?" she said raggedly. "You're safe with me." She held out her hands again.

Could Asher be the real threat to Reggie? John needed to know, and while he normally wouldn't trust someone who'd attacked him, helping Reggie was worth the risk. And if Megan was lying, he could still buy Reggie time.

"Fine," he conceded, dropping the weapons. "Just let me wipe this blood off."

"I'm sorry about that."

"Whatever," John dismissed her apology, sitting down Indian style. He clasped her small hands. "Now what?"

Chapter 21

Megan folded her fingers over Jay's, feeling guilty at the sight of his wounded arm. "Close your eyes. Picture Rhys' name in your mind. Hold it there. I'm going to count us back, okay?"

He sighed. "Wait. I guess you need my real name, huh?"

She laughed. "Yes, please."

"John."

"Here we go, John."

"I'm ready."

"Ten, nine, eight," she began, focusing on Rhys and John, linking them in her mind with her own image. Megan drew what power she could from the Earth, feeding the link until she felt something within her tighten like a tuned guitar string. The blackness beneath her lids morphed into a whirlpool, sucking her down into the Dream Realm. She flew in the void, John beside her, his eyes bulging. She silently chanted Rhys' name, hoping he would answer her call.

A room formed around their bodies, slowing their flight. Megan swayed a little as she touched the gleaming wooden floor, seeing a pink-veined marble fireplace and antique chairs. The exact construct Rhys preferred. John stared at her, mouth agape.

"Welcome to the Dream Realm." Megan gestured to one of the chairs flanking the fireplace. "Sit, before you fall down."

John walked on wobbly legs to a chair. "These are fancy digs. Now what?"

Megan sighed. "Now we wait and hope Rhys got my message. It's much harder to contact someone when they're awake. In most cases, it's impossible."

"How do I know this guy is really Rhys?"

"Question him until you're satisfied. How are you feeling?"

"You mean besides bleeding, sitting in the freaking Dream Realm, trying to help my best friend from getting killed?" He shrugged. "Some motion sickness, no biggie."

Megan sat across from him, forcing herself not to pace. She repeated Rhys' name again and again in her mind. Ten minutes ticked by. Panic started to set in when the air bent. A crack formed in the far wall of the room and a piercing light blinded Megan. When she could see again, Rhys stood before her.

John jumped out of his seat, knocking his chair back a few inches. "Holy shit!"

Rhys' eyes flicked over John. "What's happened? Who is this? Where's Reggie?"

Megan scooted to the edge of her seat. "I don't know. This is her friend John. I found him near the barrier—"

"You're Rhys?" John interrupted. "Reggie mentioned the duster, but that doesn't prove anything. What's her mom's name?"

Rhys studied him. "Arlene."

"How'd she meet Reggie's dad?"

"Arlene was lost in the woods when she ran into Sebastian. He took her home."

John was quiet. "Okay, that checks out."

Rhys nodded. "You're bleeding. Are you all right?"

John blinked, glancing at his injured limb. "I'll be okay."

"Please sit." Rhys turned back to Megan, his voice urgent. "Tell me what happened."

134

"I actually cut John. I thought he was working for Andrius," she admitted, ashamed. "Andrius has already sent someone to take Reggie back—"

John broke in. "A guy named Asher, real tall, black hair, his ears are kinda pointy, probably gets a lot."

"What do you mean 'gets a lot?'" Megan said.

"You know, he's a good looking dude. Anyway, he saved Reggie from being attacked at our school, told her you sent him to take her back to the Other. They left last night."

Rhys stilled at this information, his scar prominent. "An Indentured."

"What's an Indentured?"

"A hybrid servant. Megan, what do we know about the Indentureds in Council House?"

"Not much. We've been watching Andrius' Ravens, his trusted commanders. There are so many Indentureds in Council House . . ." Megan shrugged her shoulders, helpless.

Rhys' fist rattled the wooden mantle. "What game is Andrius playing? Why would he choose to send an Indentured?"

"And how would the hybrid know you were sending someone? Could there be a leak?"

"Doubtful. John, you said this man rescued Reggie?"

John nodded.

Rhys began pacing. "My guess is that when Asher saved Reggie, she jumped to the wrong conclusion. Believed I'd sent him. It would've been quicker to send a soldier, but there'd be a greater risk of injuring Reggie. She would have fought, and Andrius doesn't want her harmed."

"So he sends a handsome young man who plays the hero. That's brilliant," Megan said.

"Asher leads her, willingly, right to Andrius. Reggie knows nothing about the Other, so he can make up whatever story he likes."

"That son-of-a-bitch!" John shot from his chair again. "What are you going to do?"

"John, I'm going to find her. I promise you." She clasped his hand.

John looked down at her with tormented eyes. "Let me go with you." He looked at Rhys. "Can't you shoot me up me with magic or something?"

Rhys said gently, "Playing with bloodlines is a dangerous game. You'll have to help Reggie from the Real. I need to talk to Megan alone now. You're going to wake up. She'll be with you soon."

The wall behind John split open. Shadows covered him, and he was yanked away like a yoyo on a string.

Megan focused on Rhys. "Should I contact Reggie in the Dream Realm? Andrius is watching for you, not me."

"No, she'll think you're one of his agents. The only thing you can do now is track her. I'll send reinforcements to you. I'll find out all I can about the Indentureds working in Council House. Someone must have had dealings with Asher if he belongs to Andrius. If he's as striking as John said, he wouldn't easily blend in."

"People tend to look right through servants."

"Beauty attracts its own kind of attention. Once I have more information, I'll contact you. When you find them, don't approach him. Contact me first."

"You don't think I can handle him on my own?" Megan asked, her soldier's pride hurt.

"I don't know what kind of training he's received or how much power he has." He suddenly grinned. "Andrius might have been short-sighted this time."

"What do you mean?"

"To throw an Indentured and an Aether Mage together? That's a dangerous temptation. Asher has the key to his freedom walking beside him. Either the boy is evil or Andrius has one hell of a piece of leverage."

"You don't rescue someone if you're evil."

"Precisely, but we don't know what Asher's game is. Your orders are the same, let's just pray to the Mother that Asher has a conscience. Go take care of John."

"I'll do what I can for him."

"Do it quickly," Rhys said.

Chapter 22

*R*hys summoned Andrius, betting on the dark mage's curiosity. Andrius was like a cat; he could never resist swiping at a string. Rhys kept his mind blank, forcing Andrius to create the meeting place, hoping to gain insight into his mind. Suddenly Rhys landed on a white floor surrounded by gray walls. The room was sterile and cold. He smelled the sharp odor of disinfectant.

Andrius sat shirtless in a chair, his long legs spread out before him, his arm resting on a metal table. His forearm was stretched out, the vulnerable underside exposed. A tube stuck out from his vein, running to a bag hanging from a hook. Blood dripped from the bag into his arm.

"Welcome, Rhys. Forgive me if I don't get up."

Rhys leaned against the wall. "Stealing again?"

Andrius grinned. "Can't steal what was freely given."

"It's not free if it was based on a lie."

"It wasn't all a lie."

"You must be running low on supplies. I don't think your research has worked out the way you hoped."

Andrius sat up straighter. "How can I help the great Rhys Griffith tonight?"

"His name is Asher. He's an Indentured, probably one of your personal slaves. He's with Reggie Lang, making his way to you. I suppose that's why you're shooting up. Afraid of a little girl?"

"Little girls can be dangerous." He chuckled. "Asher was an inspired choice. You expected me to send a soldier. As always, you're two steps behind."

Rhys stared at this man who had been like his brother. "Even if Asher manages to deliver her, you won't keep her without a fight."

"You'd openly engage me? I didn't know your numbers were that great."

"You left an Aether Mage with an Indentured. She is his walking, talking tool for freedom. Your stolen magic has made you overconfident."

Andrius yanked the tube from his arm, standing up. Blood spilled onto the floor. "I never do anything without a guarantee that I'll get my return. Asher is quite safe from Reggie's temptation. As for my 'stolen' magic, you're not exactly an innocent."

"At least my motives were pure," Rhys said, holding his ground as the dark mage advanced toward him.

"Is that what you tell yourself? Whatever your motives, you're not pure anymore." Andrius stopped a few inches from him, blood spiraling down his arm.

"That is my greatest regret."

"I thought failing to kill me was your greatest regret."

"I haven't failed to kill you yet." Rhys severed his connection to the Dream Realm.

He needed to know who Asher was: his magical abilities, primary responsibilities, and family ties. He had to find the hammer to break Andrius' hold. Andrius was reinforcing his powers. The dark mage expected Reggie soon.

CHAPTER 23

*A*sher watched Reggie dozing across from him in a chair. They sat on the upper deck of the airship, empty plates beside them. A purple handprint tattooed her upper arm, reminding him of his failure to protect her. He wanted to punch something. But was he really any different than those guards? Once his lies were exposed, the truth would be much more painful than a bruise.

It hurt to watch her sleep, knowing how deceitful he was being. She was so open and honest. Her friendship was a gift, making him feel almost normal. When they were together, he could almost forget how Andrius had passed him around like a prostitute. Forget the women he'd serviced, who had used him like a windup toy. Lying to Reggie made him feel worse than committing those sordid acts. The guilt was unbearable.

"You okay?" Reggie asked, the sleepy question interrupting his thoughts.

"Just stop."

"Stop what?"

"Being so nice. I can't take it! Don't you understand what I am? What is wrong with you?" Asher said.

Reggie sat up, her face stunned. "What are you talking about?"

"I'm a slave and a whore for Andrius."

"God, Asher! That's not your fault. I don't care about that." She reached for him.

He pulled away from her. "You should. I'm disgusting—"

"Shut up!" Her voice rose, drawing the attention of their fellow passengers. Blushing, she whispered, "Don't say that. You've been treated horribly. Maybe that makes you think you're disgusting. But you're not. You're brave and sweet and—"

"I'm going to get you killed. Look where we're going. We're going to where Andrius lives!"

"Because he'll hunt you down. You have to go."

"To save my own hide. If I was really brave, I wouldn't care about my life."

"That's warped! I'd do the same thing in your position. I'm not suicidal, and neither are you."

"Reggie, getting attached to each other is a mistake. It's very likely one of us will die. Stop being so good to me. Stop making me feel like I can be someone different, someone normal."

Reggie jerked back. "You can be!"

"I don't deserve to."

"That's bullshit."

"We can't be friends."

"Friends don't normally make out. We're not friends."

Her eyes were shiny as she blinked. Asher felt like he'd been kicked in the chest.

He stood up. "Reggie, I'm sorry. I didn't mean to be such an ass."

"Too late," she said.

"I don't want to hurt you."

"Just go away and leave me alone." She turned away from him.

He looked at her profile, feeling ill. "I'll be in my cabin if you need me. Take some money just in case you want to buy more food." He placed four gold coins on her armrest.

She glanced at the coins, and then met his eyes. Her tears were frozen now. "Go to hell."

Asher stood still. She held his gaze until he lowered his eyes, walking away.

CHAPTER 24

*R*eggie watched Asher disappear down the stairwell leading into the interior of the ship. She was shaken, sick to her stomach. She didn't understand what had just happened, but she put her hurt in a drawer to examine later. She needed to focus on more important things. Like her father.

Was what she saw real? Her father trapped in a bubble, floating in a zombie-like state. In the Dream Realm, Reggie didn't know what was true, if anything. She knew a link had to be established between two minds, meaning her father was alive. But she had no idea what condition he was in. Reggie had been missing her father her entire life. If there were a way she could save him, she would find it.

Unfortunately, Andrius Drake stood between them like a giant roadblock. What good was having magic if she couldn't protect herself against him? She had the power, but didn't know how use it—how to bend it to her will and make it obey her, instead of reacting unpredictably to her every emotion.

A few hours later, Reggie was tucked into the narrow bunk in her cabin, staring at the ceiling, her mind spinning. She hadn't seen Asher since their fight. Kissing her had obviously rattled him. That, and the public revelation that Andrius passed him around like a party favor. If she were honest with herself, she was rattled too. Asher was a victim of abuse, and Reggie didn't know how to handle that. She was out of her depth. He believed he was damaged goods, unfit for a normal relationship.

She didn't know how to convince him otherwise or if he could be convinced.

His harsh words had wounded her, but his warning scared her more. He thought they weren't going to make it. She always knew there was a possibility she could die in the Other, but she'd hidden that thought away, refusing to dwell on it. Even after the attack by the guards, she'd persuaded herself she was safe because Asher was with her. Hearing him admit that death was close unnerved her. She felt he was holding back, unwilling to tell her the whole truth about their situation.

Reggie squirmed against the lumpy pillow until she found a comfortable spot, closing her eyes. Eventually, exhaustion claimed her mind, and she fell asleep.

Glancing around, Reggie saw she was standing in a forest with towering redwoods. Then Reggie saw her father. She lunged for him, wrapping her arms around him tightly.

"Well, hello to you too, sweetheart." Sebastian chuckled, hooking an arm around her shoulders.

"I love you, Dad." Reggie said. Sebastian tucked a stray hair behind her ear.

"And I love you. We have a little more time tonight to talk. How are you surviving the Other?"

Reggie lowered her eyes. "I pissed off some border guards."

Two fingers tipped up her chin. "Are you hurt?"

"Just a bruise on my arm, nothing major."

Sebastian examined the discolored flesh, his voice like granite. "Stupid brutes, always resorting to violence. This looks painful. Are you sure you're okay?"

Reggie nodded, stepping back.

"Why did they attack you?"

"Because they thought me and Asher—this guy I'm with—were a couple."

"That's an extreme reaction. Who's Asher?"

"My guide. He's an Indentured."

"Ahh, that explains it. Disgusting how deep prejudice runs here now." Sebastian's eyes glazed over, and his thoughts seemed to disappear to a place she couldn't follow.

"Dad?"

Shaking himself, he focused on her. "I don't remember Rhys mentioning an Asher, but our communication is unclear sometimes. Such an odd choice."

"What's wrong with an Indentured?"

He looked at her. "Nothing. I just assumed Rhys would send a soldier, someone who could protect you."

"Asher can protect me. Enough about that. Tell me what's going on with you. Where are you in the Other?"

"We'll discuss that later. First I need to tell you something."

"Let's talk about it now. I want to help you."

"What I'm going to tell you is crucial to your survival. You need to hear the story of the very first Aether Mage. It will help you understand your magic and what you're capable of," Sebastian said.

Reggie put her hands on her hips, her battle stance when rationalizing with her mother. "Now, Dad, listen—"

"You listen. Nothing is more important than keeping you from Andrius. Our time together is limited, and I can't waste a second by arguing with you."

She blinked, taken aback by this authority. "Okay."

"You must trust that I know what's best here. Let us begin." Sebastian sat on the grass.

She sank down next to him. She wanted to press him about his location, but she was as eager for knowledge about her magic as for these precious moments with her father.

Reggie woke to the sound of cursing, the interior of her cabin still dark. Angry voices echoed in the hallway. Something hit her door hard, the frame shuddering on its hinges. She shot up from her bunk, her bare feet landing on the floorboards. She hurried to the door, her hand closing around the knob. Pressing her ear against the wood, she tried to hear what was happening. She recognized Asher's voice.

Reggie cracked open the door, peering out. Asher's bare back filled her vision, his muscles knotted with tension. She smelled the fury rolling off him, the potent musk burning her nostrils.

"Like I said, Ms. Farr is not to be disturbed. You've already looked at my papers. You have no reason to be here, and I'm not letting you through that door," Asher said.

"You forget yourself, slave. Simon wants to send her his love, and we're here to see that she gets it. Now move," a man's voice ordered. He sounded like he was chewing on gravel.

"You're just a step above Andrius' rejects. Piss off."

Reggie heard the sound of flesh striking flesh.

Asher swayed but held his ground. "Hit me again. Won't change anything."

"If that's the way you want it," another guard said.

A whistling crack split the air. A fine spray of blood rose over Asher's shoulder. Her gasp was smothered by his groan of pain. Opening the door wider, Reggie dug her fingers in the back of his waist between skin and pants. Asher's spine straightened at her touch. She shoved against him but he ignored her, trapping her behind him.

148

"That's all you've got? Andrius Drake is my master! Nothing you could do to me could compare to what he's done. What he'll do to you for injuring me. A damaged servant is a useless one. So hit me again. I think he'll forgive me if I rip out your throat."

Silence rang in Reggie's ears. Then she heard the floorboards creak, and one of the guards delivered another punishing blow. She watched Asher's hand rise, slashing downwards in a blurry motion. Bones snapped. A body hit the floor.

The rough voice shouted, "You bastard! I'll kill you for this."

"It'll take more than you," Asher said.

There was movement, the sound of a grunt as extra weight was taken on. "We'll be back. This isn't over."

Asher sighed. "It never is."

Uneven footsteps echoed in the hallway before disappearing. Once they had faded, Asher turned around.

"Holy shit!" Reggie gasped. Two weal marks cut into the flesh of his upper chest. "What did they hit you with?"

"A crop. I'm sorry those monsters woke you up. You can go back to bed now. I'll be fine."

"Thanks for your permission, tough guy. But those cuts are no joke. Come in, I'll bandage you up." She gently touched the skin near his wounds.

He grasped her wrist. "That's not a good idea."

Reggie looked into his eyes. Green depths radiated anger and something that made her blush. "Don't worry. I'll just play nurse."

"I'm not worried about you," he said, his thumb caressing the pulse in her wrist. He dropped her hand. "It seems Simon's taking his revenge early."

"Shocker. Why wouldn't you let me help?"

"You've been hurt enough."

"Will you be punished? I thought you couldn't fight back."

Asher ran a knuckle down her cheek, surprising her. "I'm having a bad day. I'm just so tired of it all. Andrius won't punish me for this. But the guards will keep coming after me."

"They'll keep coming after us," she corrected.

"Us," he said and then shook his head. "I'm going to clean up. Goodnight."

"Asher! Don't be stupid, let me help you."

He smiled. "You're more dangerous than those guards."

"Idiot," Reggie muttered, going back into her room.

If he wanted to play the martyr, let him. She would deal with him in the morning. Shaky, she fell back onto her bed. Despite the violence she'd just witnessed, one good thing had come out of tonight. With her father's help, she'd taken her first steps in understanding her magic.

CHAPTER 25

*H*olden's Folly spread across the Witch Plains like a giant octopus. Government and commerce buildings formed the bulk, with markets and private residences trickling like legs from the center. Reggie viewed the city from the deck of the airship, Asher standing beside her. She could smell animals, manure, vegetables, and civilization. But something was missing. Despite the crowded city and bustling businesses, no heavy smog or automobile fumes polluted the air.

"We're going to eat like kings today. This city is the central hub for the farming community, so everything is fresh."

Reggie turned, inspecting Asher. He looked haggard, his skin pale.

"How's your chest?"

"Better."

She shook her head. "If you say so. Asher, you mentioned something yesterday that bothered me."

He raised an eyebrow. "I gave you a lot to choose from."

She snorted. "Yeah, you did. Why do you think one of us is going to die?"

He leaned his elbows on the railing. "I shouldn't have said that. I didn't mean to upset you."

"You said it for a reason. Don't keep things from me to protect me."

"You know we're in a very dangerous situation. Andrius wants you, the guards want me, and it's very likely they're going to catch one of us. Then it'll be over. But it doesn't do any good to dwell on it."

"That's all it was? Nothing more?" Reggie asked.

"You know all that I know," Asher said.

She studied his face. His neutral expression pricked her. "If you want me to trust you, you have to trust me."

"I do trust you."

"This is my life on the line too, you know."

He crossed his arms over his chest "I know that. I can't forget."

Reggie stared out at the city again. Asher's hand rested on her shoulder. She glanced up at him.

"I'm sorry for yesterday. Truce?"

"Truce. So, who was Holden and what was his folly?"

"Before the war, this used to be Market City. And then Charles Holden led the Resistance against Andrius on the Witch Plains. Tried to starve the government troops by cutting them off from their food supply. It worked for a while."

"What happened?"

"Andrius' soldiers seized the city. One of his Ravens found Holden and publicly tortured and executed him."

She shuddered. "Let me guess, they renamed the city as a warning."

"Exactly."

"Andrius doesn't mess around does he?"

Reggie admired the tall, stone buildings hugging the wide streets of Holden's Folly. Bathed in bright, primary colors, the structures were decorated with tiled mosaics forming sigils similar to the ones painted on the airship. Watchtowers sprouted from some of the buildings, trees and gardens growing on their rooftops.

Clumsy, bubble-shaped vehicles resembling bumper cars clogged the streets. They hovered a few feet from the ground with slanted sigils painted on their sides. Reggie and Asher searched for the Lilac Inn, the place Brwyn recommended. Asher had a copy of a city map stuffed in his pocket.

"What are they?" Reggie asked, pointing at the floating vehicles.

"Land cruisers."

"Could we've taken one of those to Two Cities?"

Asher shrugged. "Yes, but it would've taken us a week to get there. The airship is much faster."

Crossing a busy intersection, Reggie weaved through the cruisers. Dodging an aggressive driver, she spotted a white marble building ahead, capped with a large dome. Carved into the dome were the four symbols of the elements. Longing pierced her chest. She stopped. Suddenly she was jerked off her feet as Asher grabbed her by the waist, moving her out of the path of a cruiser. Her feet hit the sidewalk a moment later.

"What's wrong? You could've been killed!" He glanced around them.

Heart racing, she pointed toward the building. "What's that?"

"What? Oh, that's an Elemental Temple dedicated to the Mother."

"I've heard you mention her before. Who is she?"

"Goddess of the Earth. Why do you ask?"

"I feel Her."

"You do?" He stared at the Temple, then at her face. "Come on, we need to find the inn."

"I have to go there."

Asher looked uneasy. "That's not a good idea. I don't know what'll happen if you go in."

"Nothing bad." Reggie's gut burned with certainty.

"After last night, I don't want to take the chance of getting caught if something bad does happen." He took her arm, steering them away from the Temple. "We should get off the street in case we're being followed."

Disappointment bubbled as she felt her connection to the Temple thin. But he was right. "Okay."

The Lilac Inn was tucked a few blocks away from the main market on a small, winding street. It lived up to its name, its stone painted in violet hues with tiles in darker mauve creating sigils. Reggie stepped over the shin-high fence enclosing the small garden in front, and kneeled on the grass.

"What are you doing?" Asher said.

"It's a surprise." She scooped up some loose dirt, putting it in her pocket.

"That requires dirt?" Asher watched her step back over the fence.

"Yep."

He shrugged, opening the door and gesturing her inside. "Ohh-kay. After you."

A thick lavender and green rug ran down the length of the hall, ending at a polished desk where a woman sat, smiling. She resembled a crocheted grape in her purple sweater.

"Good afternoon, sir, miss. Welcome to the Lilac Inn," the woman called, her voice deep but soothing.

As Reggie neared the desk, she saw that sitting the woman was a head taller than she was. A Giant.

"Good afternoon, madam. Do you have any rooms available?" Asher asked.

"Yes." Her eyes darted between them. "How many do you need?"

Reggie didn't miss the way the Giantess' eyes lingered on Asher's exotic features before inspecting her plainer face. She tensed for battle.

"Two, preferably adjoining each other. Just for tonight." Asher's smile could have cut steel.

The Giantess' smile warmed, becoming almost motherly. "It would be my pleasure to accommodate both of you."

His face softened. "I appreciate it."

Realizing there'd be no bloodshed, Reggie relaxed. "Is there somewhere I can drop off my laundry?"

"Just give it to me when you're ready. Enjoy your stay in Market City."

Asher grinned. "I'm sure we will."

Their rooms were on the second floor, adjoined by a large bathroom. Reggie entered her room, dumping her backpack on the bed. The lavender and green quilt had too much lace, but it looked clean and comfortable. She took out some spare clothes, laying on them on the bed. Then she went through the bathroom, knocking on Asher's door.

"Hey, do you mind if I clean up first? I feel gross. I'll meet you downstairs after I'm done."

"Sure. Let me know when you're finished so I can bathe. I'm not feeling so fresh myself," he said.

She laughed. "No problem."

Reggie carefully placed the dirt in a glass by the sink, viewing her reflection in the mirror. Her hair needed washing; its normal sheen had dulled. Stripping off her grimy clothes, she turned to the tub. It was made of an enormous clamshell; not a replica, an actual shell. She felt weird bathing in the shell, trying not to imagine the creature that had occupied it originally.

After she was finished, Reggie wrapped a fuzzy plum towel around her. She knocked on the adjoining door again.

"It's all yours," she called out. "See you downstairs."

She dressed quickly and hurried to the front desk, hoping to speak with the Giantess before Asher joined her. The Giantess was still alone, writing in a ledger.

"Sorry to bother you, but do you have a map of the city?"

"Of course. Anything particular you want to see?" the Giantess unfolded a small leather map across her desk, the Inn's location marked in purple.

"I'd like to visit the Temple," Reggie said, peering at the map.

"It's a walk, but it's one of the oldest Temples standing." The Giantess whispered a word, and purple ink slithered from the Inn's location on the map, drawing a line to the Temple.

Reggie hid her delight, accepting the map. "Sounds good."

"Reggie," Asher said behind her.

She whirled around, sliding the map into her back pocket. Asher looked refreshed, his damp hair curling against his neck. She noticed the gold collar was hidden again.

"Are we going out?"

He motioned toward the door and she followed. "I am. You should stay here. I don't think it's safe for you to roam around the city. I'm going to scout the immediate area, make sure it's secure. I'll bring food back later."

She crossed her arms. "You're injured. You need someone to watch your back."

"I don't want you there if I run into guards again."

"Asher, I can help—"

"You'll distract me, and one of us will get seriously hurt."

156

Reggie wanted to argue, but his expression was rock hard. Besides, she had the map. "Fine. I'll wait here."

Asher eyed her suspiciously. "Just like that?"

"Would you feel better if I threw a fit and took a swing at you?"

"Strangely enough, yes."

Reggie gestured to her bruised arm. "No can do. I'll stay put like a good little girl; I've learned my lesson."

He arched an eyebrow. "Really?"

She shrugged. "I don't have money. I don't know the city. It would be stupid for me to wander around on my own. Trust me Asher, I'll wait right here for you."

Chapter 26

*R*eggie dug the map out of her pocket to get her bearings. She felt guilty deceiving Asher. She knew that wandering through the city was reckless, but she needed to go to the Temple. She'd just be careful not to piss anyone off, blend in, and be as boring as possible. Despite the constant danger, Reggie had never felt more alive than she did in the Other. True, the Real had been her home for her entire life— and she missed her mother and John—but some piece was always missing. Now that she'd connected with her magic, she understood what that piece was.

Keeping her eyes averted as she walked, Reggie only dug out the map when necessary. The pretty residential streets near the Inn gave way to shops and restaurants. Some of these businesses sold spell books, and smelled strongly of herbs. Others smelled of blood. She passed through Treasure Alley where the crowded main market stretched for ten city blocks. Vendors sold items ranging from food to fabrics. She watched miniature wooden dolls dancing in a line, collapsing in a lifeless heap once their spell wound down, their faces frozen in a grotesque grin. Children clapped, delighted, but Reggie stifled the urge to run away.

Suddenly she felt that tug again, a silken cord pulling her toward the Mother. Rounding the corner, the Temple burst into view. She hurried toward it, admiring the friezes she hadn't been able to see before. Detailed carvings of Elves, Giants, and

Humans decorated the sides. The massive doors stood open. Climbing the steps, Reggie hovered in the doorway, unsure.

A rectangular pool of water ran down the middle of the Temple, steps leading into the pool from the shorter sides. Light streamed from the open dome, creating prisms in the water. An altar stood a few feet away from the pool, and Reggie smelled smoke. Above the altar was an image carved out of the marble wall. The Mother.

A four-armed female reached out toward her worshippers. On three of her palms were the symbols for Fire, Water, and Earth. The Mother's fourth arm cradled a baby to her breast, and the symbol for Air was chiseled into her forehead. The Mother's features were calm, almost androgynous. Her crown was jagged, like broken twigs.

Quickly glancing around, Reggie discovered that the Temple was empty. No worshippers or priests. She stepped over the threshold. The tug became a vise, latching onto her and dragging her inside. Reggie doubled over as pressure filled her. Her bones felt as if they'd popped, her skin stretched.

Wind whipped through the Temple, groaning as it caressed her body. Water spiked from the pool, crashing down. The torches lining the altar flared to life. A tremor rippled under her feet. Unsteady from the pain, she fell again and hit the marble floor. The pressure leaked from her body, leaving a feeling of bone-deep peace. She was calm, balanced. Closing her eyes, she savored the rare sensation until she realized she was no longer alone. Someone was watching her.

Fear coiled around Reggie. She didn't hear footsteps, but she knew they were coming. Warm breath touched her neck, and she suppressed a shudder. The intruder smelled her, breathing her in.

"Ahh," whispered a familiar voice. "Aether Mage."

Her eyes popped open, meeting Brwyn's gaze. Icy blue had bled into the green of his irises. He looked drunk. He inhaled her scent again, grinning. Reggie's heart galloped so hard, she didn't hear what he said at first. She shook her head.

"I'm not going to hurt you," Brwyn repeated. He caressed her face and she flinched. Dropping his hand, he frowned. "I don't think I could hurt you in here. The Mother is clearly on your side. Let me help you up, my delicious friend."

Reggie studied him. He looked amused, his smile a little deviant. Just like the first time they'd met. She nodded.

He drew her gently to her feet, burying his face in the crook between her neck and shoulder. Reggie shivered, shoving him away. He laughed.

"Heard of personal space?"

"Not when you smell that good." Brwyn appeared civilized today. His golden hair was pulled back into a sleek ponytail, and he wore a tailored charcoal suit. He preened for her, flashing another grin. "I do naked better."

Reggie refused to banter with him. His outrageous flirtation camouflaged a very dangerous creature. "Why do you think I'm an Aether Mage? They're all dead."

He arched a golden brow. "Little darling, do I look stupid to you? All the elements reacted to you in the presence of the Mother. Add that to your unique scent, and I'm afraid you can't deny it."

"Are you going to turn me in?"

"I've been searching for someone like you my whole life! Your secret's safe with me, little darling. Such power." His voice lowered to an animal growl. Reggie took a step back. "Sorry, my Wolf got a little carried away. He likes you."

For a brief moment, the outline of Brwyn's Wolf superimposed itself over his figure. The Wolf's tongue lolled to

161

one side, his tail thumping on the ground. Blue eyes gleamed with canine devotion.

"What are you looking at?" Brwyn asked.

Reggie shook her head and the image disappeared. "Brwyn, what do you want with me?"

All the teasing and humor vanished. His eyes became solid green. "Before, I just wanted to find out what you were. Your scent intrigued me. But now that I know you're an Aether Mage, I need your help. The natural balance of magic is off. Tainted magic has control now. There's always been bad magic. Someone practicing blood rites or other black arts, but this is different. This is rotten. The balance must be restored."

"You think I can restore the balance? How?"

"Kill Andrius Drake. Don't look so alarmed. You can bend the elements to your will. Destroy armies. You're a powerful weapon, or you wouldn't have been brought here."

"What do you mean?" Reggie asked.

"You, dear Regina, are clearly not from here."

"It's that obvious?"

"Asher covers it up pretty well, but you can't hide the truth from a Wolf." Brwyn patted his nose. "You must be from the Real."

"I thought you were a big shot government official. Why should I trust you?"

"It's called survival, love. I can openly hate Andrius and get killed, or I can be clever. Use my rare Changeling status and fight him from within. And being a 'big shot' places me in an ideal position to spy for the Resistance."

"You work for the Resistance?"

"Mostly for Rhys Griffith. I'm guessing you're going to Rhys, but you're taking the long way around."

"If you work for Rhys, why don't you know about me?" Reggie wanted to trust Brwyn. She needed another ally.

"I never said I was part of Rhys' inner circle. I'm in the public eye. The less I know, the better, in case I'm discovered and tortured. Why is an Indentured escorting you through the Other? Especially one belonging to Andrius."

"You don't need to know. Like you said, if you're discovered, the less you know, the less chance there'll be to screw things up."

Brwyn laughed. "You got me there." He grabbed her wrist, tucking her arm into the crook of his elbow.

Alarmed, she tried to pull away. "What are you doing?"

"Easy, little darling. I haven't tried to hurt you, have I?"

"No."

"You're staying at the Lilac?"

"Why?"

"Because I want to escort you home like a proper gentleman," Brwyn said, steering her toward the exit.

"You're a gentleman? Try something and I'll kick your ass." Reggie's gut told her she could trust Brwyn. More importantly, she could trust his Wolf. But she couldn't let him think he had the upper hand.

He patted her arm as they stepped outside into the sunshine. "You don't know how."

"Yes, I do," she bluffed, feeling vulnerable without Asher.

"If you did, those guards would be dead. You wouldn't need Asher to protect you. I wish I could help, but I don't know how. You're going to have feel out the elements, try to identify them the way I do with scent."

"That's nice and specific."

"I do what I can."

Brwyn tucked her arm against his body as they walked down a wide avenue toward Treasure Alley. Their closeness drew stares from two male Elves striding toward them, twin sets of green eyes studying her facial features, her neck. Reggie shrank back, sliding her fingers over her naked throat. Brwyn growled, his body vibrating against hers. The Elves dropped their eyes, their steps quickening.

"Why were they looking at my neck?" Reggie whispered.

"To see if you were an Indentured. It would be more acceptable if I was screwing a slave rather than having a relationship with a Human. It's not only Andrius who wants to keep the races separate. Some Elves can be real assholes too."

"Will they make a big deal about us being together? Report you?"

"They know who I am." Suddenly he leaned down, nipping her ear lightly. "And I'm very scary."

She laughed. Eventually she relaxed, enjoying his exuberant charm as he explained the layout of the city, pointing out areas to avoid, advising her to assume someone was always watching.

"By the way, how are you dealing with your new status?" he asked.

"Which one?"

"The hybrid one."

"I haven't really thought about it. The magic thing is enough. What does it matter, anyway? I'm still me," Reggie said.

Brwyn sighed. "Yes, but be aware that others might not see you that way. Take me, for example. I was in love once, can you believe it? And my parents weren't accepting of the relationship."

"Why?"

"Changelings are rare. My parents weren't pleased when they found out my secret lover was a Human. They wanted me to continue the Changeling race."

"I guess that means you have to be with another Changeling?"

"Precisely. I really hate them for that."

"You gave her up?"

Brwyn looked at her, the sparkle in his eyes gone. "She gave me up. She said she couldn't separate me from my family. I'm still angry with her."

Reggie felt his pain. She squeezed his arm. "I'm sorry."

"I want you to understand your situation, so you're not blindsided."

"If people judge me solely on my bloodlines, then they're not worth my time, are they?"

He placed an unexpected, tender kiss on her forehead. "Good girl."

They were nearing the Lilac Inn when Brwyn stilled, his head cocked to one side, the motion pure wolf. He shoved Reggie behind him, claws slicing from his fingers. His lifted his nose, sniffing the air.

She dug her fingers into his waist. "What is it?"

"Blood," he growled. "Asher's blood."

"Is he hurt? Dead?" She clenched him tighter.

"I don't smell death. But I do smell pursuit. Stupid and clumsy."

"Asher's not stupid. He had to come back!"

"I wasn't talking about Asher." He twisted around to look at her. His eyes glowed bright blue, his canines sliding out from below his lips. Reggie fought the primitive urge to flee. "Go check on him, I have other matters to tend to. It's time I teach the valuable lesson of obeying one's superiors."

Chapter 27

*R*eggie ran. When she reached the Inn, she glanced back. Brwyn had vanished, but she could still feel his power crawling over her skin. She went inside.

Rust colored stains spotted the carpet in the hallway. Dried blood. The Giantess paced back and forth in front of the staircase, a dagger cradled in an imposing fist.

"Thank the Mother you're back!" she cried when she saw Reggie.

"Where is he?"

"Upstairs. He wouldn't let me help. He went mad when I told him you weren't here. Are his attackers still out there?"

Reggie looked up at the towering figure. "It's being taken care of. Thanks for trying to help. I'm sorry we brought trouble to you."

The Giantess took Reggie's hand, smothering it with her own. "No trouble. It's not the first time I've seen an Indentured attacked. It won't be the last. If you need anything, let me know."

Reggie nodded, dashing up the stairs. She didn't bother with Asher's door, but instead ducked inside her own room and headed for the bathroom. A torn, bloody shirt was wadded up on the bathroom floor. She jumped as the adjoining door flew open. Asher stood in the doorway, holding a letter opener in one hand. His teethed were bared. He was bleeding, the right side of his face swollen, a gash under one eye. He dropped the letter opener the instant he recognized her. Crossing the space between them, he yanked her to him, kissing her hard.

Shocked, Reggie clung to him before he abruptly pushed her away.

"Don't ever scare me like that again! Where the hell have you been?"

Placing a hand over her racing heart, she gathered her scattered thoughts. "At the Temple. What's with the letter opener?"

"I thought the guards had managed to track me." Asher sagged against the doorframe. "I told you to stay here."

New lacerations decorated his chest and arms, some closed with crude black thread like a badly stitched rag doll. Bruises colored his ribs. "You need to sit down," she said.

To her surprise, he didn't protest, sitting in the chair next to the tub. She ran water in the seashell tub, her hands shaking. She wanted to cry. But crying never helped. Squaring her shoulders, she faced him, meeting his accusatory gaze.

"I'm sorry I scared you. It was shitty of me to lie to you. But don't worry. No one is coming. Brwyn is taking care of it." Reggie dipped a cloth into the water, wringing it out.

"Brwyn? The Changeling? How—" Asher sucked in a breath as she ran the cloth over his wounds. "I've already done this."

"Just shut up and let me, okay? I should've been with you. Maybe this wouldn't have happened."

He snagged her wrist. "That's ridiculous. This isn't your fault."

Their eyes met. "It's both of ours. Brwyn was at the Temple. Something . . . happened there. He knows what I am."

His grip tightened. "What?"

"I know. He says he wants to help. He means it. Where do you think they keep the bandages?" She gently freed herself.

"I have some in my pack, but Reggie—"

168

She was already in his room, coming back with gauze and plaster. He'd stitched the largest gash, but she figured she'd wrap it to keep it clean.

"Reggie, I don't know about the Changeling. They're odd creatures."

She laughed. "So is everybody else is this place. Brwyn has come to our rescue twice. Makes him okay in my book."

"I can do this myself. I've had practice."

"So have I."

They fell silent as she bandaged his wounds. Asher sat perfectly still, surprising her once again, allowing her to help him. When she'd finished with his chest and arms, Reggie cradled his battered face in her hands, inspecting the gash under his eye. It was shallow. The swollen skin and bruises needed to be iced. The wounds transformed his face from beautiful to dangerous. Shaking her head, she sighed and stepped back.

"How many were there?"

"Five." He smiled. "They look worse."

"Good," she said, reaching to turn off the faucet. "You need food and a bath."

"There are some meat pies in my pack. I managed to buy them before I was beaten. I'm sure they're cold by now."

"They'll do."

She retrieved the pies, and they ate in silence.

"I need to show you something," she said, licking crumbs from her greasy fingers.

He wiped his hands on his pants. "Can it wait until after I bathe?"

"That water's not actually for you."

"I don't understand."

"I need it for a ritual. Do you know the story of the first Aether Mage?"

169

He shook his head. "I wasn't allowed. No one is, anymore."

It was time to lay all her cards on the table. "My father showed it to me last night."

"Your father? How have you been talking to him?"

"Apparently death doesn't stop communication here. The point is, I used to feel powerless in the Real and then I came here. Now I get what being powerless is really like. Only I have power, and so do you. Look, I think that if you see what I'm capable of, it'll help you realize that. And even though you're not an Aether Mage, you are a hybrid. This is your story too."

His eyes lit up. "Andrius has kept so much from me. Show me."

Reggie grabbed the glass of dirt off the sink, searching until she found matches and a candle. She sprinkled the dirt in the water, lighting the candle. She picked up the letter opener he had dropped. It was shaped like a miniature sword, the tip honed to a fine point. Kneeling by the tub, she pricked her index finger. She hissed as the blade slid into her flesh.

"What are you doing?" Asher knelt beside her.

"I don't know how to anchor the spell with magic. I need blood," she explained.

Red droplets swelled on the tip of her finger. Flicking them into the water, she muttered the incantation her father had spoken. Suddenly, a bleeding rainbow of colors boiled in the water, separating to form images. The liquid morphed, becoming three-dimensional like a hologram. Three figures rose before them; a man, a woman, and a boy who looked to be about twelve.

Asher gasped, and Reggie smiled, proud of her first successful spell.

"Around two hundred years ago, the races started to intermingle with each other. Make some babies. This is

Patience and Shen, two second-generation hybrids. That's their son Samuel." She pointed to the blond boy, walking through the field next to his father.

The wheat was bleached and brittle, the earth cracked. Behind Samuel and Shen was a small two-story house. Patience was in front of the house, sweeping the thick dust that coated the porch.

"Are they in the Witch Plains?"

Reggie nodded. "At first Samuel didn't seem to have a lot of magical mojo. But when he turned twelve, all that changed. That was the year a five-alarm fire started on the Plains. Have you heard of it?"

"Yes. It killed thousands. Destroyed half the Plains before it was driven to the sea."

"You're about to see how little Samuel kicked that fire's ass. Watch."

The water shifted, a billowing, black cloud forming over the horizon like a tidal wave. Ahead of the smoke, animals ran: deer, rabbits, marsh wolves, and wild boar fleeing for their lives, heading straight for the little farm. Shen shouted to Samuel, ordering him back to the house, to his mother. Samuel didn't move, staring at the oncoming fire, at the animals thundering toward him. Shaking him, Shen pushed him to run. Samuel ran, to the fire.

The terrified animals flowed around Samuel like he was a lone boulder in a fast moving stream. A two-story wall of flame rushed toward him, a fierce wind driving it. Meeting the flames, he raised his arms and commanded, "Stop! Stop, now!" The fire halted, flickering before Samuel like demons dancing in hell, stretching on either side of him as far as the eye could see. The wind stilled.

Reggie could smell the thick smoke, her mouth tasting like ashes. Asher coughed. They watched sweat roll from Samuel's forehead. Suddenly the wind whipped up again, swirling around Samuel, forming a barrier between his body and the fire. Samuel pointed to the flames. The gale hammered back the fire, forcing it into a narrow line. Like a snake charmer enticing a cobra, Samuel led the fire toward the sea.

"He's a little like me, running off of raw power and fear. But he's getting it done," Reggie whispered.

The scene before Reggie and Asher twisted again, transforming into an aerial view. They watched the fire march across the Plains, emptying into Hornsbay, the salt water swallowing its power. The hologram burst, clear water falling back into the tub once more. The candle sputtered and died.

Reggie looked at Asher, who was staring at the water.

"Asher, I have that kind of power inside me. I'm a weapon. And with Rhys training me, I can help him defeat Andrius." She gripped his forearm. "Look at me. I can free you. All of you."

Asher turned to her, green eyes blazing. "You can't save me. You have to save yourself!"

"Bullshit. I'm the last Aether Mage. Don't you see? That's why I'm here. To help you."

"Reggie, you don't have control over your magic. Don't get killed trying to play hero."

"I'm not playing hero." Reggie rose up until her face was level with his. "Rhys can teach me what I need to know. I was brought to the Other for a reason. Like Brwyn said, I'm supposed to return the balance, to right a wrong. This is what I was born to do."

"Stop, Reggie, just stop. Don't give me hope," he said, his hands fisted at his sides.

Cupping his face, she leaned against him. "Don't just give up. Asher, whatever you're scared of, whatever's holding you back, let it go."

Asher placed his hands on hers. "The things I've done—"

"You mean the things Andrius made you do. Don't let him win. Don't let him take everything from you, even your hope. How many times have you taken care of me? Trust me. Let me take care of you."

Asher stared in her eyes, emotion flickering across his face. Something in him seemed to break, forming a crack in the control he wore like armor. His lips were firm on hers. The hands framing her face trembled.

He pulled back, his expression fierce. "Listen to me. No one is going to hurt you. I promise you. Whatever I have to do, nothing is going to happen to you."

Taken aback by his vow, Reggie nodded. "I believe you."

Then he was kissing her again. They fell to the floor; the tiles cool against her back. She pulled away to slip her fingers underneath his collar, kissing his damaged skin. He shuddered. Propping his weight on one elbow, Asher used his free hand to undress her. He unveiled her slowly. She resisted the urge to squirm as his green eyes took her in, examining every inch of her skin. The admiration on his face melted her insecurities.

His eyes searched hers. "Are you okay?"

She shyly reached for the button of his trousers, helping him push the fabric past his hips. She bit her lip and touched him, smiling at his groan. "Never better."

"Wait," he gasped. He pushed away from her.

She watched in bewilderment as Asher dashed into his room. Doubts started to plague her, but he returned quickly. He held up a round disk.

"I almost forgot the scabbard." Asher gathered her in his arms.

Reggie laughed at the Other's name for a condom. "Thank God you remembered protection."

He cupped her face tenderly. "Of course."

He kissed her, touching her in places only she had touched before. He was so gentle, so patient that he made her feel safe.

Afterward, Asher ran a hot bath for them, making her get in first and asking her if she felt okay. He drew Reggie to him until her back rested against his chest. With soothing fingers, he massaged her neck and shoulders. When the water grew tepid, Asher lifted her out of the tub, wrapping her in a fluffy towel. She went to her room and he followed. He stood in her doorway, watching. She blushed at his expression, unsure of how to behave now.

"Can I sleep with you tonight?" Asher asked. He looked as uncertain as she felt.

Reggie sighed in relief. She'd wanted to ask him to stay but wasn't sure if she should.

"Yeah, come in. Fair warning, I think I snore," she said.

He walked into the room and sat on the edge of the bed.

"I can handle that."

Chapter 28

*P*ropped on one elbow, Asher watched Reggie sleep. Her shallow breath fanned strands of hair that had fallen across her cheek. He gently tucked her hair back. It was strange to want to stay in bed with a woman, as opposed to scrambling out as quickly as he could. The fleeting pleasure he usually found was bound with hatred and shame.

Peke was the first woman Andrius had given him to. He remembered that she'd been kind to him in her way, but he'd always known his place. Asher was her pet, a pretty toy she'd send for, making him perform on command. She'd reward him with gifts, like forbidden books or expensive clothing. He'd pretended he liked her gifts, liked her.

There was no pretending with Reggie. She was special. He took possessive satisfaction in being her first lover. She belonged to him the way he belonged to her. She was the first person he'd chosen to make love to. But his lies overshadowed their happiness. He needed to tell Reggie the truth, but he was afraid she'd hate him. He wouldn't be in her life that much longer, and he wanted to enjoy every moment he had with her.

Asher believed Reggie was the weapon that could destroy Andrius' poisonous grip on their world, freeing the Indentureds. He hoped he'd only be sacrificing himself and not his family as well. He pushed away those painful thoughts, focusing on contacting Rhys. He had to do it tonight. It would be risky, but he needed to give Rhys their travel route so he could intercept them and take Reggie. Once she was safely with Rhys, Asher would return to Andrius alone. Meet death head on.

Lying back on the bed, Asher relaxed his body and opened his mind. He silently repeated Rhys' name, counting back until he felt the chains of sleep drag him under. The black emptiness of the Dream Realm enveloped him. A scream in his mind shattered his concentration. He shook his head, but the scream pierced his brain like a spike, anchoring his position. With nowhere to hide, he answered the call.

Asher suddenly stood on solid ground. The room was both familiar and hated. Rectangular, with high ceilings formed by flying buttresses, the walls were lined by dozens of flickering lamps, creating a perfect path to the mahogany desk sitting at the opposite end. Asher had always believed the lamps were overly dramatic, but Andrius never missed a chance to highlight his power.

The dark mage waited for him in front of the desk, leaning back on the wood, his arms loosely folded across his chest. His casual pose didn't fool Asher.

"Come," Andrius said, flicking a hand.

Asher walked across an enormous rug covering half of the flagstone floor, magical symbols woven into the fibers. Stopping in front of the desk, he waited for Andrius to speak, diverting his gaze to the silver instruments scattered across the desk's surface.

"Asher."

Asher lifted his eyes. "Sir?"

"You were in the Dream Realm before I called you. Why?" The dark mage unfolded his arms, tapping his fingers against the desk in a slow rhythm.

Asher watched those fingers, remembering how they'd closed over his throat as a child. "I was trying to call you, Master. Report on my progress."

"You never willingly forge a connection with me. Has something gone wrong?" The tapping became faster.

There was no heat in his collar, not yet. "I had problems with border guards in the forest, and they've been tracking me ever since. I'm in Holden's Folly now. I won't be able to leave until tomorrow morning. I wanted to stay off the ley line for a day."

"That's very unlike you. You're normally discreet." His fingers stopped.

Asher regarded Andrius' hand, calculating what information he could reveal about Reggie without endangering her. "She's unpredictable. She likes to speak her mind. The guards didn't appreciate that."

Andrius' laughter grated across his skin. "Then they have bad taste. I admire a girl with spirit! I knew her father couldn't have sired a weakling. Such a valuable commodity, my little Reggie, which brings me to the reason I summoned you. Rhys Griffith has discovered Reggie is with you. It's only a matter of time before his soldiers find you. Don't come to Two Cities. I'll have a Ravens squad meet you in Pike's Crossing in two days. They'll escort you to me."

A Ravens squad! Andrius' personal guards were vicious and efficient. Could he deliver Reggie safely to Rhys in two days? Could he possibly stall? The weight of Andrius' stare hit him, and Asher realized he'd been silent too long. The dark mage's eyes had narrowed to slits. He froze like a deer hoping that the Marsh Wolf wouldn't notice him.

"What do you think of my Reggie, hmm? So pretty, so tempting. A flower just waiting to be plucked, isn't she?" Andrius' lips curved into a malicious smile.

177

Asher suddenly looked forward to surprising the Ravens when he showed up empty-handed. He wanted to see Andrius' face when he realized Asher had betrayed him, ruining all his plans. Molding his features into a calm mask, he answered, "No, Master."

"Don't lie to me!"

Asher's collar heated, warming his skin. "I'm not, Master. I know my place."

"You'd better. Only I can grant you and your family freedom. Betray me, and I slaughter them. And their deaths won't be easy, I promise you that."

Asher winced, shaking his head. "I won't, Master."

Asher kept his hands laced behind him. His nails dug into the meat of his palms. Andrius snapped his fingers. Heat seared Asher's neck, and his nails sliced through skin. He suppressed a shudder.

"So brave," Andrius mocked. "Leave at dawn. Avoid any more skirmishes with guards. My Ravens will meet you in the early afternoon on the second day, near the pool by the caves. Don't be late."

"Two days' time," Asher assured him.

Andrius severed their connection. Asher bolted upright, his body soaked in sweat, his neck aching. His ragged breathing filled the small bedroom. He glanced at Reggie, but she had her back turned to him, still fast asleep.

He had to go back in the Dream Realm and try to contact Rhys again. But he was afraid Andrius was lingering there, waiting to catch him in his web of lies. If he went in too soon, there was a good possibility he'd ruin Reggie's chance to escape.

Asher didn't know much about his magic. The only information Andrius had willingly taught him was how to make connections in the Dream Realm. However, he had

178

developed a useful talent on his own: shielding. He had the ability to construct defenses around his mind. Mental forts that deflected attempts at mind control that could ward off subtle suggestions and full-out commands.

That was the reason he'd survived Andrius so long with his will intact. Why the dark mage controlled him only in more direct ways like physical pain or threatening his loved ones. If Asher could amplify his shielding ability in the Dream Realm, then he might be able to keep a connection secure from invaders for at least a few minutes. He had to try.

CHAPTER 29

$\mathcal{R}$eggie felt Asher shift closer to her and she smiled. He was warm. His fingers were feather light as they stroked her arm. He hadn't left her side after they'd had sex, his eyes following her as if he was afraid she'd disappear. Maybe he was just as insecure as she was, despite his experience. He'd hinted she was the only person he'd slept with by choice.

Their relationship was moving at warp speed. She guessed she ought to feel guilty or ashamed of her behavior. But she didn't. Despite her questions, she knew Asher cared about her. She could count on one hand how many people had cared for her in her short life.

She gently squeezed the fingers stroking her arm. He squeezed back, and she relaxed, burying her face into the pillow. After a few minutes, she fell asleep.

Reggie walked through a meadow with her father, threading her fingers through the tall, green grass. These nightly meetings were precious to her. In the Dream Realm, she briefly got to be the child she never was. Her father was in serious trouble, but he never pushed his problems on her. He focused on shielding her from danger, but tonight she wanted the knowledge that would help him. He'd protected her long enough.

"How much time do we have?" Reggie asked her father as she slipped her hand inside his.

His fingers curled around hers. "Not much, I'm afraid. But it's quality not quantity that counts."

"Do you remember Asher? The guy I told you about?"

"Yes, of course. Why?"

"I don't know if I broke any rules or anything, but I told him the story of the first Aether Mage."

Sebastian smiled. "I'm glad you did. The poor boy has been denied all magical training or information about his heritage. He might not be an Aether Mage, but he's still a hybrid like us. How did he react?"

Reggie blushed. She couldn't tell her father that after hearing her story Asher had vowed to protect her, then lowered her to the floor and stripped her naked. Her father watched her, one eyebrow raised. She'd learned he was good at reading emotions. Was she giving off a "Hey, I just lost my virginity" vibe without knowing it?

"He was—moved by it, like I was," she said quickly. "Dad, I promised I could help free him. I'm scared I promised too much. I want to help you both, but I still don't know how to control my magic."

Her father stopped, putting his hands on her shoulders. "You will help, sweetheart. Believe in yourself. Now, tell me how your magic is reacting to your emotions, your environment."

"I make things happen when I'm scared or angry, and that isn't good enough. And sometimes I'm in pain. The pressure builds or I react with new magic, and bam! I'm lying on the ground, easy pickings for anyone."

"Don't block the flow of magic, it's like water being trapped by a dam. When the dam breaks, you're left defenseless. Think of your body as a conduit for magical power. Relax and let the Earth's energy flow through you. As an Aether Mage, you feel the Earth's components more strongly, that's why you can influence all the elements. The first step is to learn to identify the individual element you want to manipulate."

"How? When I make things happen, there's no warning. It's not like I'm reaching for Water to make it rain."

Sebastian tilted his head. "Think of it like this. Every element has a . . . sort of flavor to it. You need to practice separating those flavors. When you're able to distinguish one element from another, experiment with it."

"What do you mean?"

"Focus on the element you've isolated. Slowly push energy into it. You've already been doing it, albeit accidentally. Really concentrate, think about what you're doing, about how the world works around you. Believe it or not, your magic is instinctual."

"Okay, but what happens when I'm in a real fight? I'll be pissed or scared, is that always a bad thing?" Reggie asked, grabbing a fistful of grass.

"Sometimes emotion makes your magic stronger, makes it hit harder. But if you're not in control, you lose the ability to handle your power with finesse. You can cause a lot of destruction. It's a critical time for you now because you're so young, and your emotions are chaotic"

Reggie sighed. "Yeah, I've got some anger issues, no doubt. Dad, how much power do I really have?"

Sebastian started walking again, and she fell in step beside him. "Some Aether Mages have more power than others, but I was very powerful, and you are my daughter. Your magic was felt in the Real."

She shivered. "Aether Mages can do weird stuff sometimes, right? Do things beyond the four elements?"

Her father observed her. "Yes, sometimes our talents evolve. Why do you ask?"

"I got busted because I was bringing things back to life."

He stopped. "That is an unusual talent. The Harbinger of Death meets the Life Giver. No wonder he's afraid of you."

"You mean—"

"Your powers oppose one another."

"I guess that's a good thing?"

"It makes you a stronger opponent."

"I'll know just how good I am when I start practicing this stuff. I hope I don't disappoint you." Reggie bit her lower lip.

"Impossible," Sebastian replied. He leaned over, kissing her on the forehead. "I have faith in you, Reggie. I want to show you something. Look, this is my home now."

The terrain around them changed. A redwood forest now stood in their path, the massive trees stretching toward the heavens like nature's skyscrapers. A pearly mist cloaked the lower trunks, concealing the ground from view. The stark beauty distracted her, and Reggie didn't see the enemy at first. An encampment of soldiers littered the vast edge of the forest. A group of them entered the trees armed with swords and torches, disappearing into the mist.

"What's going on?" she asked.

"The dark mage's men. They keep trying to burn the forest down, send me to my final resting place. The mist swallows them, driving them mad like all those who have gone before them. But still they come."

"That's Hornsbay Forest?"

"Yes. That's where you're going. Rhys needs you to save us all. I'm so angry with him." Sebastian turned to her, his face full of anguish.

Reggie wrapped her arms around him, looking up. "Why? Don't you trust him?"

He squeezed her tight. "Yes, I trust him. He wants what's best for us all, including you. But he's placing so much responsibility on your shoulders. And I'm not much use to you like this. You're so young—"

"Believe me, Dad. If there's a chance I can set you free, bring on the hard stuff. I can handle it."

"My brave girl. It's meant the world to me, you know," her father said, releasing her. "To spend time with you, I never thought—"

His words died, and he went still as if listening for something.

Reggie glanced around, but she didn't see anyone. "Dad?"

Sebastian looked at her. "Reggie, you have to leave now. He's found me. I can't allow him to see you with me. But if he thinks I'm weak here—there's a price for what he has done."

The air around them rippled just like it had the last time she'd been with Rhys. Andrius was here. Fear clamped onto her like a pit bull she couldn't shake. "Dad?"

A fierce anger tightened her father's face, his fists clenching. "He won't get you. Leave, Reggie!"

"Dad!" Reggie screamed.

She woke up frightened, her heart racing like a revved up engine. When an arm snaked around her, she instinctively slammed an elbow into the muscled body behind her. There was a sharp grunt. Reggie rolled over to find a startled Asher rubbing his chest.

"You're stronger than you look. Are you okay?"

"Shit Asher! Sorry." She patted his chest.

"It's nothing. Tell me what happened."

"I was with my father. Andrius found us." Reggie sat up, leaning against the headboard. "What if he's hurt my dad?"

Asher pulled her into a tight hug. "Your father has survived Andrius once. That makes him pretty damn remarkable. If he couldn't kill your father before, I don't think he can do it now or he would've done it."

185

She lifted her face from his shoulder, blinking back tears. "My dad is—I don't know what he is, exactly. I think I've been talking to his spirit. I saw his body once in a dream, just an empty shell floating in the ocean. I have to get his spirit back to his body somehow. I can't let Andrius take him from me again."

"You won't."

Could Andrius hurt her father's spirit? She wanted to charge back into the Dream Realm, fight alongside her father. But she couldn't even form a Dream connection, and what Asher had said made sense. If Andrius had the capability of truly destroying her father, he would've already done it. He didn't seem the type to leave an enemy alive.

"Maybe you're right. Maybe Andrius can't truly kill my Dad. The not knowing still sucks."

Asher kissed her gently. "I know."

"Dammit!" Reggie beat her fists against the bed in frustration. No, she wouldn't focus on the things she couldn't do, she'd focus on the things she could. "Asher, my dad told me how to practice my magic. Your magic can't be that much different than mine. Want to learn how to kick ass with me?"

Asher's face lit up. "Yes."

CHAPTER 30

*J*ohn leaned on the doorframe, watching as Arlene tore the attic apart. Earlier that morning, he had dumped out every liquor bottle in the house. He couldn't take any more chances after he had found Arlene so drunk she was almost comatose, with a hidden bottle of vodka in her bedroom. She'd scared the hell out of him.

When he told her last night that Reggie wasn't coming back, she had crumpled, a piercing scream escaping her lips. John didn't know a human could make that sound, and the hairs on his neck stood up just remembering it. She'd cowered in a corner, rocking back and forth, whispering Reggie's name over and over again like prayer. He'd never felt so helpless. He had a whole new respect for Reggie. She'd dealt with this shit most of her life.

He had told Arlene this morning—when she'd finally come around—the truth about where Reggie was. She had fled to the attic. Now here they were, with Arlene tearing up everything in sight.

"Don't you want to talk about where Reggie is? You at least gotta think my story is nuts," John said.

Arlene paused. "I've always known about the Other, John."

"What?"

"Sebastian was my husband. We loved each other. Do you honestly think he'd keep something like that from me? Reggie was never supposed to find out about the Other. She was supposed to stay here where she'd be safe."

"So you've been lying to her, her whole life?"

"I've been protecting her. Look what happened the moment she learned about the Other."

John shook his head. "I still think you should've told her. What are you looking for, anyway? Maybe I can help."

"No, it'll take too long." Arlene rifled through a box, stopping to rub her temples with her fingertips. She'd been doing that after every burst of movement.

John didn't point out that if she had told him from the beginning what she was looking for, they would have probably found it by now.

"This is all my fault. If I wasn't such a bad mother . . ."

John crossed the room. "You're not a bad mother."

"I am. I'm so weak, so weak!"

"Hey, Reggie loves you. She does, believe it. Listen, I know it's bad. But we have to have faith that she's going to be okay."

"Faith?" Arlene snorted. "I had faith that Sebastian would come home. That his powers could conquer anything. And now look, he's gone and I couldn't protect the best part of us. Letting Reggie protect me." She buried her face in her hands, crying.

John shook her. "Pull it together. Reggie is being strong for you, and you've got to be strong for her, okay? She needs you. Hell, I need you. You've got more info than I have."

Arlene dropped her hands. Her pale skin was mottled. "You're right. She's not dead, she's not. I'm going to help her."

"I'm guessing that's why we're up here. Care to let me in on the plan?"

"I need to—" Her eyes narrowed and she became still.

John arched a brow, following her line of vision. She was staring at the old metal daybed. Pushing away from him, she stumbled to it. Kneeling on the floorboards, she reached under the bed and pulled out a large box.

188

"Aha!" She glanced back at John, waving a hand. "Come here, I found it!"

John weaved through the disarray she had created, kneeling beside her. "What is it?"

Arlene opened the box and smiled. "These things belonged to me and my husband before he disappeared. There are things in here that will help us."

"Really? Like what?" he asked, peering over her shoulder. It looked like the same box Reggie had rifled through a few days ago.

"Well, all my old camping stuff and my . . ." Her voice trailed off and she frowned.

"What's wrong?"

"My backpack is missing. But I'm positive it was in here. Where the hell else could it be?"

"Wait a minute. Was it an old army backpack?"

Arlene turned to him, surprise wiping away her frown. "Yeah. How did you know?"

"Reggie took it when she went to the Other." John was jolted by the look of panic on her face. "What?"

But she had already turned away from him, digging frantically inside the box, tossing aside cups, old clothes and what looked like a compass. "Shit. I wonder if she saw it."

"Saw what?"

Arlene didn't answer him, tipping the box over. Searching through the debris, she pushed things aside muttering negatives.

"You're freaking me out. What could she have seen?"

She raised her head, the movement jerky like a bird's. "My gun!"

"It was your gun! Why would you have a gun?"

Her eyes narrowed. "I used to take it when I hiked with Sebastian, just in case. Reggie was never supposed to see it. The questions she'd have."

John grinned a little. Maybe she wasn't supposed to see it, but Reggie wouldn't have gone into the Other without some sort of back up. "I hate to break it to you, but she took it to protect herself. She didn't know a whole lot about her magic. It was damn smart."

A sigh puffed out Arlene's thin cheeks. "That does sound like my girl. I'm surprised she didn't find this." She picked up the discarded compass.

John looked at it, shrugging. "It's just a broken compass."

"John, do you really think I'd search through all this junk for a broken compass?"

Arlene shook her head, prying open the back of the compass with her fingers. The metal back popped open. A piece of paper—folded many times over and yellowed with age—burst out of its directionless prison. She threw the compass aside and began unfolding the paper with careful hands. John scooted closer to her.

"What is that?"

"A map. See," Arlene said, spreading the map between her hands so the paper stretched taut.

The map was hand drawn, but the black ink was clear and concise. Places John had never heard of were marked: cities, mountain ranges, landmarks. And in the corner, he saw small but distinct hand-drawn symbols. The only one he recognized was a flame, which had been on the badge Megan flashed at him. He thought these must be Earth symbols. Maybe they represented Reggie's magic.

"Is that the Other?"

"Yes, but it's an old map. Things have probably changed since Sebastian drew it for me. But it's all I have to work with when I go."

"You mean when we go," John corrected her, picking up on the omission.

Her mouth pressed into a firm line. She faced him. "John, listen to me. I know Reggie is your best friend and you love her. But she's my daughter. My responsibility. A responsibility I haven't been living up to. But you have a mother here—"

"I'm coming with you."

"No. My child is missing. I can't tell you how much it hurts, the hole here." Arlene thumped a fist against her chest. "I won't do that to your mother, John."

John felt desperate. He'd promised Reggie he'd look after her mother. There was no way he was letting Arlene go to the Other by herself. "You don't get to decide. I'm not your kid. And you have . . . other problems. You need me there to keep you in check. I don't trust you to go alone."

A flush swept from Arlene's pale neck, filling her cheeks. John scooted back. Maybe he'd poked the mother bear too hard, but he had to hold his ground.

"I would never let my—my problems stop me from finding Reggie."

"I don't believe you," he shot back. "I told you she went missing and instead of talking about it, you turned to the bottle. How can I be sure that at the first sign of trouble, you won't start drinking?"

Arlene shot up from the floor, John following. "I won't, I promise. You have to trust me. I can't be responsible for you!"

"You won't be responsible for me. I can take care of myself. I have wilderness training, so if you have a way into the Other, I'm coming with you."

She squared her shoulders. "I'll tell your mother."

She had him there. John thought quickly. "No, you can't. She'll believe Reggie's missing, but I'll tell her what you told me. She'll think you're crazy, that you've finally lost it."

Arlene let out a short scream, startling John. "Why won't you let me protect you? I didn't protect Reggie, but at least I can get you out of harm's way." Tears filled her eyes.

John's voice softened. "I'm not yours to protect. I made a promise to Reggie that I'd watch over you. I'm going to keep it. How do you plan on crossing over, anyway? Do you have magic?"

Suddenly Arlene smiled, her face lit with triumph. "No, but I have a way to get it."

"How?"

She dropped the map, and walked to the opposite wall of the attic. Stopping in front of a large, wooden wardrobe, she turned to look at him. "My magic is in here."

John made his way to her side, staring at the cabinet. It just looked like an old wardrobe to him. "Do you have an invisibility cloak stashed in there somewhere?"

"Listen, John. You hear it?"

Did she drink more when I wasn't looking? He sighed in frustration, but he listened. After a few moments, he heard it. "What is that? It's like an electric hum or something, like from a . . . a refrigerator?"

Arlene nodded, opening the wardrobe's door to reveal the inside of a refrigerator. A single box sat on the middle shelf. "I bought it from a lodge that had it behind their bar. The owner thought this old icebox looked classier than a normal fridge, and I thought it looked a lot less conspicuous."

"What's in the box?"

192

She reached for it. With an almost reverent air, she lifted a vial of red liquid from inside. "This is from my husband," Arlene whispered.

"You've kept your husband's blood for seventeen years? Wow, impressive, and a little creepy."

Arlene rubbed her thumb over the vial. "He had me keep it in case of an emergency. He told me to only take a little, just enough that the barrier could detect magic. If I took too much, my body would be tainted. He said people who changed their blood too much lost their ability to cross over."

John was afraid. "I hope there's an exact measurement. I don't want to be stuck in Never-Never Land."

"That's just it, John." Arlene removed a syringe from the box. "I don't know what's safe for you, and I'm definitely going. Guess you'll have to stay home after all."

John looked at her, then at the vial. He didn't need the needle. He could just drink some of the blood. Bile rose to the back of his throat, but he swallowed it down. No time to get queasy. He lunged for her wrist. Arlene drew her hand back, but her reflexes were slowed by her hangover, and he caught it in a firm grip.

"What the hell are you doing?" she hissed, fighting against his hold. "You'll break it!"

Her bones felt fragile. John hated himself for putting pressure on her delicate frame. "I won't if you let go!"

He entwined his fingers with hers and pulled, yelping as her fingernails cut into his skin.

"Let go, let go! I don't want to hurt you!" she said.

John pried one of her fingers loose. "Then stop fighting me." Two fingers, there went the fourth, and he broke the vial free from her grip. "I guess we're both going after all." He took a few steps back from her, the vial clutched in his hand.

Arlene lunged for him but he dodged.

She waved the syringe in front of him. "I still have the needle. You can't take the blood without it."

"I plan on drinking it. Needles freak me out." He fingered the vial's rubber stopper.

"No! That's not the way you're supposed to do it. Sebastian was clear about that." Arlene's face went white.

"I guess this is what they call a Mexican standoff," he said. She inched closer and he uncorked the vial, holding it near his lips. "One more step, and I drink."

"No, John, please. I don't know what it will do to you like that. Just give me the blood. If you drop it, I won't be able to help Reggie." A sob caught her voice, but she swallowed, trying to be strong. In that moment, her resemblance to Reggie was clear.

John hated hurting her. But she wasn't stable enough to go after Reggie on her own. "Give me the syringe. I'm going to drink it or inject it, but either way, I'm coming with you." He held out his hand.

The electric hum of the refrigerator seemed almost grotesque in the tense silence. Then, without a word, Arlene slowly handed him the syringe. He reached for it, keeping the vial pressed to his lips in case she planned to trick him. But she simply held the needle out palm upturned. Fingers closing around the syringe, John moved the vial from his lips.

"How do I do it?"

Arlene explained the procedure, but she wasn't sure how much blood he should take. John placed the needle against the blue vein running alongside his inner elbow. Suddenly he felt lightheaded. "You sure you don't want to help?"

"You want this, you have to do it."

"Fair enough." John pushed the needle into his skin. He watched the foreign blood go into his body. His stomach clenched, the ground spinning. When it was over, he dropped the syringe, keeping hold of the vial as his legs collapsed. A hand gripped his shoulder.

"Are you okay? John, answer me!"

He blinked up at her. "I'm okay."

"How do you feel?"

"I don't know yet."

"Will you be okay if I leave you for a minute?"

"I think so," he replied.

"Give me the blood," she said and he handed it to her. "I need to sterilize the needle. I'll be right back."

He nodded and heard her footsteps leaving the attic. John clutched his chest. A burning sensation began building in his body like the blood was burrowing into his DNA, transforming it. Wave after wave of pain lapped over him. He curled on his side, waiting for it to pass.

A hand covered his. John looked up to find Arlene had returned, the vial empty. Her eyes were filled with pain. They gripped each other's hands until the storm passed. Magic now flowed freely in their blood. There was no going back.

Arlene helped him to his feet.

"How'd you recover before me?" he said.

Her smile was self-depreciating. "That hurt like hell, but my hangover hurts worse."

John laughed, swaying a little. "Now what?"

"We gather some supplies together, take the map, and we go. John, are you sure you want—"

"I'm sure."

She sighed. "Go to your house, pack some things, and meet me in an hour. We need to make it to the crossing before nightfall."

"Remember, if you leave without me, I'll just follow you."

She gave him a sad smile. "I won't leave without you. We're in this together now, for better or worse."

John nodded. "For better or worse."

Chapter 31

*P*ikes Crossing was a decadent resort town that catered to Two Cities' politicians and wealthy entrepreneurs. It let them indulge in vices that the various resorts provided with a level of discretion not found elsewhere. Located an hour away from the capital, it was close enough for politicians to keep an eye on their powerbase while at play.

Reggie observed the town from the airship's deck. Built near a large spring, the buildings resembled log cabins, their dark wood blending in with the forest. The town's rustic appearance didn't fool her. She recognized quality when she saw it. Luxury dwelled beneath that simple veneer. Shops clustered in the town's center, with large hotels leading away to more secluded areas.

"'Morning," Asher said, sliding his arms around her from behind. He rested his chin on her head. She was surprised at his open display of affection, but it was early and the deck was deserted.

She snuggled into his warmth. "'Morning. So why are we stopping here?"

"Outside the town is a cluster of caves. There's a secret path that we can follow into Two Cities. It gets us off the road, and away from the guards."

"And a step closer to Rhys."

His muscles tensed and he lifted his head. "Yes, today will bring you closer to Rhys."

"What do you mean by 'today?'" Reggie twisted around to look at him.

His smile was a blade. "Nothing."

"Asher—"

"I accidentally blew my bunk over."

"What?" They'd been practicing their magic together. Reggie gaining more control of her power, and Asher discovering that he had an affinity for Air.

"I lost control. I didn't know I had so much power."

"That's amazing! Who knows how much power—"

His lips covered hers, his hips pressing her against the railing. Her fingers tangled into his silky hair as she kissed him back. She momentarily lost sense of time and place as his hands roved over her, spreading liquid warmth. Then sanity punched her in the face. They were out in the open, vulnerable to attack. She released his hair, but he was already retreating.

"Forgot myself," Asher said, leaning his forearms on the railing, his shoulders slumped as if he bore a heavy weight.

Catching her breath, Reggie studied him. He'd been acting strange the past few days, happy one minute and withdrawn the next. She was worried about him, but when she asked questions it usually ended with both of them naked. As much as she enjoyed their newfound intimacy, she couldn't shake the feeling that something was wrong. Yawning, she leaned against the railing next to him.

He flashed a grin. "Tired?"

"You know you've been wearing me out. Stop being smug about it," she said, elbowing him in the side. "You sure you're not a Changeling Rabbit?"

His grin broadened. "I'm nineteen and you're beautiful. You're lucky you can walk," he teased, but Reggie saw the sadness in his smile.

"Barely." She watched him, a scary suspicion forming in her mind. "It's almost like . . . like you don't think you're going to see me again."

His easy manner vanished. "That's ridiculous. Once we get to Two Cities and I hide you somewhere, I won't see you for a few days. But then we'll be on our way again."

Reggie shook her head, crossing her arms over her chest. "I don't buy it. Something's off. You're not that happy despite all the crazy sex. I realize I don't have your experience, but I don't think it's me."

Asher pushed from the railing. "Nothing's off. I'm just anxious about facing Andrius again. It's never pleasant."

She mulled over his words, sensing she was getting a partial truth. "Andrius sucks. Don't worry. You won't be alone this time, you'll have me."

"Right. I'll have you." He pulled her into his body again, hiding his face from her.

Asher led Reggie into Pikes Crossing. He had flicked open the top three buttons of his shirt, revealing his collar fully. The gold gleamed in the morning sunlight like a beacon.

"What's with that?" she asked, nodding toward the collar.

"I want to blend in. Many Indentureds come here with their masters. Sometimes to serve, sometimes to be traded as a favor."

As they walked through the streets, Reggie noticed that the few people out were Indentureds, their exposed gold collars announcing their identity. They glanced at her a few times, but she and Asher were generally ignored.

The surrounding shops sold colorful potions promising enhanced sexual pleasure, true love, and a firmer ass. A life size replica of a female Elf stood in a box on the sidewalk outside one storefront. Her curvy naked body was made of plush velvet. Beside the Elf, a sign read: "Have an unforgettable night with Elektra."

"What is that thing? The Other's version of a blow up doll?" Reggie whispered.

"She's a famous singer. The body comes alive with an incantation and for an hour, you get to screw the beautiful Elektra," Asher explained.

"That's disgusting and creepy as hell."

"Welcome to Pike's Crossing."

They moved quickly through the town, coming into a wooded area that had strange, circular patterns embedded into the forest floor. At the center of these circles, steel posts were driven into the ground. Attached to the posts were chains ending in handcuffs.

Reggie stared at the handcuffs. "Do I want to know?"

Asher glanced at the metal rings, shuddering. "No."

Past the circles, a worn trail wound deeper into the forest. Asher's head swiveled around, his eyes sweeping the area. He pulled out a small pocket watch from a chain, checking the time.

"Are we on a schedule?" Reggie asked, her unease accelerating.

"We've been on a schedule since the day we met. The springs are this way. The caves are behind them. Come on." Asher tugged at her hand.

The trail followed a clear stream, and Reggie shivered as the air became chilled. Large gray boulders sprouted up, dotting the terrain on either side of the path, green lichens staining the rock like smears of paint. A fine mist rose, clinging to their ankles.

Asher broke into a light jog. He kept looking around like a nervous cat waiting for something to jump out at him.

"Asher, spill. What the hell is going on?" Reggie demanded, running beside him.

"You can't come with me to Two Cities. I'm going alone. We're meeting one of Rhys' teams near the springs. They're going to take you back to Hornsbay Forest."

Her steps slowed at his words. "What? Why didn't you tell me this sooner? How long have you been planning to leave me?"

"It's not like that. I'm doing this for you."

"I don't understand. I thought being with a group of soldiers was too conspicuous. But now it's okay?"

"We don't have time to discuss this. I hear the springs. We need to move." Asher grabbed her hand.

Reggie jerked away, stopping. "Make time. I'm not going anywhere until you give me an explanation."

He faced her. "Andrius came to me in the Dream Realm a few days ago. He's suspicious about why I'm off schedule. He's sending his Ravens for me right now. I knew you wouldn't want to leave me, so I waited to tell you."

"I can help you—"

"No!" Asher straightened to his full height, towering over her. She stepped back. "I know you made a promise to me, but I made a promise too. I promised to keep you safe. Andrius isn't going to get his hands on you."

"I hate when people lie to me, Asher."

He flinched as if she'd struck him. "You think it's been easy keeping this from you? I don't want to leave you. Being with you has been like a dream. But I don't have a choice."

201

"Maybe you don't, but you still should've told me. I'm not stupid. If it really isn't safe for me, I'd understand."

He reached for her, but she evaded him. "No, you wouldn't. You're brave and you've just discovered how powerful you really are. But you're untrained, and Andrius is a monster. I won't allow you to get hurt because of me."

Reggie was so angry that she felt her magic tug at her, begging to be set free. She reined it in sharply, looking into Asher's eyes. He met her gaze, the green depths like molten metal. He wasn't going to bend.

"Let's go then. We have a schedule to keep, right?"

His jaw clenched and he nodded. They resumed their quick pace in a thick silence. Asher's tension infected her, and she tasted his fear, acrid on her tongue. He was afraid for her, but it was more than that. She sensed there was going to be a reckoning between Andrius and Asher that would result in worse injuries than burns.

"Here we are. Stay alert," Asher warned.

They rounded a bend in the trail and a large, bubbling pool of water came into focus. Behind the pool, a deep half-circle was carved into the rock forming a cave. In front of the opening stood four soldiers dressed in form-fitting camouflage uniforms: one woman and three men.

Asher pushed Reggie behind him. "Rhys sent you?"

Reggie felt his muscles coil as she peeked around his side.

A slender, flame-haired woman stepped forward, nodding. "I'm Megan Treston and you must be Asher. Hello, Reggie. Rhys will be glad to see you."

Reggie nudged Asher, and he moved to the side. "I'll be glad to see him too. It's been a hell of a couple of days. Thanks for coming for me." She smiled despite the knot that twisted her stomach. Asher was leaving her to face Andrius alone, and she had to let him.

"You're welcome. This is Thomas, Finch, and Cole." Megan said, gesturing to the men behind her. "I'm sorry there isn't time for small talk. It's dangerous here, and we can't linger. Asher, before we go, I need to look at your collar."

Asher shook his head. "No, I told Rhys I'm staying behind."

"And he told me to examine your collar."

"Look but it won't change anything." Asher walked toward her, Reggie following.

Megan and the three men watched her closely as she approached. The youngest one—Finch—looked disappointed. "I thought you'd be bigger," he said.

"I was thinking the same thing," Reggie replied.

"She's an Aether Mage. She can handle you just fine," Asher added.

A snarl twisted Finch's bland features. "Seems like you've been handling her, convincing her—"

Megan held up her hand. "Enough! Really, Finch, we're all on the same side here. There's no need for that."

Finch sneered as he looked at Asher. "If you say so."

"What the hell?" Reggie said.

"Finch, we are." Megan's eyes darted from Reggie to Asher, her eyes widening for a moment.

Asher's face turned to stone. "I'm here to make sure Reggie is safe, just like you are."

"I know you are," Megan interjected, reaching for his collar. "Let me look at this abominable contraption."

Tension crackled like a live wire between the soldiers and Asher. Reggie moved closer to Asher, glancing at the three men in front of her. They wouldn't meet her eyes. She didn't know what was going on, and she didn't like it. Her magic stirred

203

within her and patches of moss crawled toward her like huge hairy spiders. Everyone stared at her. Reggie clenched her fists, nails cutting into her palms. The immediate pain allowed her to gain a measure of control. The moss stopped.

"You okay?" Asher asked. Megan's hands were frozen on his collar.

Reggie shrugged. "Don't worry. I've got it under control now."

Megan nodded once more, focusing on the symbols embedded in the gold. She frowned. "The sick bastard knows his binding spells," she muttered, running her fingers over the metal. "I can't do anything with this. Rhys will have to look at it when we get to Hornsbay Forest."

Asher shook his head. "No, I'm staying."

Reggie grabbed his arm. "Asher, come with us. If Rhys can take the binding spell off, you'd be free. You don't need to play double agent anymore. There's no reason to go back to Andrius."

"She's right. My orders are to take you back with us," Megan said.

Asher stared at Megan, his eyes jade flints. "Rhys isn't my Master. He and his orders can go screw themselves. Andrius' Ravens will track me and be after us from here to Hornsbay, and you know it. They have a larger force, and we'll be overrun. She matters, not me." Asher pointed at Reggie. "Get her out of here."

"I'm not arguing with you. You're going with us," Megan began, then stilled. "Do you feel that?"

Magic brushed against Reggie with cold slimy fingers and she shivered. "Yes."

"It's coming from the cave. We need to leave. Now," the one called Thomas said; a deep scar bisected his chin.

The third man, Cole, sniffed the air. "The magic smells."

Reggie tasted something sour on the air, like spoiled milk. Tainted magic.

"Damn it! Andrius' men are coming. I thought we had more time. Reggie, get in the middle. You'll be safer there. Move out." Megan turned to Asher. "Protect Reggie."

Asher grasped Reggie's hand tightly. "I won't let them get her."

"I can look after myself," Reggie said, but she folded her fingers over his.

The Resistance soldiers formed a loose diamond around her, with Megan at the lead and Thomas at the rear. They were close enough to shield her, but far enough away to fight without injuring each other.

Suddenly Megan unsheathed a long, curved blade from her belt, plunging it into the empty space in front of her. A high-pitched scream rent the air and then the veil ripped apart.

CHAPTER 32

*R*eggie gasped as a man materialized in front of Megan, blood spewing from his chest. He fell to his knees. Twisting around, she saw they were surrounded. Eight soldiers boxed them in. Ahead lay the forest, to the left the water, and the cave at their backs. The soldiers wore black uniforms with a red insignia shaped like a bird above their hearts: Andrius' Ravens. Their weapons were drawn, short swords that gleamed in the morning sunlight. Reggie hadn't seen or heard them. The sour taste and oily cold of their magic had been the only sign of their presence.

A hard voice bit out, "You should've left the slave. You might've had a chance." A tall, rugged man stepped behind his fallen comrade. His muscles strained against the black fabric of his uniform. "It's amazing any of you have survived this long if you can't detect a veil sooner than that."

"Your associate might still be alive if you didn't stink so badly," Megan said. She flicked her wrist and the Resistance soldiers pushed away from Reggie, drawing their weapons.

The Raven captain smiled. "You can't win. Give us the girl and I'll kill you quickly. Master Andrius plays with his food before he kills it."

Reggie was tired of being threatened. "Come on. Try to take us! The only dead guy I see is one of yours," she said. Finch looked at her and grinned. Asher squeezed her hand.

"I think you have your answer," Megan said.

The captain smirked, feral hunger in his eyes. "I like her. It will be a pleasure to watch the Master break her."

Asher released Reggie's hand. "He won't touch her."

"The traitor speaks. He'll touch her all he wants to, slave," the captain said.

Asher bellowed. The guttural cry sent shivers down Reggie's spine. Leaping past the gap between Finch and Megan, Asher launched himself at the captain. The captain calmly held out his hand, muttering under his breath. An invisible force swatted Asher like a fly. His body flew backward, smashing into the rocky surface behind Reggie. The Resistance soldiers erupted into motion.

Thomas shoved Reggie to the ground. The impact knocked the air from her lungs. Gasping, Reggie tried to get her bearings. She sensed magic blooming and fading in bursts of power. The Ravens' magic possessed an unclean quality that clung to her skin like spider silk.

She saw Cole directly in front of her, wielding a long knife and chanting. Reggie propped herself on her elbows, looking around Cole's legs in search of Asher. He wasn't in front of her. She twisted to see Finch bleeding but still on his feet. His lips moved silently. Two Raven soldiers hit the air in front of him. Their swords drew sparks.

The Resistance soldiers' diamond widened as Megan and Cole pushed a few of the Ravens back into the forest. Reggie scrambled after them on all fours. Soft soil replaced sharp rocks. Finch moved next to her, flanking her left side. Reggie rolled back into a crouch. She needed to do something. These people were bleeding because of her.

"Stay down!" Megan's harsh voice ordered. Reggie glanced at her. She was dueling with the captain. The air between them was blurry, as though looking through gasoline fumes.

Frustrated, Reggie remained huddled on the ground as battle raged around her. The Resistance soldiers held the ground they'd gained, but they were tiring. The Ravens were too many. She had to help.

Finch swore loudly beside her. Reggie turned as a Raven breached his defenses, stabbing him in the shoulder. She leapt up, planning to aid Finch when Asher crashed into his attacker. Wrapping his arm around the Raven's neck, Asher choked him. The man sputtered. Another Raven rushed Finch, punching him in the face. Finch landed beside Reggie, his eyes closed. Then the second Raven thrust his blade into Asher's back.

The world slowed to a trickle as Reggie watched the Raven slide his blade free, preparing to strike Asher again. Her own safety forgotten, she rose to her feet. Elemental power surged through her. The forest seemed to go silent, awaiting her call to arms. She unleashed her rage.

The wind wailed, the sound eerily human like an echo of her voice. The Raven assaulting Asher stopped, staring at her. His face whitened. Roots burst from the Earth, coiling around the Raven's body like a constrictor. Reggie felt the roots squeeze the man, and heard his screams as he was dragged underground. The Earth shook. Water shot from the springs' pool like a miniature tidal wave, slamming into the fighting bodies. The icy water pushed Reggie down, but didn't cool her anger. She looked around, no longer recognizing friend from foe. She only saw Asher lying on the ground. The sight of his blood shredded her control.

Stumbling to her feet, Reggie gathered more power to her. Her father's warning about letting her emotions control her magic flashed through her head, but she ignored it. She was tired of seeing people she loved get hurt. The boulders embedded in the side of the trail trembled, bursting from the soil. As if in slow motion, Reggie watched the soldiers dodge the deadly rocks. A few didn't make it. They were crushed, bone sticking out of pulpy flesh. A boulder sped toward her, but her legs wouldn't move. She stared at it, picking out the pockmarks in its surface as it rolled closer.

Closer . . .

Suddenly Reggie was hit from two sides as Asher and Finch knocked her out of the boulder's path. Asher spun away in time. Finch wasn't so lucky. The rock rolled over his midsection and lower body. He coughed blood. Reggie crawled to Finch, tears clouding her vision. She took his hand in hers.

"I'm so sorry," Reggie cried, clenching his hand. "I didn't mean to..."

Finch smiled, blood staining his teeth. "I know. You're a good kid."

She shook her head. "I can fix you. I bring things back to life."

"Reggie," Asher said gently. "This isn't the same thing."

Reggie turned to him. "Yes it is! He's just bigger, that's all."

"It's too late for me," Finch whispered.

"No." Reggie refused to believe him. Pulling her hand from Finch's grasp, she laid both of her palms on his chest. She heard the sounds of fighting again. "I know you're hurt, Asher, but can you keep them off me?"

"It takes more than a little toothpick to stop me," Asher said. He put a reassuring hand on her shoulder. "Don't kill yourself."

"I'd deserve it if I did," she muttered, focusing on Finch.

Reggie didn't understand how she'd brought those things back to life in the Real. And she had no idea how to do it in the Other. But she had to fix Finch. Closing her eyes, she tasted the elements as her father had instructed. The body was mostly water, so she began there, seeking out Finch's injuries.

210

He was fading. She felt his light going dim, just like she felt the blackness inside the frog and the moth.

She found his ribs embedded in his lungs. Forcing air into the spongy tissue, she breathed for him as she sought to repair his ribcage. A ragged cry escaped Finch's lips, his desperate pain urging her on. When Finch began breathing on his own again, Reggie focused on the internal bleeding. There was so much of it. Stemming the flow and directing the blood back to its proper channels sucked her energy like a leech. Sweat ran into her eyes, and her back bowed.

This was a thousand times harder than bringing back the frog. Reggie wasted half of the magic she drew from the Earth because she didn't know how to direct it properly, like pouring a gallon of water into a shot glass. Despite her clumsy efforts, she felt the spark of Finch's life force growing brighter. Reggie opened her eyes. Red bubbles had stopped foaming from Finch's mouth. His breathing was uneven, but he was no longer starved for air.

Finch looked at her, trying to speak. She laid a finger on his lips. "Don't talk, just nod. You feel better?" Reggie's voice was raspy.

Finch nodded. She smiled.

Asher's voice sliced between them. "Reggie, we need to move him. Now!"

The sounds of battle came roaring back. Reggie looked over her shoulder. Asher stood with his back facing her, his feet spread in a defensive stance, blood soaking his shirt. Megan and Thomas double-teamed the captain; their swords whirling like fans. Reggie felt the Raven captain's power. His magic was strong and carried the taint of corruption, like rotting flesh. Reggie pulled her eyes away, turning back to Finch.

"He's not well enough to move."

"We don't have a choice," Asher said.

She turned around again, watching as the captain sliced into Thomas' side with his knife. The captain then shoved Thomas into Megan who went down under his weight. The captain sprinted toward them. Reggie surged to her feet, her fatigue forgotten as fear replaced it.

Asher put an arm out in front of her, backing her up. She crowded against Finch.

"He's used a lot of magic. And I'm stronger than him, even with my wound," Asher said.

"I'll back you up," she replied. But she felt empty and afraid to use her magic again defensively. She could accidentally kill them all.

The captain had both knives drawn, ready to strike. Asher rushed to meet him. Suddenly Asher fell to his knees, screaming. Reggie stared, shocked as the engraved figures on his collar glowed. The Captain swept past Asher, delivering a snapping blow to the back of his head. Asher slumped forward, hitting the ground. The captain grabbed Reggie, pulling her into his body with her back to his chest, his arm hooking around her neck. Cold steel pressed against her throat.

"Stay back!" the captain ordered Megan and Thomas, who were running toward them.

They skidded to a stop. A surviving Raven soldier limped behind them.

"You won't kill her," Megan said, stepping closer. "Your master won't allow it."

Reggie gasped as the knife pierced her skin, warm blood trickling down her neck. Megan stopped.

"He didn't say I had to bring her back whole," the Captain said. "Wex, come here. Take the slave."

Despite the danger, Reggie bristled. "Leave him alone!"

"I'll do whatever I want to with him, little girl," the captain warned. She hissed as the dagger pricked her skin again. "Let him through!"

Reggie met Megan's eyes, beseeching her to act, but Megan shook her head.

"It will be all right, Reggie. We'll come for you," Megan said.

"I'd love to see your ragtag army try to take Two Cities," the captain chuckled, and Reggie hated him even more.

Megan bared her teeth as she and Thomas stepped aside, letting Wex through.

Frustrated and angry by her helplessness, Reggie reached for her magic. But instead of her power igniting inside her, she felt only a flicker like a sputtering candle. Healing Finch had drained her dry.

They all watched in silence as Wex struggled with Asher's weight, finally managing to wrap a limp arm around his shoulder. Reggie stole a glance at Finch. He was alive, but barely.

"I can't keep my master's prize from him any longer," the Captain said, loosening his grip on Reggie. Something slammed into her skull. Everything went black.

CHAPTER 33

*R*eggie woke in a dimly lit room with a throbbing head and a mouth like sandpaper. Propping herself up on her elbows, she fought waves of nausea and looked around. She was lying on a huge, four-poster bed with a red velvet canopy that dripped gold tassels. The coverlet was also red velvet and wickedly soft to the touch. Reggie closed her eyes, convinced she was dreaming. When she opened them again, the decadent bedroom was still there.

"What the hell?" she said aloud.

She thought she'd be in a cell somewhere. But it looked like she was inside Versailles, or a really upscale bordello.

Exploring her skull with careful fingers, Reggie discovered a large knot. That explained the nausea. Slowly she scooted to the edge of the bed, trying not to vomit. It took a long time. The bed gave "king size" a whole new meaning.

She wondered why Andrius had put her here and not with Asher. God, Asher! "Please be alive!" she whispered fiercely, as panic tightened her chest. Reggie took deep breaths. She needed to keep a level head, figure out what was happening.

She looked at the floor, grimacing as a bout of dizziness swept over her. A thick, multicolored carpet resembling a Persian rug stretched before her. Gripping one of the bedposts, she lowered her feet onto the plush softness. Her head didn't like the idea, and Reggie swayed, trying to find her balance. Once she'd steadied herself, she released the bedpost. She realized the room wasn't dimly lit; the bed's canopy was just the size of a small circus tent. The sudden light wedged a splinter of pain in her skull. It was so intense that it took her a few moments to realize the lump on her head wasn't the only thing wrong with her.

Reggie couldn't feel her magic. The connection she felt to the Earth had been cut. It was as if her soul had been severed from her body and she was reduced to a thin, wraithlike shadow. She sank to her knees. What had Andrius done to her? She quickly stripped off her shirt and jeans, examining her body for any signs of abuse. Nothing except the wound on her neck. Not even a needle track marred her skin.

"Dammit!" Reggie said, climbing back into her clothes.

A large vanity stood across from the bed with an oval shaped, gilded mirror. She stumbled over to the vanity, landing on the stool's velvet cushion. Her eyes reflected pain, but the pupils weren't dilated. No signs of drugs. How had Andrius separated her from her magic? Her father had never mentioned anything like this to her. Had both he and Rhys underestimated just how powerful Andrius had become?

Reggie looked around. Near the double doors to the bedroom was a settee with her backpack lying on top. She staggered across the room, plopping onto the settee, and rested her head against the padded arm until the room stopped spinning.

Reaching for her backpack, she prayed that the guards hadn't stolen her gun. Maybe they wouldn't have known what a gun was. She'd seen plenty of blades in the Other, but no guns. Magic was just as deadly.

The memory of boulders crushing bodies, blood soaking the ground, flashed through her mind. The weight of their deaths was like a heavy stone pressing on her chest. Don't think about it, she told herself. Focus on the here and now. Opening the zipper, she rummaged through her clothing.

"Oh, thank God," Reggie whispered when she saw the gun.

Clutching the gun in one hand, she checked to see if it was still loaded and then clicked the safety again. She dropped the gun back into her pack, snagging a bottle of aspirin. Slipping the pack on her shoulders, she stood up. She needed water. There was a narrow door near the far corner of the room next to the bed. Reggie crossed the room and turned the knob, peering inside.

The bathroom was just as luxurious as the bedroom. Blue and ivory tiles layered the floor in a mosaic pattern. An enormous tub rested on one side of the room, its claw feet, faucet, and handles gleaming with what looked like real gold. Andrius was evil, but he had taste. Reggie went to the two-basin sink, splashing cool water on her face and neck. She popped open the aspirin bottle, swallowing a couple of pills. She hoped the aspirin would kick in soon. The way her body felt now, she didn't know if she could run. Standing upright was a challenge.

Medicated and armed, it was time to test the doors. The tall doors looked heavy, their handles made of brass. Sigils were painted on the door in swirling patterns of gold. Reggie reached out for the handle, but hesitated, her hand hovering over the brass. Changing direction, she picked up a silk pillow from the settee, tossing it at the door. No magical sparks, no wailing alarms. Nothing. Cautiously she pushed down a handle.

The doors jerked open, sending her sprawling on the wooden floor. Pain shot down her hip and elbow. Of course there was no carpet here. A guard stepped into the bedroom and stood over her. His body was encased in a black uniform.

"You're finally up and moving around," he said. "Or maybe not."

Reggie examined his uniform. No red. He wasn't a Raven. "The door's booby trapped."

217

He raised his eyebrows. "I'm not sure what 'booby trapped' means, but it's warded to detect motion. When you tried to open it, an alarm was sent to me."

"Just my luck," Reggie said, pushing herself to her feet with care. The fall had made the pain in her head worse. "What now, Jeeves?"

"Jeeves?" the guard asked icily.

Reggie shrugged. "I don't know what to call you. Are you here to hurt me?"

"So eager to experience pain, are you?" he asked, and something dark flashed in his eyes. She stepped back. "Unfortunately, I don't have that privilege. I would like to. You killed one of my friends."

"I didn't mean to kill anybody."

The guard's face was glacial. "This is war. Kill or die. Come, Master Andrius wishes to see you now." He made a shooing motion with his hand.

Reggie didn't want to confront Andrius when she was so weakened. She hesitated on the threshold, sizing up the guard. He had the build of a prizefighter, sculpted muscle and hard lines. She couldn't take him without her magic. Her mind briefly went to the gun, but she'd never shot anything in her life. And killing in self-defense was one thing, killing in cold blood quite another. She needed to save her bullets and formulate a better plan.

The guard watched her, smiling as if he could read her thoughts. "Are you going to come with me like a good little girl, or are we going to do this the hard way? I'd prefer the hard way."

"Let's go," Reggie said and followed him out of the bedroom.

CHAPTER 34

*A*sher was wedged in the corner of a prison cell. He leaned his head against the cold stone wall and closed his one good eye. The other was swollen shut. Blood crusted under his nose and around his mouth. The guards had enjoyed kicking, stomping, and punching him. It was a miracle all his teeth remained.

Having the heritage of Giants ensured that his broken ribs would knit in a few days. But right now it was agonizing to breathe. He couldn't straighten three fingers on his right hand, and his legs throbbed with pain. He wished for numbness, for his nervous system to be overwhelmed and switch off.

Asher raised his hands to check the skin under his collar as the sound of clanging metal echoed against the walls. His manacled wrists pulled up chains that looped through a reinforced steel ring that was welded to the floor. The flesh under his collar was blistered, and of all his wounds, that burned flesh hurt the most.

He'd come so close to getting Reggie to safety. He'd thought he was out of Andrius' range, but underestimating Andrius proved to be a fatal mistake. He would die here in this dank cell, useless, and unable to protect Reggie.

A memory of Reggie's raw power at Pikes Crossing flashed through his mind. She wasn't helpless. He didn't know if she had the control to challenge Andrius in a direct fight, but maybe she could out maneuver him enough to escape. He clasped his hands together and did something he hadn't done since he was a child. He offered silent words of prayer to the Mother, begging Her to protect Reggie.

Chapter 35

*J*ohn and Arlene trudged through the forest, following the path he'd taken previously with Reggie and Asher. Arlene was lagging behind, her breath coming out in loud huffs. She was clearly out of shape, and John shook his head, knowing this was the worst rescue team ever. But he couldn't sit home and do nothing. And neither could Arlene. Suddenly Arlene cried out.

John whipped around. Arlene lay on the ground, clenching her knee. Blood seeped through her torn jeans. He rushed to her side, kneeling on the ground beside her.

"You okay?" he asked.

Her eyes were shiny. "I'll be fine. Just fell is all."

"Let me take a look." He peeled back the torn material of her jeans, revealing an ugly gash under her kneecap. "Hand me the first aid kit."

Arlene dug through her backpack, passing him the little plastic box. "Sorry."

"For what?" He poured hydrogen peroxide over her cut. She winced.

"For slowing us down."

"Don't worry about it." He bandaged the wound.

"Some rescue team we are." Her face was dark, drawn.

John helped her stand. "We've got an old map and some kitchen knives. We're ready to kick some serious ass."

She laughed. "I'm glad you're here. I wouldn't have been able to make it on my own."

"Come on. We need to keep moving."

This time John detected the gateway to the Other before he heard it, the new magic in his blood acting as a homing beacon. That magic felt wrong, but he pushed his worry aside. He gripped Arlene's arm tightly, guiding her up the steep hill. She was limping slightly, and John was afraid that she wouldn't last long once they crossed over into the Other.

"You feel that?" Arlene asked.

"Yeah, almost there. Pretty soon we'll be able to hear it."

The buzzing began as they climbed, and he spotted the wavy patch of air between the two oak trees. John glanced at his melted sneaker, swallowing. God, he hoped this crazy blood transfusion worked.

"I haven't been here in years," Arlene whispered. "I tried to forget, but I never could."

They stood before the doorway. "So you've seen this done before? Going in, I mean?"

"No, but I used to say goodbye to Sebastian here."

John heard the fear in her voice. "Listen, this freaks me out too, but we'll go in together, okay? It'll be a tight fit, but we'll make it. Feet first, follow me."

Arlene nodded, clenching his arm hard. His body burned as it was drawn to the gateway. Together they stepped through the barrier. The air parted, letting them pass through to the Other. John swayed as his feet found solid ground, Arlene's weight almost tipping him over. The magic in his body became lighter, less of a burden, as it connected with its natural environment.

"You all right?" he asked, steadying Arlene.

"Give me a minute, I'll be fine." Arlene bent over, her hands resting on her knees.

John nodded, looking around. The forest resembled the one in the Real, but it felt different. Being lost in the woods in fairy tales never boded well. If he saw a gingerbread house or the Big Bad Wolf, he'd run like hell.

"Take out the map. Let's figure out where we are." John rolled his shoulders. He didn't like the stillness.

Arlene straightened, digging into the old satchel snug against her hip. She unfolded the map. He stepped closer, taking one end. She tapped a finger on a small ring of trees. "We're here and we need to get . . . here."

John's eyes widened as he looked at the vast space between the two points. "Two Cities? Shit, that's far. Are you sure?"

She nodded. "Sebastian told me it's the capitol. That's where Andrius is, and that's where Reggie will be if he's got her."

"How are we getting there? It'll take months if we walk! We don't have that kind of time." The edge of the map crinkled under his fingers.

Arlene tugged the map from his grip, folding it. "Sebastian told me about airships we can take. When we get out of this forest and find the Witch Plains, we should be okay."

John's head spun. "Airships? Goodbye, Kansas."

"You okay?" Arlene's voice was gentle.

He shrugged. "Stellar. Which way to the Witch Plains?"

"Southeast," she said, turning around. "That would be . . ."

He watched her spin in circles and sighed. "Maybe my compass will work here." He dug out the compass, comparing the position of the needle to the position of the sun. "What do you know, something is going our way." He pointed straight ahead.

Arlene smiled. "See? It's a sign—"

John clamped his hand over her mouth. Her eyes darkened in anger. Voices drifted through the trees like ghosts, soft and unnerving. He removed his hand from her mouth, putting a finger to his lips. Arlene turned toward the sound, which grew louder. John stood frozen as he listened, his heart knocking against his chest.

"Simon, forget about that little bitch. There's nothing you can do about her or the slave," a feminine voice said.

"Made a fool out of me! I should've castrated him right there, Andrius' slave or not. It was obvious what they were doing!" a man said.

And here came the Big Bad Wolf. John grabbed Arlene's arm, whispering, "I think they're talking about Reggie and Asher. We need to go now. Run!"

She wrenched her arm free. "They might know something. We should ask them—"

"Are you crazy? They just mentioned castration! We're getting out of here." He took her arm again, dragging her along. Arlene relented and they broke into a run.

A branch snapped in the distance behind them, loud like a gunshot. "Do you hear that? I think we have some fugitives!" A gleeful voice shouted. John heard bodies crashing through the underbrush and coming fast.

Arlene's eyes rolled with terror, echoing the fear in his. He grabbed her hand. "Run faster!"

John sprinted blindly through the forest, weaving around trees, jumping over fallen branches, never letting go of Arlene's hand even when she stumbled. The assailants followed, their footsteps growing closer.

CHAPTER 36

*T*he guard stopped in front of towering twin doors, their wooden surface lacquered with black paint and inlaid with silver carvings of elemental symbols. Reggie waited beside him as he rapped three times. Those respectful knocks were like hammer blows. Her heart lurched. The guard paused for a moment, listening for something that Reggie couldn't hear. Nodding to himself, he pushed open the door.

The guard smirked as he made a mocking bow. "In you go, my lady. Beware of the lion."

Reggie ignored him, crossing the threshold. The door closed behind her, the soft click confirming that she was trapped. She looked toward the opposite end of the room. Andrius Drake stood, tall and imposing, behind a huge desk, his hand outstretched toward her. He crooked his finger.

"Come, Reggie Lang," Andrius said. "How good it is to have you here at last." His voice carried in the large space, smooth, deep, and perversely charming.

Reggie wanted to resist his command, to spit on the polished stone floor, but his power crashed into her like waves pounding against the shore in a hurricane. There was something so familiar but so wrong about his magic. It was laced with the same sour scent that had clung to the Raven captain.

Reggie observed the room as she walked, taking silent inventory of the man waiting for her. On her left, the walls were lined with bookcases stuffed with leather bound tomes. The bookcases were so tall that spiral staircases and platforms had been built to allow access to the upper shelves. A high vaulted ceiling curved over the room with a fresco of the Mother resting like a jewel in the center.

To her right, a fire blazed in an enormous fireplace of black marble shot with veins of ivory. A map hung near the fireplace, but she couldn't make out much detail. As Reggie neared Andrius, her feet left stone and sank into a thick, plush carpet with a swirling pattern of the elements. Lifting her eyes from the rug, her gaze met the dark mage's. Her fear skyrocketed. She stopped in front of the desk, her feet rooted to the rug.

"I realize there's no need to introduce myself, but I believe courtesies must be observed. I am Andrius Drake, Master Mage and Head of the Council of Two Cities. It's a pleasure to have you in my home."

A giggle bubbled up her throat at his gracious display, and she cleared her throat. "I can't say it's a pleasure to be here." Reggie bit her lip at her audacity.

Andrius' eyes narrowed. "You wish to dispense with the pleasantries so soon? Very well, then, sit." He gestured to the high-backed chair next to her.

Reggie shook her head. "I prefer to stand." Standing would give her a better defensive position.

"I said sit." His voice was like a whip. Reggie's behind hit the chair hard, the force of his will overriding hers.

Andrius waited until she was seated before taking his seat. He leaned back, placing his elbows on the armrest, his fingers coming together in a point like a church steeple. "That's better. I admire spirit, but it doesn't excuse bad manners."

"Should I have said 'no thank you, I prefer to stand?'" If Reggie wanted to survive, she needed to figure out the rules to this game.

"Precisely." They fell into silence as his eyes probed her.

Reggie sat on the edge of her chair, hands clenched in her lap under his leisurely perusal. Intelligent eyes drilled into her as if seeking answers to very important questions. His mahogany desk—littered with silver instruments—didn't provide enough space between them.

"I've heard tales that you've grown powerful. Tell me."

Reggie blinked. "I don't know what you mean."

"Tell me what you did to my soldiers."

"I killed them."

"Obviously. Tell me how."

"You want details? No."

"Are you intentionally provoking me?" he said coldly. His power surrounded her, squeezing.

Choking, she shook her head. The pressure faded and she gasped.

"Good. Now, indulge me."

Taking deep breaths, Reggie sputtered, "I-I w-was pissed. Then the boulders came out of the ground. I don't remember much after that. Just people being crushed."

"Clumsy, but effective. Congratulations on your first kill. We have more in common than you thought." Andrius grinned. "I'm a killer too."

His words struck her like a physical blow. "I'm not a killer. It was an accident—"

Andrius laughed. "You wanted those men dead. You hated them."

Reggie studied her hands, thinking about the power she'd wrenched from the Earth. She hadn't thought about the consequences. She had just wanted the people she cared about to stop being hurt. But Andrius was right. A dark secret part of her had wanted those men dead, wanted them to suffer. She felt sick.

227

"You've tasted power. Death. You're no longer innocent."

Her head snapped up. "What I did was to protect myself. Doesn't make me a murderer like you!"

"Murderer? That's much too simple a word for what I am. What do you know about me? Only tales that Rhys and Asher have told you." He leaned forward, resting his elbows on the desktop.

"You attacked me in my dreams. You killed my father and all my kind! And I've seen what you did to Asher. That's everything I need to know about you."

Andrius just smiled. "Ah, yes, Asher. You've grown quite fond of him, haven't you? Not that I don't understand the attraction. Women have gravitated toward him since he entered puberty."

"You took advantage of him," Reggie said bitterly.

"You must always learn to use your weapons, Reggie. Unfortunately for me, Asher carries the burden of having a conscience. It's rather annoying. Gets in the way at the most inconvenient times. I've tried breaking him of the habit. Well, I'm sure you've seen the scars."

"You must be proud."

"It's just a standard punishment. Like your mother taking away a toy when you've misbehaved." Andrius shrugged. "Emotional pain, now there's an effective tool." He paused, tapping the desk with his fingertips. "His parents were heroes for the Resistance. I sent them to the mining Pits in Hornsbay Mountains to slowly die."

"Should I wait for the movie or is there a point to this?" Reggie asked.

Andrius frowned at her. "Patience is a virtue, as are good manners. We really must have a lesson later, don't you think?"

Magic slithered over her skin, like slimy fingers. She shrank against the chair, shivering, wanting it to stop. She ground out, "Please go on."

Andrius released her. "Freedom and family are important to Asher. He would do anything for his family. Anything for his freedom. You understand, don't you?"

Reggie stared at him as dread seeped into her heart.

"Holding his family makes him more cooperative, but he still balks at hurting innocents. Despite rather brutal punishments for his refusal." Andrius paused, watching her like a cat about to unsheathe its claws. "Imagine how eagerly he responded to my offer to free him and his family if he would bring you to me unharmed."

She shrugged off his attack. "Asher's already told me he's been working with Rhys behind your back. You're just trying to get me to turn on him, but it won't work."

"Stupid girl, Rhys sent her." He produced a crystal orb with a moving image inside. Reggie saw a blue-eyed young woman with a scarf covering her hair. It was Megan. Andrius handed her the orb. "She does retrievals for Rhys. Asher got to you before she did. I spoke with him two days ago in the Dream Realm. I'm the one who told him to take you to Pikes Crossing. How do you think my Ravens knew you'd be there? All this time you've trusted him with your life, and he's been working for me."

His words knifed into Reggie. She took the orb, staring at Megan. She remembered Brwyn's surprise that an Indentured was guiding her to Rhys. She remembered the hostile undercurrent between Asher and the Resistance soldiers. But Megan had insisted that they were on they same side. She didn't know what to believe anymore. The fragile glass slipped

229

through her numb fingers, shattering on the floor. She shook her head. "He wouldn't do that," she whispered.

"I promised freedom on your delivery. What price would you pay for freedom?"

Reggie's heart cracked, but something didn't ring true about his story. "The Resistance soldiers met us before we were ambushed. Asher must've told Rhys that. He must've turned on you."

Andrius wagged an accusing finger at her. "Because of you. I underestimated what a temptation you'd be. He knew if he failed me that I would kill him and his family. Not quickly, either, oh no. When he chose you and contacted Rhys, he sealed his fate. I'll be dealing with him shortly."

That meant Asher was still alive somewhere. Could she save him? Did she want to? The pain of his betrayal crippled her. Asher had lied to her, but he had chosen to save her in the end. If she could, she would save him. She owed him that. Unwanted tears tracked down her cheeks.

"Tears? I'm disappointed, Reggie. I expected more from you."

"I'm happy to disappoint you." Reggie rubbed her face with the back of her hand.

"You insult me, I hurt you. That's how the game is played," Andrius said. "I think I've been rather accommodating. I gave you a beautiful room, treated you as a guest, yet I receive such little gratitude."

"Do guests normally get their heads bashed in?"

"That was unfortunate. Captain Julian is being punished for his disobedience."

"I actually feel sorry for him."

"Don't. I went to a lot of trouble to bring you here unharmed, Reggie. If only I could have gone myself, things would've been much simpler." Andrius watched her, waiting.

Reggie bristled, tired of his games. The silence stretched between them. "Why couldn't you come?" she finally asked.

"Good girl, you want to play after all. Your father and I were friends a long time ago. Did you know that? You look like him."

"What?" she stammered.

"He and I were school friends. A brilliant Aether Mage, Sebastian. He had so much raw power he was frightening. They all were. Rhys was our friend too. Pure human, but he could manipulate the elements almost as well as an Aether Mage. We were inseparable, learning everything we could about magic until I went seeking a different kind of knowledge." He leaned back in his chair.

"You were friends with my dad and Rhys? Friends?"

"I was one of the few to know he married an Outsider, but I didn't know he had a child. That he kept secret from me. I suppose he had a premonition of what was coming," Andrius mused, tapping his fingers on his desk again.

"None of this makes sense. Couldn't he tell something was wrong with you? The way you smell—" she bit her tongue until she tasted blood as his eyes turned smoky.

"Smell like what, Reggie?" Andrius asked softly.

"Nothing."

"You're lying. Most can't sense what's different about me. I wasn't like this when your father and Rhys agreed to work with me. I was pure then." Andrius stretched his hand out in front of him, studying his palm. "Not anymore. When I was younger, I saw that although each race was magically talented and powerful, the Aether Mages' raw power couldn't be matched.

231

And there were more and more of them and they were gaining influence."

"So what?" she asked, ignoring her darkening suspicions. His eagerness to chat concerned her.

"People worried about the power the Aether Mages possessed. They were outnumbered, but their magic was so immense they could have controlled the Other. As their influence grew, I went to Rhys with a proposition. I told him we needed to dissect the magical properties of the Aether Mages, figure out the exact genetic combination needed to create their power to protect ourselves. It was the perfect opportunity."

"For what?"

"To conduct my experiments. Your father, along with Rhys, was my greatest supporter. We took blood samples from all the races, studied them, attempting to recreate the perfect combination. Your father was our only Aether Mage donor." Andrius' smile was menacing as he pushed the sleeve of his shirt past his elbow on his right arm, exposing the delicate blue veins. He tapped the veins with his fingers, meeting her eyes. "Your father's blood is in me now. Feeling cut off from your magic?"

Reggie sucked in a deep breath. "I knew you did this to me! I just can't figure out how."

"I'm using your father's blood against you. Because you're younger, his blood is stronger than yours. I can lock your magic away from you. He gave the gift that truly keeps giving."

"You don't have the right to use my dad's blood. That's how you're getting your power boost!"

"I gave myself a fresh injection just for you. Who knew I could use the father to control the daughter this way, hmmm?" He made a fist and the veins protruded farther from his skin. "Think of it as making weapons. Isolate the magical properties

232

in the blood, figure out the right combination, and increase your power. We did this so we wouldn't be helpless against the Aether Mages."

"Maybe it started out that way, but then you took the blood to help yourself," Reggie guessed. Andrius' little game of truth or pain started making terrible sense. He'd shared a lot of sensitive, and most likely secret, information. It probably meant she didn't have much longer to live.

"Rhys and I started taking the blood. Why do you think he didn't come to the Real to get you? The same reason I can't. We've tainted our magic." Andrius rolled his sleeve back down. "Your precious Rhys is just as polluted as I am."

The knowledge that her father and Rhys played a part in this man's rise to power knotted her stomach. "Maybe Rhys is polluted, but I bet he and my dad didn't know what you were really about."

"They didn't suspect anything until I started taking Sebastian's blood. His natural combination increased the artificial one I had forced onto my body. The power was . . . intoxicating," Andrius said, his fingers dancing along one of the silver instruments on his desk. "I could control things I never could before, convince people that the Aether Mages were more dangerous than they feared."

"You brainwashed them?"

"I didn't have to. Violence is a persuasive instrument," he said, his cool expression reptilian.

"You pretended to be an Aether Mage and attacked people," Reggie deduced.

"I had little control in the beginning, so the destruction was devastating," Andrius admitted with that same coldness. "Let me show you."

He waved his hand. The air between them swirled like liquid. Images formed, painted with vivid color. The air smoothed out again, and it was as if a projector had shined a film in front of her. A section of a city was in ruins, and bodies were strewn under the rubble, blood seeping into the ground. People were running in the streets, tripping over body parts. A tall, cloaked figure pursued the fleeing crowd, making sharp movements with his hands. The buildings in front of them burst into flame, trapping the victims between the rubble and the inferno. Some caught fire, their bodies engulfed in silver flame. Reggie closed her eyes, covering her ears so she wouldn't hear their agonized screams.

"Look! See how terrified they are." Andrius' soft voice managed to pierce through the screams. "They needed a hero to save them." The scene of destruction vanished and a younger Andrius appeared. Handsome and tall, he addressed an assembled group in what looked like an outside auditorium. "I became that hero. I was a successful graduate of the academy and a powerful mage in my own right."

"You murdered all those innocent people. What is wrong with you? Why didn't my father and Rhys stop you?" Reggie was so angry by what she'd witnessed that she forgot to be afraid of him.

Andrius didn't seem to take insult. He just shook his head. "By the time they suspected me, it was too late. The war against the Aether Mages had begun. I do regret the loss of their friendship. They would've made excellent allies."

As she stared into his eyes, Reggie searched for signs of insanity but only found intelligence. But his foul stench held proof that he'd paid a price. "What did the blood do to you?"

"Made me more than what I was. I've always been an ambitious man, the blood just multiplied it."

Reggie scooted to the edge of her seat, her backpack straining at her shoulders. She had no doubt he was going to kill her, but she needed to know why.

"Why do you want me so much?" she asked. "You have magic like mine. You killed my kind. Why am I a threat to you?"

He paused for a moment, flashing her a wry grin. "You see, dear Reggie, I wasn't exactly able to kill your kind . . ."

CHAPTER 37

*H*er brain shut down. Reggie struggled to breathe as her surroundings spun in a circle.

"Put your head between your knees. Take deep breaths," Andrius ordered.

She bent over, resting her elbows on her knees, and closed her eyes, inhaling and exhaling. Her head felt too light and her chest too heavy. When her breathing became even again, she raised her face.

"What did you say?" Reggie whispered hoarsely.

"You heard me."

Shaking her head, she leaned into her backpack, a comforting presence between her body and the chair. "I don't understand. My father didn't come back to us. He said he would've—" She clamped her mouth shut, glancing at Andrius.

He became very still. "He said he would have come back?"

Reggie remained silent. She felt rage leaking from his calm façade. His oily magic brushed against her skin again.

Andrius' laughter held no humor. "I've been prowling around in what's left of Sebastian's mind in the Dream Realm. He attacked me a few nights ago, but I didn't really believe it was possible. But you are his blood. I guess Rhys was able to reach Sebastian after all. Well played, Rhys, well played," he murmured, switching his laser focus back to her. "You probably thought he was some sort of spirit contacting you."

"I didn't know what he was." Reggie rolled her shoulders, trying to free them from the invisible slime touching her.

"That explains the focus you were able to give your magic. Given a little training and time, you'd be a very dangerous opponent," he said.

A light film of sweat coated her body as his magic seeped into her pores. He watched her struggle for a few seconds and then his magic retreated. She slumped back, relieved.

"As you can feel, Reggie, blood magic is a very dark and dangerous thing. A powerful thing. I created a spell using my new blood to rip the magic out of the Aether Mages. But it didn't kill them the way I'd planned. Although, I'm sure they wish they were dead."

She remembered the bodies floating underwater in her dream. "What did you do?"

He grimaced as if swallowing something bitter. "I tore their souls from their bodies. It was a mistake, but one I'll soon rectify."

Reggie was like an amateur boxer in the ring with a heavyweight contender. Andrius kept delivering punishing blows, and all she could do was hold onto the ropes to keep from being knocked out. "What does that mean? Are they in pain?"

"To have the very consciousness severed from your body must be the worst kind of agony. Your sanity would surely wane, don't you think?"

Hot tears trickled down her cheek as Reggie remembered her father telling her that it had been years since he'd felt the sun on his face. "So you didn't kill the Aether Mages, but they're no longer a threat to you. I don't get it. Why do you want me?"

"The Resistance collected their bodies, and Rhys channeled their spirits into the trees of Hornsbay Forest. The bodies rest in a Stasis bubble in Hornsbay, waiting for you."

"Me?" she sputtered.

238

"Your magic can reunite body with soul. Rhys isn't a fool. He knows I'll never be able to use that spell again. The Aether Mages will rise and my time will be over. I can't allow that to happen."

"You are going to kill me," Reggie said, frantically thinking of escape plans. She couldn't let him murder her. She needed to find a way to Rhys.

Andrius shook his head, baring his teeth. "I'm going to use you to give the Aether Mages their final death."

"Screw you, I'm not killing my father! If you want them dead so badly, why don't you just burn down the forest?" Pain exploded along her skin like it was being rubbed off with a sandblaster.

"If I could do that, I would just slit your throat, drain you dry, and use your blood. It would save me the trouble of disciplining you into an obedient servant," Andrius said. "Rhys protects Hornsbay Forest with powerful confusion spells that make it impossible for my soldiers to invade or burn the forest down."

"You're the big bad now. Just take Rhys on," Reggie said through clenched teeth.

"Rhys isn't a weak opponent, and I cannot go near Hornsbay."

"Why?"

"Because I can't. The spells are too strong for living soldiers, so I plan on using dead ones."

Reggie's mind connected the dots, and she stared at him, horrified. "I've never brought back a dead person before! How's that even gonna help? You said the spells are too strong for the living."

"Come with me," Andrius commanded, rising from his chair.

Reggie shot to her feet. "Where are we going?"

"Don't look so terrified. I want to show you my map of the Other." He pointed to the map hanging by the fireplace.

Reggie reluctantly moved toward the map, Andrius strolling beside her. He was tall and solid, moving with a fluidity she associated with trained fighters. Even without magic, he would crush her. They stopped in front of the map. Made of rich leather the color of buckskin, the map stretched across the wall with black stitching detailing the landmarks and cities of the Other. She spotted Hornsbay Forest. Rhys and her father waited for her there, needing her help. Narrowing her gaze, Reggie noticed the map also marked battlegrounds of the Other. Dates were placed there with a body count.

Andrius tapped his index finger on a battleground near the Hornsbay Mountains close to the Pits. "These warriors have been buried almost five hundred years, too old to be completely reanimated. It's quite a daunting task, but I believe with a little help, you can raise them all."

Reggie stared at the black stitches marking the burial ground. "What do you mean they're too old to be totally reanimated?"

"Their souls have left long ago. They won't be capable of independent thought or action. I don't want living soldiers, I want animated corpses."

Reggie's stomach lurched. "You want me to make an army of zombies? I don't think I work like that. No spark, no army."

With blinding speed, Andrius cupped her skull in one big hand, his fingers tangling into her hair. Reggie expected pain, but his hold was gentle on her scalp. "I'll help you. All I need is a few drops of your blood to connect us, and you can feed power from me to create my army."

Reggie shuddered. "You're going to feed off me too?"

"It's not necessary. But your blood gives me power, and I need to replenish my blood stores, continue my experiments. I used the last of your father's blood to confront you." She filed that piece of information away as Andrius reached out with his free hand and stroked the burial marker with his fingers. "When you draw energy from me, my blood magic will infect your power and awaken the soldiers. They will be an army unlike any the Other has ever seen. Indestructible and mine."

She glanced at the map and then at his face, which was uncomfortably close. "No," she said, gasping when his grip tightened.

"What did you say?" Andrius said quietly.

"I won't help make your zombie army. I won't kill my father."

Andrius lifted the hand tangled in her hair to drag her up onto her toes, a few meager inches between their faces. His breath was hot on her skin. "Reggie, have I given you the impression that you have a choice? The only real choice left to you is how painful it will be. You're such a lovely, talented young woman. You can obey me and be taken care of," he said, raising his other hand to rub his thumb lightly over her cheek. "Or you can defy me and be broken into pieces."

Agony ripped through Reggie's body, buckling her knees. But the hard hand on her skull held her upright as the pain increased, tremors racking her body. Tears rolled down her cheeks, dripping off her chin. Andrius kept pitiless eyes locked onto her face. He finally released the grip on her head, only to dig his fingers into her backpack. She folded over, and he dragged her limp form across the stone floor back to his desk. He dropped her. She hit the floor hard.

"Shit," Reggie groaned. The stone felt like ice.

Andrius bent down, yanking her to her feet and shoving her against the desk. Her knees banged into the wood. "Stay."

Stay upright? She didn't know if she could. Swaying, she held onto the corner of the desk, the wood slippery in her sweaty hands. "What are you doing?"

Rummaging around the silver instruments, Andrius held up a needle and a glass vial. "Give me your arm."

Reggie clutched her right arm to her side, leaning her hip heavily on the desk. She wanted to run, but her body felt like it was made of gelatin. "No," she shook her head.

"No?"

Sudden pain splintered her spine, bowing her back.

"Shall I do it again?" he asked.

"No!" Reggie slid back to the floor. Shaking her head, she tried to clear away the fog of pain, to think. The desk hid her from him. Quickly she stripped off her backpack, thrusting her hand inside and groping with her fingers until they closed around the smooth handle of the gun.

"You're testing my patience," Andrius warned.

"Okay, okay." Reggie drew the gun to her hip, thumbing the safety off. Breathing deeply, she pushed herself to her feet. She faced him, wrapping both hands around the gun and raising it to shoulder level. Despite her shaking hands, the move was lightning fast.

"What are you doing?" Andrius asked, his gaze narrowing on the gun.

Reggie squeezed the trigger. The first shot boomed like thunder, the sound ricocheting off the high ceilings. The bullet missed Andrius, hitting the wall behind him. Pain lanced through her again, and Reggie knew Andrius had recovered from his initial shock. The muscles in her hands twisted. She almost dropped the gun. Blood seeped from her nostrils and ears, but she steadied her hands. Locking eyes with Andrius, she squeezed the trigger again. This time she didn't miss.

CHAPTER 38

The bullet ripped into Andrius' right shoulder. His eyes widened with stunned disbelief but remained locked on Reggie's face. Blood sprayed behind him, splattering on the floor. She lowered the gun, tasting burnt copper. Andrius' magic gnawed at her fingers, and the gun fell from her hands. Suddenly, he toppled to his knees and the connection was broken.

Magic rushed through her with the force of a mudslide. Reggie collapsed on the chair behind her as power filled up her empty places, making her whole again. She focused on Andrius' crumpled form. She hadn't killed him, but she'd wanted to. His eyes snapped open. He focused on her. She felt his magic gathering around her, oily and dark.

Her survival instincts kicked her hard, pushing her into action. The guards would be coming soon. She slipped on her backpack and ran to the door, the gun forgotten on the floor in her haste. Andrius' angry voice bit at her heels.

"I'm already healing myself, Reggie. I'll enjoy punishing you," he shouted from behind her. "Why don't you come back and finish me? Never leave an enemy alive, you stupid little bitch!" His power lashed at her like invisible claws raking over her flesh. "You'll never get beyond the grounds. I'll come for you!"

Reggie jerked open one of the large doors, peering outside. She was surprised to find the hallway deserted. But Andrius hadn't expected her to be able to gain back her magic or be any real threat. Stepping out, she closed the door quietly behind her and surveyed her surroundings.

The long hallway stretched before her. How to get out? Floor to ceiling windows formed the left side of the hallway, and the right side had doors leading off the main corridor. Should she break a window, or see where one of the doors led?

She needed to find where Andrius kept his prisoners. She wasn't going to leave Asher behind. Looking around at the luxurious hall, she couldn't imagine Andrius would sully his lair with the stink of prison. Footsteps echoed from a distance, drawing closer. She'd figure out where Asher was later, first she needed to hide. Reggie dashed to one of the large diamond-paned windows and looked out.

She was on the second floor of a château. The outer walls were made of white stone inlaid with a slate blue pattern. A thick, manicured lawn surrounded the castle with planted gardens full of blood-red roses. Large trees dotted the landscape, their wide trunks interrupting the formality of the gardens. Reggie pressed her face against the window, craning her neck to the left. She saw a small cluster of outlying stone buildings, with armed guards manning the largest structure. Soldiers were posted at the entrance and around the perimeter. Score. There was the prison.

The footsteps down the hallway grew louder, multiplying as others joined the first pair. The sounds came from different directions now. Reggie felt like a fox being cornered by hounds. She glanced at the lawn with longing, the heady taste of freedom teasing her tongue. But she couldn't go that way. She didn't know if she could survive the drop. And even if she could, the guards would quickly figure out where she'd gone. She'd immediately have to defend herself, and she was weak right now. Random door it was.

"She escaped the Master?" The sound of an incredulous voice floated down the hall.

"She's still in the manor. We need to find her now," another voice commanded sharply.

"But she escaped the Master! How is that poss—"

"Enough! Do you want to die?" the other man said.

Reggie had only seconds before she'd see the heads belonging to those voices. She crossed the hallway to the first door. Door number one locked, door number two jammed, door number three, just right. Pushing open the heavy oak door, she quickly shut herself inside.

Whirling around, Reggie braced for an attack, but the room was empty. A long, gleaming table dominated the space, lined on both sides with leather chairs. A machine that looked like it was the lovechild of a typewriter and a brass telephone sat on the table. Maps covered the walls, with silver pins pushed in certain locations. Shelves full of large leather books framed a stone fireplace.

No windows. Muffled voices drifted from beyond the heavy door. Reggie searched for a place to hide. Under the table was out. She hurried to the fireplace, kneeling in front of it and searching for a secret handle like in the movies. No such luck. Her eyes landed on the maps. She lifted them up, hoping for some hidden passageway. Solid wall. What kind of castle was this?

"Check all the doors. She couldn't have gone far!" a man yelled, right outside the room.

"Shit!" Reggie muttered.

Her eyes went to the fireplace again. The base was large and the hearth mercifully unlit. She crawled inside, looking up the dark chimney. It seemed large enough to accommodate her frame. Biting her lip, she pushed her head and shoulders into the gloom. Sweat broke out on her back as images of being trapped in that tight blackness froze her in place. But then she heard the doorknob turn. Cursing silently, Reggie's fingers found purchase on some uneven stones. She pulled her body up just as she heard the door bang against the wall. She braced her feet on the stone, her fingers clinging to her unstable holds made slippery with soot and sweat. She listened as guards entered the room.

"Check everything and be careful. The captain says she's dangerous," a woman's voice said.

A man snorted. "Can't believe she got away from the Master."

Reggie heard them pulling out chairs away from the desk, then a loud scraping sound. Did they think she'd be stupid enough to hide underneath the table? As if answering her question, the woman said, "Check the compartment under the table. She could fit in there."

"It's clear."

Light footsteps approached the fireplace. She watched the dim light below her feet. Her muscles ached with strain and her breathing was impossibly loud in her ears. The footsteps stopped.

"What are you doing?" the woman asked.

"This fireplace is movable. It's one of the Master's escape routes," the man replied.

Reggie had searched all around the base of the fireplace and had found nothing. The fireplace started moving. She dug her fingers deep into the stone, trying not to fall. She grunted as the rock cut her fingers. Stone scraping against stone smothered the betraying sound as the fireplace rotated.

"Come on," she heard the man say.

"See anything?"

"No. Check the windows. I'll take the bathroom and the closet."

Hope surged through Reggie. There were windows in this new room. She strained to hear what the guards were doing, but the stone muffled their movements. If they didn't leave soon, she'd fall out of the fireplace, hand-delivering their victory.

"Nothing. Not a trace that she was here," the woman called.

"I didn't see anything either."

She heard the guards step back on the fireplace. It rotated again, stopping in the original room. Reggie waited, suspended in the dark like a spider, listening as the guards left the room.

Then only silence remained, but she still waited. Andrius' guards might be hanging around to see if she doubled back. Minutes ticked by slowly. Her muscles cramped in agony, the tissues on fire. When she was certain the guards weren't returning, Reggie straightened her legs and released her grip.

She crumpled when her feet hit stone, shaking. Dropping to her hands and knees, she crawled out of the fireplace. Soot coated her arms and clothing. Blinking at the light, she looked up. What had the guard done to make it move?

Her gaze fell on the bookcase to the right of the fireplace. It stuck out more than its twin. Reggie stood up, inspecting the back. A lever was embedded in the wall. She smiled as she pulled the metal handle down. Stone rumbled as the fireplace began to move. She ducked back into the large hearth. A loud thud filled the room as the fireplace finished rotating. Reggie winced, but no guards burst through the door. She climbed out of the fireplace.

She was in a parlor. Two settees and four chairs occupied the space, with a few coffee tables scattered about. The furniture was covered in bold, sapphire blue brocade shot through with silver thread. A silver tea set sat on one of the low tables.

Reggie quickly touched the teapot. Cold. Ignoring the door, she hurried to the windows. She was finished playing hide and seek in the castle.

The windows opened onto a small balcony. Reggie gulped in cool air as she crouched, looking through the balcony's railing. The prison was no longer visible, but she had a good idea of where it was. Unfortunately, more guards patrolled the grounds, their black clad figures swarming like militant ants. Another balcony lay directly below her. It was a fifteen-foot drop. If she could climb down to it, she could make it to the ground without killing herself. But the moment she made a move, the guards scurrying below would spot her.

With a fearful heart, Reggie reached for her magic. To her relief it swelled up inside her immediately, warming her body. She pushed away the pain and fear, concentrating on the taste of the earth. At first she couldn't detect it, but then a rich spiciness saturated her tongue with the promise of green buds and fertile soil. Delving beyond the surface, she discovered the hot lava and tectonic plates that formed the Earth's crust.

It was the dark power she focused on, the violent motion of creation and destruction. Reggie plugged into that darkness, creating a link between her body and the Earth. Once she was sure she had control of the connection, she channeled all her fear, anger, and pain down the bond. Power jolted her body, electrifying her bloodstream. The Earth roared as the lawn split open like a gigantic maw.

Reggie gripped the railing as the ground shook, forcing her eyes open. The guards scrambled for footing on the shifting ground. One of the castle turrets crumbled. White powder formed a mushroom cloud as stone was crushed, pelting the grass. Screams cut through the confusion, beating against her skull. She was killing people.

She corked the bitter flow of her emotions, her muscles straining with effort. Her rib cage felt like it was being shattered from the inside out. Reggie fought to take in air, her lungs burning. Letting go had felt so good. Too good. But she wouldn't allow herself to become a monster. She battled the pain, wrestling with her magic. A few agonizing moments later, the Earth calmed.

Reggie slumped against the railing, viewing her handiwork. Clumps of guards lay on the ground while others ran toward the fallen turret searching for injured people. She stared, stunned at the destruction before her. A dark power brushed against her skin, snapping her from her stupor. Oily fingers reached for her magic but were still too weak to take hold.

Andrius was feeling her out, trying to pinpoint her location. She quickly pulled herself to her feet. Taking advantage of the confusion, Reggie climbed down to the lower balcony. She had to rescue Asher and find a way out of there.

CHAPTER 39

The prison building was squat and wide. Its musty air was layered with the scents of rotting food, sweat, and human waste. Reggie crouched against the wall inside the kitchen, hiding beside a large cabinet. The bony cook shuffled back and forth in front of the kitchen door, his hands twisting a metal spoon. The crash of the turret had drawn most of the guards away from the prison. She'd managed to slip inside during the chaos. Only the cook and two guards remained, standing between her and the cellblock door. The warden's office behind her was empty.

Keeping her eye on the cook, Reggie snatched a rolling pin off the top of the cabinet. She stood on silent feet. The cook continued to pace, focused on the prison entrance. She had one shot at this. Springing forward, Reggie brought the rolling pin down on the cook's skull. He folded over. She grabbed him as a flash of silver whizzed by. She fell to the floor, muffling a grunt as the cook's dead weight landed on her. Reaching out with her hand, she snagged the spoon before it could hit the floor.

Laying the spoon gently beside her, Reggie pushed the cook away. She dragged his body behind the large cabinet, sitting beside him. Only the two guards remained, but she didn't know how she was going to get past them. Fatigue weighed her down. Throwing heavy magic at them was out of the question. It would draw too much attention, and if she managed to free Asher, she'd need all her energy to get them away from the castle's grounds and into Two Cities.

Reggie did a quick mental inventory of her weapons. She had the gun. Shooting the guards wouldn't be like shooting Andrius, but her options were limited. Slipping her hand in her backpack, she rummaged through her clothing and food but couldn't find the gun. Where had she left it? She stilled when she realized the gun was with Andrius. All she had left now was her magic and her fighting skills.

She crawled to the doorway and peeked out, sizing up the guards. Both were male, with carved muscle bulging under their uniforms. Bullies in the schoolyard she could handle, trained soldiers were another matter.

Seconds ticked by. Sweat trickled down her brow. Reggie knew she lacked the finesse for a subtle magical attack, but she had to act soon before Andrius realized that she was here. Physical force was the only remaining option. One of the guards jerked his head around, glancing toward the main corridor past her hiding place. She shrank further back into the shadows.

The taller of the two guards, an Elf with feline green eyes, turned to his partner. "Master Andrius wants us to join the others outside, help create a perimeter around the prison. She might be headed here."

The shorter guard shook his head. "What about the prisoners?"

"They aren't going anywhere. Master Andrius doubts she'll come for that half-breed piece of shit. But if she does, we'll take her."

They trotted toward her. Reggie ducked back into the kitchen, hiding behind the cabinet once more. She waited until the sound of their footsteps had faded before hurrying to the kitchen door. This was going to be tricky. She needed to cross in front of the main corridor to reach the prison block. Her sneakers were soft on the stone floor as she peered past the warden's office and down the hallway. The guards' backs faced her. She scampered across the corridor and stood in front of the cellblock door. It was locked.

"Come on," Reggie whispered.

She tilted her head toward the corridor, listening hard. The guards' movements were faint. She turned toward a metal cabinet hanging on the wall next to the cellblock door. Reaching for the handle, Reggie pulled gently. The cabinet door opened with a high-pitched squeak. She stilled as the footsteps stopped. Reggie waited, her heart tap dancing against her chest. If they came for her, she'd open up her magic with both barrels and damn the consequences. But after a few moments the footsteps resumed and she exhaled.

Four different sets of keys hung from metal hooks in the cabinet. She lifted each key set off the hook, taking care not to jangle the metal. She tried four keys before the fifth slid into place. Turning the key in the bolt, she pushed the door open, cringing when it scraped against the floor. She wiggled her body through the small crack, shutting the door behind her. The cellblock stretched before her.

Reggie gagged as the rancid smells of unwashed bodies and human waste slapped her. Ignoring the startled glances of the first two prisoners, she raced down the cellblock until she found Asher. He gasped when he saw her.

"Reggie, is that really you?" Asher rasped.

Reggie stared at him. The flesh around his neck was raw. Purpled and swollen skin gave his normally beautiful features a misshapen edge. One of his hands was mangled, the digits hanging at odd angles. Her anger melted away as she looked at his wounds. Andrius had a lot to answer for.

"It's me. I've come to get you out of here."

Asher stood as tall as his manacles would allow. "Forget me. Andrius will torture you if you're caught. Run, Reggie!"

"I'm not leaving you behind. Can you walk?" Reggie stuck a hand in between the bars. Asher gripped it like a lifeline.

"I think so. Are you okay?" His good eye examined her features. He squeezed her hand. "Did Andrius hurt you?"

"Yeah, but I survived."

"Reggie, I'm sorry that I—"

"Don't worry about that now. We have to get the hell out of here, no arguments. Do any of these keys look familiar?" Reggie released his hand, thrusting her other hand through the bar with the keys.

Asher nodded, taking the keys from her. "I think this one will open all the cells." He separated another key with his thumb. "This will unlock my manacles. I hope." He handed the keys back to her.

Reggie took the keys he had indicated, pocketing the rest. "Let's see if this works." She slid the key in the lock and turned. The door popped open. She stepped into his cell. The other prisoners were murmuring all around them, their voices rising at an alarming rate.

"Quiet!" Asher hissed. "Do you want the guards to come back? As soon as she frees me, we'll get you out."

Reggie turned to look at the other prisoners. They clutched the bars of their cages. Their faces were pressed against the iron, men and women gaunt with fatigue and hunger. "Yeah, we will. But pipe down or we'll never be able to pull this off."

"Why should we trust you?" a woman cried.

"Because I just got away from Andrius Drake. You felt that earthquake? You can thank me for that," she said. Murmurs and whispers flitted around the cellblock. Reggie knelt in front of Asher.

254

"You escaped Andrius?" questioned one.

"I don't believe it," said another.

"But the earthquake! That doesn't happen in this part of the Other!" came another voice.

"You've started something now," Asher whispered.

"It's about time," Reggie said, fitting a key into the lock holding his manacles. "Got it. Your legs don't look so good." She lifted his pant leg, gasping at the sight of mottled flesh.

"They're just bruises. Nothing's broken. I'll heal."

Reggie freed Asher's legs, quickly moving to his wrists. She had to get them out of there soon. Once Andrius recovered, he would use what was left of her father's blood to trap her again. "Done." She stood. He pulled himself up. When she went to help him, he shook his head.

"Don't," Asher said, swaying on his feet.

Reggie hooked his arm around her shoulder. "Don't be such a martyr. Come on. Let's help these people." Asher nodded. He tripped as they moved out of his cell. She clutched his side, flinching at his hiss of pain. "What's wrong?" His mouth was pulled tight. White lines bracketed his lips.

"Broken ribs. Give me a minute to adjust. Free the others. When you're finished, I'll be well enough to help you."

"Okay, rest."

Reggie hurried through the cellblock, unlocking doors until all the prisoners were free. After looking at the pitiful condition they were in, she wished she had shot Andrius in the head instead of the shoulder. Some were more skeleton than living flesh. And the smell! Decay, stale sweat, and shit. Reggie pushed back her queasiness. She didn't want to deliver another blow to the prisoners' dignity by puking. She returned to Asher's side.

"Can you move now?"

He nodded. "What can I do to help?"

Reggie bit her lip, surveying her troops. "All the guards are outside the prison. They're waiting for me. It's going to be a hell of a lot harder to get out than it was to get in. Asher, can you carry me?"

Asher's brows rose. "Yes, why?"

She took a deep breath. "It's time to create another magical disaster. I don't know what that will do to me." She was putting her life in his hands once again.

His green eye was determined in his battered face. "I'll take care of you."

Reggie nodded, believing him. She focused on the prisoners before her, six in all. "Once the magic kicks in, we're not going to have a lot of time. I need you to run as fast as you can. Understand?"

There were nods. A female Elf stepped up, her once wheat-colored hair matted around her head. "Who are you?" she asked.

Reggie stared into her dingy green eyes. "I'm an Aether Mage." She ignored the gasps around her. "When I get out of here, I'm going to find a way to kick Andrius' ass and help all of you."

The Elf searched Reggie's face. She nodded. "I believe you. What's your name?"

"Reggie Lang."

"Reggie, you're what we've been hoping for. Don't worry about saving us," she said.

"What?" Reggie asked, her eyes darting over the other prisoners who nodded. "I don't understand."

The Elf reached out her worn hand, clasping Reggie's. "Call whatever power you can, but we'll distract the guards for you. Give you more time to escape."

Reggie recoiled. "No! Don't sacrifice yourself for me! I'm getting you out of here alive—"

The woman squeezed her hand hard. "We want freedom. We want change," she said, her eyes holding the fiery promise of revolution.

"But—" Reggie began when Asher closed his hand over her shoulder. She glanced up at him. He shook his head slightly.

The woman brushed back a stray hair behind Reggie's ear. "Good luck, my young friend. Come on." She gestured with her hand. The five other prisoners followed her like drones following their queen.

Asher's hand kept Reggie in place. "They're Resistance fighters. They feel they're doing their duty to the Other."

Their courage humbled Reggie. "I'm not worth that."

"Yes, you are."

The prisoners had left the cellblock door open. Reggie heard them running down the main corridor. They were screaming, their voices echoing off the walls. She looked around, thinking hard.

"Besides the main entrance, are the any other exits?"

"No. And the windows are barred," Asher said.

"Dammit!" Reggie paced back and forth. Causing another earthquake would likely kill them. What could she do? Then it hit her. She'd noticed Andrius had built his castle around large, old trees. Two shaded the prison building. Their roots ran deep. "Doors and windows are overrated."

"What?"

She smiled, holding out her hand. "We're busting out of here. Anchor me, okay?"

He closed his good hand over hers. "Okay."

Reggie clung to his hand, both comforted and hurt by his touch. But she needed that. She needed the conflict in her emotions. Like a dangerous chemical cocktail, it would make her magic explode. She felt the dampness of the earth as her magic snaked its way through the soil, curling against those powerful roots. Channeling energy through her body, she spoke to the wooden limbs. She urged them to rise, to pull the wall down. Dark power vibrated beneath the floor. The stones shook, cracks forming.

"Reggie!" Asher shouted.

His arm wrapped around her waist, pulling her away from the cellblock's outer wall. The floor groaned. Roots speared through the stone like knives through flesh. Large fractures formed in the wall. Concrete began to crumble. The damage traveled beyond the cellblock's wall. The whole side of the prison was tumbling down.

"Reggie, you're going to trap us. The prisoners' sacrifice will be for nothing if we can't escape!" Asher yelled over the noise.

Running a soothing hand over his arm, she continued to talk to the tree. The buttery taste of oak burst into her mouth. Her heart sang as she bonded with that life force, slipped inside its skin.

"Asher, take me outside."

Asher stared at the falling debris. "It's not safe. The guards are here."

Reggie heard muffled shouts over the roaring of the collapsing building. "Do you trust me?" Her voice was strained. He bent down close to listen.

"Yes." He clutched her body tighter to him.

"Then take us outside. Grab on when it swings by," Reggie whispered. The amount of control she was maintaining made it hard to speak.

"When what swings by?"

"Go! Now!"

258

Scooping his arm under her knees, Asher lifted her to his chest. Her arms clung to his neck. He sped through the debris, flinging them outside the prison walls. Sunlight hit her eyes, burning. But she didn't break her hold on the tree. Through her hazy vision, she saw black uniformed guards surround them. Terrible screaming filled her ears. The prisoners.

A rough voice barked, "You actually came back for this piece of shit slave."

An oily sensation licked her skin. Andrius. Even though his magic felt slightly different, the sliminess managed to worm its way inside her. Her magic snapped back from its touch. Her link to the oaks wavered. Reggie gritted her teeth, pushing her magic outward again.

"Reggie, whatever you're going to do, do it now!" Asher said.

"Grab hold!" she said.

Suddenly a thick tree limb whipped toward them. Asher reacted with cat-like quickness, slinging Reggie over his right shoulder. She felt the muscles in his back bunch as he held onto the branch when it lifted from the ground. Shocked faces filled her vision as the tree branch swung back. She used her last spurt of magic to make one more request. This one was going to hurt.

"Asher, hold on tight to me!" Reggie screamed into the wind. "We're going for a ride."

"The Mother save us!" he shouted back, clenching her to him.

The tree branch sped up, catapulting them over the wall that enclosed Andrius' estate. Reggie slipped from Asher's shoulder, wrapping her legs around his waist. He gripped her closer as they sailed through the air.

Buildings zoomed near as if magnified with a looking glass. A river cut down the side of the hill. Its rocky bank grew closer and closer. Reggie felt Asher shifting, positioning his body to take the hit. She hugged him tighter in gratitude. Straightening her legs, she closed her eyes.

The impact rattled her teeth and shook her bones. She held onto Asher as they skidded down the bank toward the water. Pain lanced her body. Asher shouted as he extended his legs, his muscles straining. They finally slid to a stop. Aware of his broken ribs, she rolled off him. She ignored her pain, examining Asher. His golden skin was pale, his body soaked in sweat. Hearing his ragged breaths hurt her.

"Asher, are you okay? Can you move?" She hovered over him, afraid to touch him in case she hurt him more. He mumbled something. Reggie lowered her face to his. "What?"

"I'm not okay. But we have to move. They'll be coming for us. We need to get lost in the city," he gritted out. "Can you—"

"Yeah." She hooked his arm around her shoulder, wincing as she helped pull him up. He was heavy, but with his help she managed to get him to his feet.

Asher twisted, panting, "How bad is my back?"

Reggie's mouth fell open. The back of his shirt fluttered in tatters, blood soaking through the ruined material. Strips of skin were missing. "Cut to pieces. If we had more time, I'd try to heal you. What can I do now?"

"Nothing. We'll lose them in the city and then I'll take care of it." He held out his hand. Her brief hesitation caused a different kind of pain to cross his face. "It will be easier if I guide you."

She silently cursed herself, grabbing his good hand. Her fingers slid between his in a familiar gesture. "I trust you."

CHAPTER 40

*A*s they hurried away, she glanced back at the hill they'd just sailed down. Large estates clung to the side, interwoven with government and commerce buildings. Two different structures caught her eye. One rested near the highest point, its white marble twisted into arches and spires. The second was a Temple. Just looking at it calmed her.

Asher led her into the heart of Two Cities, his pace relentless despite his injuries. The buildings closed in on them, the streets narrow and crowded. He kept them to the shadows, keeping her close. Bookstores, alchemy shops, and restaurants surrounded them. But the paint was faded, everything a little shabby.

"Where are we going?" Reggie asked.

"To the Pleasure Zone. We can hide there. I used to run errands for Andrius in the Zone. Courtesans make good spies for both sides. I know someone who might be able to smuggle us out of the city and cut this collar off me, for the right price."

Jealousy suddenly pinched her. "What would that be?"

"Information. I know a lot about Andrius. I'm more than willing to trade."

"Are they tracking us with your collar now?"

He grimaced. "Yes. I should leave you, face Andrius' guards by myself. But you don't know the city like I do. They'd find you." They ducked into a narrow alley.

"So willing to leave me again," she said, her shoulders brushing against the side of a brick building.

"I'd kill to stay with you," Asher said. She stared at him. "After everything, do you really want me with you?"

"I risked my life to save you. Of course I want you with me." His eyes widened. She squeezed his hand. "How fast can they find us with that thing?" She gestured to his collar.

"There are many Indentureds in the Zone. All those collars and magic make it hard to distinguish who is who. It will buy us some time."

"I need to contact Rhys. He has to know I'm coming to him. I need somewhere safe so I can sleep, catch him in a Dream."

Asher nodded. "I'll do my best, Reggie."

"Thanks for taking the hit." They exited the alley, emerging on a shaded street as overhead canopies competed for space.

"It was the least I could I do." Asher looked down at her. "I'm so sorry I lied to you. You have to believe me."

The sincerity and regret in his voice moved her. But she slipped her hand out of his, keeping up with his long stride with an effort. "I know Andrius promised you freedom. I get why you did what you did. But the other stuff...when was it real for you? How long were you playing me?" She could forgive him for taking her to Andrius because his life was at stake, but she didn't know if she could forgive him for making her love him.

Suddenly Asher stopped, gripped her elbow, and pulled her into the shadows of an overhanging canopy. The smell of overripe fruit assaulted her. He bent his forehead down until it touched hers. "It was always real. How I feel about you, the things I said. I knew I was in trouble the moment we met. You're the kindest, bravest person I know. It was real for me."

Reggie blinked back tears at the raw emotion on his face. She recognized what it was, but words wouldn't come. She needed time to think. This thing between them couldn't be resolved now.

She ran the back of her hand down Asher's cheek. "I believe you. But I have to focus on saving my father and the other Aether Mages now. Andrius has trapped them."

His eyes lit up. "Just point out who you want me to kill."

The heaviness in her heart lightened and she laughed. Without the lies, they'd be true partners. She wouldn't be alone. "Let's find this friend of yours."

Asher nodded and took her hand once more, leading her into the maze of streets. He brought her to an arched entryway set in a brick wall. The arch was constructed of brass with carved friezes of naked figures twisting around each other. Reggie stared at the more acrobatic positions, knowing she'd never be that flexible.

"Welcome to the Pleasure Zone," Asher said.

They crossed the threshold and entered the Zone. Cinnamon and ginger spiced the air, along with the smoky sweetness of incense. Reggie breathed deeply, discovering the fragrant smells covered earthier odors, ones of musk and stale sweat. She caught a whiff of something that smelled like pot.

Reggie hoped they would find safety here. If they didn't get that collar off Asher soon, their escape from Andrius would amount to nothing. Crowds clogged the narrow, cobblestoned streets as Elves, Humans, and Giants bustled back and forth. Every available piece of real estate was in use, leaving only the bare minimum of space for walking. There were no bubble cars here. She wondered how the peddlers brought in their merchandise.

Asher moved swiftly through the crowd, pulling her along through the throng of bodies, deeper into the Zone. Ahead she spotted a couple of scantily clad Elves lounging on chaises in

263

a window. As they passed a few more brothels, Reggie noticed that what distinguished one brothel from another were their awnings. Each was a different color, with some sporting symbols such as half moons, while others had images of animals such as stags or birds painted on them. Peddlers in tiny carts dotted the streets, selling condoms, drugs, food, and those creepy velvet dolls. Reggie guessed if you couldn't afford to get off with a real person, the doll was the next best thing.

A giant bumped into her. Reggie tilted her head back, gazing into bloodshot eyes. "Beg your pardon," he slurred, grinning. "Aren't you a pretty little thing?"

Asher stepped in front of her. "Move along, friend. There's nothing for you here."

The Giant put up his hands. "Meant no harm."

Asher shoved him back a few steps, tugging Reggie forward again. "We need to hurry. My collar is heating up. What exactly did you do to Andrius?"

"I shot him," she said.

"You shot him? With what?"

"A gun from the Real."

"Was he injured badly?"

"Yeah, I put a big hole in his shoulder."

"That explains why I haven't felt any pain before now. But he's starting to get his power back. Soon I won't be able to handle the pain."

Reggie's chest clenched. "I'll help you with pain if I can. Like how I helped Finch."

His smile was grim. "I know."

A few moments later, Asher stopped in front of a red brick, three-story brothel. A crimson awning with a crouched, snarling black wolf hung over the doorway. They entered into an empty foyer decorated with velvet chaises in jewel tones. A curved staircase made of polished wood dominated the space, lending the house an antebellum air.

A super-sized Giant stepped into their path, with shoulders so wide Reggie wondered if he fit through a normal doorway.

"You look like hell, Asher," the Giant said, his eyes roving over Asher's injuries. "She isn't expecting you."

"I've come to trade information for a meeting with the Drunk. Tell her it has to be now or it will be too late," Asher said.

The Giant looked her over. "Who's the little bite?"

"She's with me," he said.

"That's a first. Wait here." The Giant disappeared up the winding staircase.

"Who's 'she?'" Reggie whispered as soon as the bodyguard was out of sight.

"Neelie is the madam here. Her clients are people with influence. She's always looking for an advantage with them. If I give her something good enough, she'll let me see the Drunk. He's my best chance at breaking the binding spell on my collar."

"You're getting help from somebody named the Drunk?"

"You'd be surprised."

"If this Drunk guy is so powerful, why haven't you asked him to do this before now?"

Asher sighed. "I was too afraid. I knew if I escaped, Andrius would murder my family. Even if I broke the spell and kept the collar on, pretended to be bound to buy some time, I was afraid the information I'd have to give Neelie would've been traced back to me. Either way, my family would've died. But now Andrius already knows I betrayed him. There's nothing to keep me from spilling his secrets."

His family. Reggie's throat tightened. "I'm so sorry. Andrius said, but I—maybe there's still a chance I can—"

"Don't." Asher cupped her cheek. "I made my choice. All I can do now is hope and know that I did the right thing."

The Giant returned. "She'll see you now. She's real curious to meet your little lady. Follow me."

They followed the Giant up two flights of stairs. Reggie did her best to ignore the noises coming from the closed doors. On the third floor, the Giant led them down a long hallway carpeted in plush red velvet. He knocked briefly on the last door. She heard a voice bidding them to enter. The Giant thrust open the door, nodding with his massive head.

"No trouble," he warned Asher.

"I wouldn't dream of it," Asher said.

The door closed behind them. They stood in a large bedroom. An overgrown canopy bed decorated in blue and white striped silk filled one end of the room. At the other end, an ivory couch sat in front of a marble fireplace. Next to the couch, an Elf rose from a white desk in the corner. Her pale blue trousers and matching blazer were molded to her curvy figure; the effect was both professional and feminine. Reggie blinked, surprised. She'd been expecting a silk negligee or leather, not something that looked at home in a boardroom. The Elf's green eyes stood out against skin the color of molasses. Her lips were overfull and her nose a shade too long, but when she smiled, all Reggie saw was beauty.

"Asher, Micah tells me you have information for me." The Elf held out her hands. "What happened to you? You look awful."

Asher crossed the room, folding his fingers over hers. He kissed her on the cheek in a practiced motion. "I've been to hell and back. Neelie, I'm here to trade for a favor."

"What does Andrius want in return?"

"I'm not here for Andrius. I'm here for myself."

266

Neelie's eyes widened. She stared at Reggie, her expression calculating. "I see. Who is this, Asher? She's lovely, but it's not like you to bring guests."

"She's the reason I need to trade. I want the Drunk to neutralize my collar," Asher said. "And I'm willing to pay your price."

"Does Andrius suspect you're here?" Neelie's eyes remained fixed on Reggie.

"Not yet. But he will if I don't get this collar off."

Neelie looked sharply at Asher. "I don't need trouble brought to my house, Asher. I might not like Andrius, but I'm not dying for you."

"If you hurry, there won't be any dying," Asher promised. "I know you've been interested in Councilman Thorton for a long time."

Reggie held her breath as Neelie tilted her head, considering. Time slowed. She watched Asher tug discreetly at his collar, wanting to scream at the courtesan to get on with it.

"Tell me, and if I like what I hear, I'll call the Drunk," Neelie finally agreed.

A few minutes later, a smiling Neelie summoned the Drunk. Reggie paced back and forth, biting her lip as sweat glistened on Asher's brow. An old man entered the room with an unsteady wobble. His black garments hung on his bony frame, and his long gray braid swayed behind him.

"You rang, Neelie?" His voice was as sloppy as his movements.

Neelie pointed at Asher. "Look at his collar. See if you can neutralize it."

The Drunk raised his eyebrows. He stumbled over to where Asher sat on the couch. He touched the gold, snapping his hand back. "That's hotter than hell, boy! How come you're not screaming?"

"It's hot! Asher, you lied to me. Get out!" Neelie yelled.

"It's too late. If he doesn't disable it now, we'll all get caught," Asher said. Then he doubled over, gasping.

Reggie rushed to his side. "Hold on."

"You should go," he grunted.

"I'm not leaving you."

"May the Mother damn you, Asher! Fix it," Neelie ordered the Drunk.

"What do you think I'm trying to do?" the Drunk said, turning his attention back to Asher's collar. He began muttering things to himself. Steam rose from the gold as if it had been submerged in cold water. "Whom do you belong to? These are the best binding spells I've ever seen."

Reggie heard shouting in the distance. She ran to the window. People were fleeing down the street, trampling each other in their terror.

"Fix that thing now!" Reggie screamed at the Drunk.

"I'll just turn you over myself." Neelie sprinted toward the door.

Reggie was on her in an instant, driving her to the ground with a knee between her shoulder blades. "You're not going anywhere. You try anything, and I'll bring this whole building down. I swear to the Mother."

Neelie twisted her head around. "Who are you?"

"Someone who has no problem killing you." Reggie dug her hand in Neelie's hair, dragging her from the ground. She felt the Elf's magic begin to pulse around her. Reggie reached into the Earth again. The building began to shake. Neelie's mouth gaped open and her magic vanished. "The whole building," Reggie repeated, marching Neelie closer to Asher.

The Drunk stared at Reggie, his old face scared sober. "Young lady, I have an idea. I need some of your blood." He grabbed the penknife off the desk, making a quick slash across Reggie's forearm. Blood spilled onto the white carpet.

Reggie yelped, releasing Neelie. To her shock, the courtesan didn't try to escape, but stayed next to her. But why would she run? There was a wealth of information to be gleaned from this encounter. The Drunk smeared her blood on Asher's collar and began chanting again. The chaos outside grew louder. Reggie hurried back to the window. Black uniforms were visible now.

"Hurry!" Reggie shouted.

"Yelling isn't helping me," the Drunk said. A loud pop broke the tense silence, like a cork being released from a bottle of champagne. "Hell, I think that did it."

Asher snapped the collar off his neck. The skin underneath was bubbled and raw. "Open the window."

Reggie fumbled for the handles, swinging the window open. A flash of gold sailed past her head, landing in the alley below. A ragged figure lying in the shadows crawled over to pick it up. The soldiers changed direction, rushing toward the alley. Reggie pushed back from the window, closing and locking it. But she could still hear the sound of flesh striking flesh. She felt sick.

"I thought you neutralized it!" Reggie said.

The Drunk shook his head. "Couldn't break the tracking spell, so I concentrated on the binding one. You've got strong blood."

Neelie studied her, eyes brimming with fascination. "Is it love, Asher, or something else?"

"It's love," Asher said, standing up. "Reggie, we need to get out of here. It's not safe."

They started toward the door when Neelie stepped in front of them.

"Get out of the way," Reggie said.

"I can hide you. You're wounded, Asher. You need help. If you leave now, you'll get caught," Neelie said.

"It's a nice offer, but I don't trust you." Asher moved around her.

Neelie grabbed his arm. "I'll hide the Drunk with you. That way you'll know I'm sincere."

The sounds in the alley stopped. The guards must've realized they had the wrong person.

"I guess we don't really have a choice," Reggie said.

Asher sighed. "I guess not."

Neelie's enormous closet was stuffed with clothing ranging from silk dresses to leather corsets. Reggie brushed a feathered boa off her face as she followed the madam through the cavernous space. In the back of the closet, Neelie slid a piece of wall paneling to the side revealing a small room. Reggie stared at the tight space, sweat beading on her upper lip.

"You okay?" Asher asked.

Reggie nodded. "Fan-freaking-tastic. Let's get this over with."

She ducked into the room, pressing her back against one of the corners. Asher settled in beside her. The Drunk squeezed in next to Asher, making the already crowded space unbearable. He smelled like sour alcohol and sweat, his scent conquering all the fresh air. Reggie watched as Neelie slid the wall panel shut, the blackness pouring over her like dark water.

She felt trapped, helpless. She strained her ears, listening for every noise. Muffled shouts drifted from downstairs and then quieted. The silence plucked at her frayed nerves. If they were going to be attacked, Reggie wanted some warning. She tried not to focus on the walls that seemed to press closer or on the eerie silence that had descended. Cool lips touched her forehead.

"It'll be okay." Asher whispered, his voice soothing. "We'll be out of here soon."

Reggie concentrated on him in the gloom, clenching his hand hard. He'd said he loved her and she believed him. They would survive this. Time slowed to a trickle. The darkness was getting to her. Asher's arms were wrapped firmly around her, caging her body and preventing her from rocking back and forth. It seemed like hours had passed, when footsteps broke the stillness. Reggie tensed as the wall slid open.

Neelie stood alone and unharmed. Pushing past Neelie, Reggie escaped to the larger space of the closet. She sucked in air, stomping her feet to get the blood back into her toes. Neelie and Asher helped the Drunk out of the closet. Reggie stumbled after them into the bedroom. They laid the Drunk on the couch.

"What happened?" Asher asked, shaking out his legs one by one. "Are they gone?"

Neelie smiled. "Yes, I gave quite a performance. I offered to let them search the house, of course. But I was quite insulted that they would think I, a known loyalist to Andrius, would help his Indentured and his prisoner escape. What did you do to make that man angry, dear girl?"

"You don't want to know."

"I have a good idea," Neelie murmured.

"Why the change of heart, Neelie?" Asher asked. "You might like me, but you wouldn't risk your own hide for me."

"She's the most interesting thing you've ever brought me," the madam said. "Her blood broke the binding spell. Andrius' binding spell. I offer you a safe haven for tonight and passage out of the city tomorrow. All I ask in return is that she tells me what she is."

"No!" Asher said. Neelie's eyebrows shot up.

Reggie glanced at his wounds. He needed treatment or infection would set in, and she didn't have energy left to heal him. They both were exhausted. "It's okay, Asher. I'll tell her."

"Reggie, you can't trust her—"

"We need help and she's all we've got." Reggie turned to Neelie. The madam wore a hungry expression. "I'm an Aether Mage. Now give us a room."

Neelie's mouth dropped open. "You can't be!"

"Can."

The Drunk popped up like a Jack-in-the-box. "That explains the tremors. Even if Earth is your element, it's damn hard to do that. That's why I thought your blood would work on the binding spell."

Neelie shook her head like a dog shaking off water. "An Aether Mage. I never thought—come, let's find you a room."

CHAPTER 41

*J*ohn ran, clinging tightly to Arlene's hand. She was faltering, pulling him down. Their pursuers were closing in. They remained hidden, but John knew they were out there. He heard twigs snap and heavy breathing. That frightened him more than anything. When they hit, he wouldn't see it coming. He wouldn't be able to defend Arlene.

"John, you have to leave me," Arlene wheezed. "Just take my things and go."

He glanced back at her, shocked. "There's no way I'm leaving you behind. We'll make it."

Arlene stumbled, her injured knee folding under her. John slung her arm around his shoulders, taking her weight. His eyes darted from side to side, searching for their hunters. Why weren't they attacking? He and Arlene were easy prey, wounded and lost. The footsteps behind him slowed. His ears strained to pick up any sound.

A woman dropped from a tree in front of him, rolling gracefully to her feet. John shoved Arlene behind him. He watched as the woman pulled a knife from a leather belt around her slender hips.

"Going somewhere?" she asked, baring her teeth. "Simon, Jensen, come on out!"

John's hand fumbled for the kitchen knife he'd brought, his eyes never leaving the woman's face. Her smile widened at his clumsy movements. He felt like a kid dressed as a warrior for

Halloween meeting the real thing. And the real thing wanted to kick his face in. Arlene shifted behind him, placing her back against his. John hoped she'd drawn her own knife. The leaves rustled behind him. He resisted the urge to spin around, knowing he might wind up with a knife in his back.

"These are piss-poor examples of witches," the deep voice he'd heard before said. "No confusion spells, no veils. Just ran through the woods like animals. Made enough noise to raise the dead."

"How many back there?" John whispered to Arlene.

"Two men and they're big," she whispered back.

"Great," John muttered, considering the odds.

Maybe they could fight their way through three people. But if the other two men handled weapons with the same ease as this woman, their odds had just taken a sky dive sans parachute. His heartbeat rocketed as the woman moved closer. He raised his knife. She kept coming, stopping an arm's length away. Her stance was easy, loose. John wasn't fooled. He knew that the minute he moved wrong, she'd carve him up like a Christmas ham.

"So young," the woman said softly to him, eyes bright above a hawkish nose. "I don't know what these two are, Simon. But they're sure as hell not witches."

"This one doesn't look like a witch either," another male voice said.

"If they were witches, they'd already be throwing curses at us," the deep voice replied.

A large man came around to the side where he could study both John and Arlene. He carried a knife. His eyes focused on Arlene, leering at her. His gaze roved from the soles of her feet to the top of her head, lingering on her breasts. John bristled, but kept his mouth shut. The guy looked like he punched holes in walls for a living. The man's eyes flicked to John, taking an inventory of his thin body. John lifted his chin, meeting those cold eyes. It might be stupid, but he couldn't let on how scared he was. He knew they were just looking for an excuse to tear Arlene and him apart.

The man sneered. "This all you got for protection, sweetheart? Couldn't you find anything better?"

Arlene leaned harder against him, staying silent. John pressed back, hoping to offer her some comfort.

"Wait, Simon. Doesn't she look familiar?" the man behind him said.

John felt invisible rocks sink in his stomach. Reggie didn't look exactly like her mom, but there was enough of a resemblance to identify a connection.

"We've never seen you before," John said. Simon's head snapped toward him.

"Well, the piece of shit can speak," Simon said. He nodded at the woman. "Friegbert, teach him some manners. It's not polite to interrupt a man when he's talking with a lady."

Friegbert closed the distance between them. John lashed out at her. She dodged his swipe, delivering a solid kick to his knee. Pain lanced his kneecap, dropping him to the ground. His head was jerked back, cold steel pressed against his throat.

"Drop your little toy," Friegbert purred in his ear. "Slowly now. We wouldn't want any accidents."

John looked up, meeting Simon's cruel grin. He relaxed his fingers, letting the knife drop. Friegbert rubbed closer to him. The intimacy of the motion penetrated his fear-clogged brain. She was enjoying this way too much.

"Dear Maxim, I never thought this would happen to me," John muttered. Suddenly the blade pricked his neck. He sucked in a breath.

"What was that?" Friegbert said, her breath hot against his face.

John bit his tongue until he tasted blood. Arlene was staring at the knife at his throat. Horror reflected off her pale face. Horror and something far more dangerous. He recognized that look. He'd seen his mother wear it a couple of times when she found out he had been bullied in elementary school. He sent Arlene a silent plea with his eyes, but he knew it was too late.

"Now, where were we?" Simon asked, turning back to Arlene.

Arlene ignored him, her body shaking. She pointed at Friegbert's face. "How dare you attack him? He's just a kid! We haven't done anything to you. Get the hell away from him!"

Arlene reached for John with one hand, brandishing a knife in the other. Friegbert gripped him tighter, stepping back. The man behind Arlene lunged forward but missed. Simon snatched Arlene's arm. She jerked back, slicing him across his forearm. His roar sent shivers over John's skin.

In a blur of speed, Simon had Arlene flat on her stomach. Her knife arm was pinned uselessly behind her back. Simon ripped the knife from her grip. She whimpered. John struggled against Friegbert's hold. He felt a sharp sting in his neck. Blood trickled down his skin.

"Where you going?" Friegbert said.

John watched as Simon twisted Arlene's arm, bending it a vicious angle. Her face contorted in pain. Rage settled into John's stomach. He wanted to kill Simon more than anything he'd wanted in his whole life. Simon yanked Arlene's hair back from her face, studying her.

"Jensen, what do you think?" Simon asked the other man.

Jensen, a beefy blond man, came around and observed Arlene. "Looks like her."

John tensed as he felt Friebert look at his backpack. "I've never seen these labels on their packs before."

"What do you know about Regina Farr?" Simon said to Arlene.

"Reggie," Arlene murmured. John swore under his breath.

"What was that?" Simon said, but Arlene remained silent. Simon put more pressure on her arm. She screamed.

"Stop! You're going to break her arm," John shouted, ignoring the press of Friegbert's blade.

"What have you done with my daughter?" Arlene gasped. "You son of a bitch—"

"Daughter?" Simon repeated.

Friebert moved them closer to Simon. "They were by the barrier, do you think that they—"

"Shit! You think Andrius' slave went into the Real?" Jensen said.

"Why would he send his slave into the Real? It's forbidden to go there," Friegbert said. "What could he want there?"

"Maybe Andrius didn't send him. That bastard was too uppity. Probably went behind Andrius' back." A mad grin spread across Simon's face. "And if he did go behind his back, it had to be for a damn good reason. These two could be our key out of here. Our key to moving up again." He dropped Arlene's arm. She cradled it to her body. He glanced at John and Friegbert. "Looks like we got ourselves two prisoners."

John stared at Simon, his heart plummeting. There was no hope for them now.

Chapter 42

*R*eggie checked Asher's bandages, careful not to jostle him. He was stretched out on the large bed next to her, lying on his chest. Clean bandages covered the wounds on his back and his neck. His fingers had already started to heal and had to be broken again and then reset. Neelie's physician had given him a salve to put on the burns, administering a mild sedative so Asher could sleep through the pain. When she'd gained enough energy back, she'd tried to speed up his healing process.

Before he'd succumbed to the sedative, Asher had instructed Reggie on how to enter the Dream Realm. Sinking back into the fluffy pillows, Reggie counted back in her head. She silently chanted over and over, letting her mind slip under. A shadowy vortex opened before her. Suddenly she plummeted down through the emptiness; terrified at the speed she was falling. Asher had told her she needed to create an anchor, carve a place out of the nothingness.

A forest grew around her. Massive trees shot up, shading the ground below. A dead boar lay on its side, wolves tearing into the carcass. She landed beside them, afraid to get too close. She scolded herself for her foolishness. They couldn't hurt her. They were her creations. Leaning against a tree, she waited.

Her construct split open, like a rip in a painting. A familiar figure came zooming toward her, his long golden hair flying behind him. He landed lightly, a saucy grin plastered on his face. "Little darling! You rang?"

"Brwyn!" She held out her arms, relieved that he'd answered her call. He pulled her into a hug.

Brwyn inhaled sharply. "Even here, you smell delicious. What's going on? Are you all right?"

"I need your help. You have to get word to Rhys that I'm coming to him," Reggie told the Changeling, releasing him.

"I can do that. But why don't you contact him yourself?"

"I don't want Andrius to find me. He'll be watching for me to contact Rhys."

"Why?"

"He captured me, and I escaped. I shot him with a weapon from the Real. He's really pissed at me."

Brwyn's eyebrows shot up. "Well, aren't you full of surprises. I'm impressed. Where are you now?"

"Hiding in the Pleasure Zone. I'm leaving tomorrow."

"Alone?"

"No, Asher's with me."

He laughed. "Ahh, the tragic hero. Don't worry. I'll pass along your message, little darling."

"Thanks, Brwyn." Reggie hugged him again.

He wrapped his arms around her, resting his hands just above her rear. "My pleasure. I'll be seeing you soon."

She moved his hands away from her butt, sliding them to her waist. "You will?"

He grinned. "Sweetheart, you're going to need all the help you can get. Andrius is going to come after you openly now, and in full force."

Reggie shivered. "I know. Thanks again, Brwyn."

"Like I told you before, I like you. You're a force of change. Wake up now, so you can get some real rest."

Reggie's eyes blinked open. She sat up, feeling better. Her list of allies was growing. With Asher and Brwyn helping her, she'd find a way to Rhys. Punching the pillow, Reggie snuggled back into the blankets. She needed sleep. She had to be at her best for the journey ahead.

"No! I can't get in there—I just can't." Reggie stared down at a large, black trunk. She stood in the middle of Neelie's bedroom. It was early morning, the sun still asleep.

"You don't have a choice," Neelie replied, elegant and fresh in a red crushed velvet robe. "This is the only safe way to smuggle you out. I'm going to Pikes Crossing today. This is the perfect opportunity to get you out of the city without being seen. Besides, you'll only be in the trunk for a little while. Until you're loaded into the Cruiser," she said, referring to the hovering bubble cars.

Chills ran over Reggie's skin as she stared at the open maw of the trunk. "Fine. What about Asher? You have a trunk big enough for him?"

Asher was lying facedown on Neelie's bed, the physician changing his bandages. "I can't fit inside that," he muttered, lifting his head to stare at the trunk.

Neelie rolled her eyes. "Of course not. You'll be going out in that one." She pointed to an enormous square, black shape near her door.

"That's a trunk? I thought it was a table!"

The madam shuddered. "Ugh, like I would keep something like that as a table. My clients sometimes request special things, and this is a very special client. It's best to be prepared."

"So all these trunks won't look suspicious?" Reggie asked, crossing her arms over her chest. Just a few minutes, she told herself. She could handle a few minutes in that dark space.

"I always carry luggage. Besides, you won't stay in the trunk. There are two hidden compartments under the Cruiser's seats. You'll both hide in there until we get out of the city."

Panic stole Reggie's breath. "How big is it?"

"About two feet longer than your trunk. You'll be fine, but poor Asher will be miserable." Neelie reached over, running her fingers through Asher's inky hair. "Sorry, my darling."

"I've been in worse." Asher winced as the physician plastered bandages to his skin. He caught Reggie's alarmed look, frowning. "Reggie, you okay?"

Her heart galloped in her chest like a spooked racehorse. "How long are we gonna be in there?"

Neelie stretched. "I'm not sure. This early there shouldn't—"

"How long?" Reggie demanded. The window shattered next to her. The physician yelped, linen dangling from his fingers. Asher shot to his knees.

Neelie stilled. "I'll get you out as soon as I can. But I know Andrius. He'll have patrols checking every route out of the city. Once we reach a safe distance, I'll let you and Asher out. Then you're on your own. I understand you find this upsetting, but this is the only way you'll be safe." The madam stepped forward slowly, tucking a strand of hair behind Reggie's ear. "Trust me. I've gotten you this far, haven't I?"

Her touch was soothing and Reggie's chest eased. "Yeah. Sorry about the window."

"It's only a window," Neelie replied. She nodded toward the physician. "Have you finished with him?"

The pale man pulled his eyes away from Reggie to focus on his boss. "Y-yes, almost."

"Come," Neelie said. "We need to get the remainder of your things. It's not safe for you to linger here."

Reggie nodded. "We should go before the Ravens decide they don't believe you."

Reggie had discovered a new hell. Although roomier than the trunk, the hidden compartment was black as pitch. It ran the length of one of the long bench seats in the back of the Cruiser. She could stretch her legs out, but couldn't shake the feeling she was entombed. Her fingers gripped the release lever on the inside of the compartment that would spring open the seat top. The compartment was hard to detect because it couldn't be opened from the outside. Neelie only used this coffin when she wanted to smuggle the living.

They'd been traveling for a while. Reggie knew that she and Asher couldn't stay hidden much longer. Eventually their oxygen would run out. Taking another slow, shallow breath, she recited a Shakespeare sonnet in her head. She would've had a test in a few days. It was funny to think only last week the most dangerous thing in her life was getting a B on an exam. Reggie slammed into the side of the box as the Cruiser suddenly stopped. Pain exploded in her shoulder, and she bit back a shout. Neelie's voice was loud, penetrating through the seat cushions.

"Why have you stopped us? I have places to be," the madam demanded.

"That's not my concern. Out of the Cruiser. We need to search it," a male voice said.

"Sergeant, that's no way to speak to a lady. How are you, Ms. Neelie?" another male voice said. He was quieter, and Reggie had to strain to hear him. "We're looking for two fugitives. Very dangerous. Would you mind stepping out?"

"Captain Panko! It's been too long," Neelie said. "Surely you don't think I'm hiding fugitives?"

The cushion above Reggie's head groaned with added weight. "No, sweetheart, I don't. But you know how it is, no special treatment. Come here, I've missed you."

Soft smacking noises and Neelie's rich laughter invaded her box. Reggie really hoped they weren't having sex right on top of her.

"You're very persuasive, Captain. Very well, help me out of here. I want to hear more about you missing me."

There was a brief rustling and then they were gone. The seat dipped again. Something scraped against the surface as if hands were running along the cushion, searching for abnormalities. Reggie held her breath. Panic seized her when she heard a loud thump. Did they find Asher? But the sound was quickly echoed and she relaxed. They were just tossing out the luggage in the back compartment.

Time flowed as slow as honey. The box seemed to shrink, its walls narrowing. Reggie kneaded her nails in and out of the flesh on her stomach like a cat flexing its claws. Finally Neelie's laughter rushed past her again.

"You will come see me soon?" Neelie said. There was a thump above Reggie's head.

"I have some time off in the next few weeks. I'll be along then," the captain said. "Be careful. I wouldn't want any part of you damaged."

Reggie heard the door slam shut. The Cruiser began moving. Gulping a breath of hot air, her muscles relaxed. Then they went limp. Everything felt fuzzy. She shook her head but heaviness pulled on her eyelids, tugging them down.

She heard shouting. Angry, loud voices pressed against her. They seemed far away. The twisted scream of metal being wrenched from wood hammered her ears. Light hit her eyes, but they refused to open. She couldn't speak. Her voice was hibernating, and she couldn't rouse it.

"May the Mother damn you! How long has she been in here?" someone growled, the pretense of humanity gone from his voice. Gentle hands lifted her from the box.

"A little over two hours. She should've been fine." Reggie recognized Neelie's voice. Her normally smooth tones were pocked with fear.

"She doesn't like small spaces. Probably panicked," Asher wheezed.

"Asher's having problems, but you thought she could handle it? Come on, little darling. Take in the fresh air. Wake up!"

A cool breath filled her mouth. It was foreign, the wild magic tasting of something primal. Reggie felt the breath escaping and she gulped, sputtering, wanting to take it back in. Opening her eyes, she met Brwyn's blue gaze. He held her tight as she coughed, one large hand stroking her back.

"Easy, sweetheart, easy. You're okay now. You're safe," Brwyn said.

Reggie blinked, focusing. She was sitting across Brwyn's lap. Asher knelt beside her, his golden skin tinged with gray. He tangled his hand with hers when she met his eyes. Neelie and her Giant bodyguard stood near, their faces masks of concern.

"What happened?" Reggie rasped. Her head flopped against Brwyn's shoulder. Her muscles felt weak, useless. She didn't like being helpless in front of Neelie.

Neelie met Brwyn's eyes, shifting from side to side like a child in front of an angry parent. "I don't know. You must've panicked and fainted. I'm so sorry."

Reggie knew the madam had risked a lot to bring her here, wherever here was. Looking around, she saw they were in a forest. "You got me out of the city. You did what you said you would."

Neelie lifted her chin, glancing at Brwyn. "I always keep my word. Now that she's in your capable hands, I'll be on my way."

"Yes. And Neelie, in case you're ever tempted to whisper in Andrius' ear, remember who your silent partner is." Brwyn smiled wide, flashing elongated canines.

Neelie took a step back. "No need to doubt my loyalty. Until we meet again, Reggie. Asher, take care of yourself." She jerked her head at her bodyguard. Then they were gone, slipping into the Cruiser and driving away.

"Silent partner?" Asher asked.

Brwyn shrugged. "She's a good investment and a great source of information."

"That's why there was a wolf painted on her house." Reggie pushed at Brwyn's chest to let her up.

Brwyn stood, taking her with him. "Sometimes the best way to hide is in plain sight. Feeling better?"

Reggie nodded. "A little. I wasn't expecting to see you so soon." The ground was uneven and she swayed on her feet. Brwyn and Asher each grabbed an arm.

"I like to surprise you; I wouldn't want to become boring and predictable." Brwyn grinned, his hand firm around her elbow.

Reggie steadied herself. "That's not possible. How did you find us?"

"When you told me you were in the Pleasure Zone, I made some inquiries. It was damn lucky that you were with Neelie.

286

She told me where she was dropping you off, and I let my nose do the rest." He tapped his nose.

"You could smell me in the Cruiser? That's kinda creepy. So what now? Do you have a plan? Asher and I are winging it."

Mischief sparkled in his eyes. "Little darling, you have no idea."

CHAPTER 43

*T*he airship was tied to an enormous tree in front of them. Wide and squat, the tree rested on the ground like a giant toadstool in a clearing. Ropes strained and creaked as the airship swayed. Smaller than the commercial craft Reggie and Asher had taken, this was built along the sleek lines of a clipper ship. A crouched, crimson wolf stained the black canvas of the ship's balloon, overwhelming the slanted sigils painted alongside it. Leaning against Asher, Reggie stared at the ship. Hope expanded through her like the air filling the balloon.

"You know how to travel in style," she told Brwyn. "Wow."

"You're taking us all the way to Rhys?" Asher asked.

Brwyn opened his mouth to answer when a rope was thrown over the side of the airship. A woman slid down it, landing gracefully on her feet. Reggie recognized her fiery mane. "Megan!"

The Resistance soldier bowed. "Good to see you alive and whole. Both of you. You took longer than expected. I was getting worried," Megan said to Brwyn.

Brwyn stiffened, lifting an eyebrow. "I can handle myself. You of all people should know that. Reggie had a little trouble, but she's fine now, aren't you?"

Reggie nodded as Megan crossed her arms over her chest. "I'm sorry my concern offends you. We should get going, we're behind schedule."

"Right. Need help climbing up, little darling?" Brwyn asked. This time it was Megan who tensed.

Asher came to her rescue. "I've got her. Hop up on my back." Asher knelt down, wincing as Reggie locked her arms around his neck and slid her legs around his waist.

The rope was thickly woven and tough. Asher made quick work of the climb, pulling himself over the side. He put Reggie on her feet. Megan and Brwyn followed. The deck had a full crew waiting, and Reggie recognized the Resistance soldiers who'd come to her rescue earlier. Finch was there, pale but standing. She smiled at him.

"Cast off," Brwyn barked, delaying a reunion. "Come with me." He gestured for Reggie and Asher to follow him. He took them to a narrow staircase and below deck to the captain's cabin. Megan followed.

"It should take me three days to get you to Rhys." Brwyn leaned against a wooden desk shoved into a corner. "We shouldn't run into any trouble, at least not until we get to Hornsbay."

"Why—" Reggie began when Megan's harsh voice cut her off.

"You're not taking us all the way to Hornsbay. It's too dangerous."

"It's much safer than you trying to slip past Andrius' soldiers."

"What about you and your family? What will happen to them once Andrius knows what you've done?"

"As always, your concern for me and my family is noble but misguided. I've told them what I plan to do. They're distancing themselves from me as we speak."

"Brwyn!" Reggie protested.

"Brwyn, you're their only child!" Megan reached for him. The gesture was intimate in its familiarity. The underlying tension between them became clear. Megan was the one he loved.

He shrugged her off. "I've made my choice."

"But—"

"Enough!" Asher interrupted. His eyes were bright with anger. "We don't have time for this. We need to do what's best for Reggie to keep her safe." He pulled her against him, nodding at Brwyn. "Thank you, brother, for everything."

Brwyn smiled at Reggie, his rakish charm returning. "No need to thank me. I'd do anything for the little darling. She's such a tasty bite."

Reggie and Asher shared a cabin with a tiny wardrobe and attached bathroom. Compared to the commercial ship, the bathroom was cruder, running water a rationed supply on the smaller ship. But the food was good and the bed comfortable despite its small size, which was a blessing since she and Asher spent most of their time below decks. Megan and Brwyn didn't want to take the chance of them being spotted above by a Raven squad.

Reggie lay plastered against Asher, his body heat like a mini furnace. "I need to check your bandages. You should let me try to heal you."

He rolled onto an elbow, his face above hers. "I'm a fast healer. I'll be okay."

"You're just afraid I'll give you some payback, accidentally re-break something."

He snorted. "The thought did cross my mind."

"I wouldn't actually do it on purpose, but my lack of control is a valid concern."

"You handled our escape pretty well."

"That's easier. I'm still letting the magic rip. Healing Finch was hard. If he hadn't been so far gone, I don't think I would've been able to do it. Pinpoint accuracy is still not my strong suit. Now roll over, so I can have a look at you."

His wounds were healing rapidly, patches of fresh, shining skin slowly zipping the cuts closed. His neck was the worst. She rubbed salve on the burns with careful fingers. Brwyn had assured her that eventually the scars would fade.

"It's strange not to have it on," Asher said. "I didn't realize how heavy it was."

Her fingers stilled. "I'm sorry about your family."

"Andrius kept them in the Pits. That's where he put his greatest enemies. They lived in filth. They were slowly starving, being worked to death. Sometimes I felt guilty."

"About what?"

"Andrius abused me, but I was being fed, cared for. When he let me visit them, I could see them fading away, but I was healthy."

Reggie stroked his hair. "No, you weren't. It was just a different kind of torture, that's all."

Asher turned over, facing her. "I wanted to save them. I know it's not an excuse for lying—"

She placed her fingers against his lips. "It hurts that you lied. But you lost your family by choosing me. How can I ever make up for that?"

Pulling her down on top of him, he kissed her. It was the first time they'd kissed since she'd found out the truth. She melted into him, letting the intimate sweetness take her under.

Reggie was applying salve to Asher's back on the third morning when phantom fingers brushed over her skin, an eerie sense of foreboding filling her chest. Strangely, she thought of her mother, fear seizing her heart. But her mother was safe in the Real, and John was taking care of her. Andrius couldn't get to them there. Brwyn burst into their cabin, interrupting her troubling thoughts. She jerked her head up. Asher bumped her against the wall as he rolled onto his side.

"We're coming up on Hornsbay Forest. I spoke with Rhys last night. He's waiting for us. He's going to remove the protective spells, so we can fly over the forest without going mad. This is where you come in, little darling."

Reggie climbed over Asher, scrambling to her feet. "What can I do?"

"Andrius' soldiers are going to try to shoot us from the sky. They might even have a fighting class airship. This ship has good wards, but it will be hard to keep us afloat and stop the soldiers from entering the forest once the spell is down. I need you stop them."

Asher swung his legs over the side of the bed, slipping an arm around her waist. "Are you up for this?"

Reggie nodded. "What's the plan?"

Brwyn's smile was hungry, his wolf peeking out in the blue-green of his eyes. "I hear you work wonders with trees."

CHAPTER 44

*R*eggie stood on deck in the cold air, her hair whipping back in the wind. She held heavy, gold embossed binoculars to her eyes. The redwoods of Hornsbay Forest stood tall like giant ship masts. A mist hid the boles of the trees. There was a small army of men on the ground below, their camp running along the edges of the tree line. She didn't spot any black uniforms. This wasn't Andrius' personal guard, but that didn't make them any less dangerous. She focused on the trees again. She didn't know if she had the magical skill set to play puppeteer with that great a number.

"What do you think?" Asher asked. He snapped an arrow into a large crossbow attached to the railing.

"I don't know. I had trouble controlling two trees. This is a whole other level. Guess I don't have a choice."

He shook his head. "Take your time, I'll keep you safe. I've looked at the defensive wards. They're solid. Megan and some of the others are good with Fire. If there's an Air mage below, we'll be in trouble. But I think the Changeling can handle it."

Reggie dropped the binoculars, glancing at Brwyn. He stood behind the ship's control console, tall and confident. A feral grin slashed his mouth. "Handle it? He's enjoying every minute of it."

Asher shrugged. "He's a wolf."

A swirling fog appeared before Brwyn, solidifying into an image of a woman. She was older, with silver hair pulled into a severe braid. "Representative Cavill, Hornsbay Forest is a restricted air space. Is there something wrong with your airship? Do you require assistance?"

Brwyn laughed. "No assistance necessary, Captain Marrow. I'm on my way to see a good friend."

The woman's stern expression slackened. "Sir?"

"You heard me, Captain."

"Sir, if you continue your course I will be forced to fire on you."

"Do you worst, Captain," Brwyn replied. The image dissolved.

"Here we go," Reggie whispered, looking back over the bow.

The soldiers below were loading crossbows similar to Asher's, only much larger. Suddenly, a dozen metal bolts zoomed toward the ship, aiming for the vulnerable canvas.

"Incoming!" a man to the left of Reggie shouted.

Asher grabbed her, wrapping his arms around her body. They ducked below the railing. Reggie watched as the lethal points smacked into an invisible force, falling harmlessly to the ground. The airship shuddered. Reggie clung to Asher.

A group of soldiers gathered in a circle. They stood still, fixating on the airship. Reggie felt magic building around her. It tasted of smoke and heat. Streaks of blue flame assaulted the airship's defenses. The fireballs sizzled as they hit the wards, dissolving into steam. Heat penetrated the defenses. Reggie gasped as it painfully licked her skin. Behind her someone screamed.

"Megan, prepare the fire! I'm dropping the wards. Ready the weapons to be released on my count!" Brwyn yelled. Asher let go of Reggie, grabbing his crossbow. "One. Two. Three. NOW!"

Megan, Finch, and three others conjured fireballs. The dancing flames rocketed from their hands, whipping toward the soldiers below. The fire exploded against the enemies' wards.

A rain of arrows followed, soaring over Reggie's head. Back and forth, the two sides slugged it out like a deadly tennis match.

Another wave of bolts flew at the airship. The wards shuddered again, becoming a misty orange as they flickered. A single bolt pushed through. The razor edge ripped a small tear in the canvas. The damage was minimal, but Reggie knew the defenses couldn't take much more punishment.

"Son-of-a-bitch!" Brwyn snarled. His eyes glowed bright blue. "Reggie, it's your turn! Rhys has dropped the mist. We're almost over Hornsbay Forest. Keep them from getting in."

Reggie stood on trembling legs. Smoke billowed from the soldiers' camp. The acrid smell filled her lungs. But the flames didn't stop the fighters from reloading their weapons. She glanced over at Asher. He aimed his crossbow. He looked at her, waiting. They were all waiting for her to live up to her heritage.

Closing her eyes, Reggie focused on the redwoods. Her magic probed the roots like delicate tentacles. It hurt to keep her power on a leash, not to push too quickly. She linked her magic from tree to tree like a web, injecting power into the gnarled wood. She felt it travel up through the roots of the tree line. A collective moan rippled through the trees. They began to sway, rumbling, but Reggie held them in place. She opened her eyes, tears curving over her cheeks. The battalion below had stopped concentrating on the airship. They stared at the redwoods.

Rocking back and forth, Reggie watched the trees mimic her movements. She twisted at the waist. The trunks bent, their bodies straining. She fed more magic into the web. Curving her fingers into claws, she swung her hands back and forth. Roots erupted from the ground. They scooped up bodies and weapons, hurling them from the forest like an Olympian throwing a discus. A Giant screamed as he zipped by the airship, narrowly missing the hull.

Reggie's control slipped. Enemy soldiers were smashed to pulp. Gritting her teeth, she pulled back. Her vision blurred. Strong arms encircled her as she staggered. She rested her head against a solid chest. The tops of the trees were under her now. Someone whispered in her ear. Asher.

"Let go, Reggie. I've got you. We're clear now. Lean on me."

Reggie released the trees. Her body folded like a lawn chair. Asher scooped her up, and she snuggled into his warmth.

"I love you too, you know," she whispered. He tensed, tipping up her chin. He searched her eyes. Then they were kissing.

Brwyn's laugh rang out. "Look at that. Seems like sex and death always go together." Reggie broke the kiss, glaring at Brwyn. He grinned at her. "Rest, little darling, you'll have plenty of time for that later. We're almost there."

Asher continued to hold her. She turned her head to gaze at the forest. Salt tinged the air, clean and tangy. She saw the gray waters of Hornsbay. White, foamy riffles broke out over the surface, pushing toward shore. Seagulls floated on air currents searching for food. A beach came into view. A lone man stood in the shallow foam watching them. Reggie narrowed her eyes. His leather jacket flapped around him, standing out like a beacon.

"Rhys," she said. "Asher, it's Rhys!"

"Throw over the anchor, I'm taking us down!" Brwyn called out.

Reggie watched impatiently as the airship was stabilized and ropes were thrown over. Asher gently put her on her feet. She grabbed his hand, pulling him toward the side. Megan and her team were already climbing down. Brwyn was waiting for her. He looked as cocky as always. But if she looked hard enough, she could see the protective streak he hid. Reggie let go of Asher. She walked to Brwyn, hugging him hard.

"Thank you so much. Are you coming with us?"

"Of course. I'm here to stay," Brwyn said. "Take her down. I'll be right behind you."

Asher shimmied down the rope, Reggie on his back. Anticipation curled her stomach. As soon as his feet hit the sand, she swung off his back and ran. Rhys stood tall and straight, his scar pulled tight from his smile. Stopping in front of him, she hesitated. But when he opened his arms, she went into them.

"Welcome home, Reggie," Rhys whispered.

"It's good to finally be here," Reggie said.

About the Author

Rebecca Jaycox grew up in the tiny town of Berryman, which borders the Mark Twain National Forest and the Courtois River, about 70 miles south of St. Louis. The beautiful landscape fed her imagination, and she began writing stories at age 10 and never stopped.

Always seeking adventure, Rebecca moved to France after she graduated college with a journalism degree to teach English at a French high school. Bitten by the travel bug, she has recently visited Italy, Greece, Austria, Spain, and finally made it to her bucket-list destination of Istanbul last summer.

Rebecca now lives in New York City with her husband, Gregory. She enjoys reading and writing fantasy, urban fantasy, steampunk, and science fiction. The Other Inheritance is her first novel.

Learn more at rebeccajaycox.com

Printed in Great Britain
by Amazon